Praise for Paul Watkins'
The Story of My Disappearance

"A fascinating premise for a novel....Watkins' *Story of My Disappearance* is a thriller, a love story, and an inquiry into the nature of identity."
—*Newark Star-Ledger*

"Subtly evocative...Watkins uses the most extreme circumstances to test the identities and obligations of his displaced characters as he confides their stories gradually, building sympathy and suspense and conveying a textured picture of the gray world of people caught between two cultures...Ingenious."
—*Publishers Weekly* (starred review)

"*The Story of My Disappearance* captivates....[Watkins is] a gloriously endowed young author."
—*Ft. Worth Morning Star Telegram*

"A fine psychological adventure-mystery....*The Story of My Disappearance* will add luster to Watkins' reputation as an accomplished young writer."
—*Flint Journal*

"Paul Watkins' first-person narrative is startlingly compelling."
—*Salem Press*

"*The Story of My Disappearance* pounds with a passion for all things Rhode Island....Riveting."
—*Rhode Island Monthly*

Also by Paul Watkins

The Story of My Disappear- ance

Paul Watkins

Picador USA

New York

Picador® is a U.S. registered trademark and is used by St. Martin's Press under license from Pan Books Limited.

For information on Picador USA Reading Group Guides, as well as ordering, please contact the Trade Marketing department at St. Martin's Press.
Phone: 1-800-221-7945 extention 763
Fax: 212-677-7456
E-mail: trademarketing@stmartins.com

Library of Congress Cataloging-in-Publication Data

Watkins, Paul.
    The story of my disappearance : a novel / by Paul Watkins.
        p.   cm.
    ISBN 0-312-17995-2 (hc)
    ISBN 0-312-20026-9 (pbk)
    I. Title.
PS3573.A844S76   1998
813'.54—dc21

97-33410
CIP

First Picador USA Paperback Edition: May 1999

10 9 8 7 6 5 4 3 2 1

The Story of My Disappearance

One

IT HAD BEEN A LONG TIME SINCE I'D SEEN A MAN KILLED.

I was sitting with Suleika in a place called Bad Joe's Bar, down by the docks on Thames Street in Newport, Rhode Island. Suleika was not talking to me again. She pulled her shoulder-length blond hair down in front of her eyes and inspected each individual strand. When she did this, I knew she wanted to talk. But I'd have to gouge it out of her. It was like opening an oyster with my fingernails, working them between the bony halves, twisting and pulling, until at last in the yawning of the shell, I'd see what was on her mind. This time, I already knew.

Suleika is a name you don't see very often. Soo-lay-ka. It took awhile before I became fond of the name, and then I fell in love with it—the way the word slipped out of my throat and silenced itself with the *ka* at the end. Suleika was tall, six foot in her oil-stained work boots. She made some people nervous with her height. In winter, her pale skin was clear, but now that the sum-

1

mer was approaching, her freckles had returned. They made her blue eyes stand out more. The blue was ringed with a band of gray, which could be seen most clearly when you glanced at her, not if you focused hard. The only part of her that had suffered from the years out working on the water was her hands. They had lost their delicacy, and contained instead a kind of smoothed-out muscularity. It was the same for all of us. A fisherman can break bones with his grip, but the feeling in his palms and fingertips is dulled by calluses.

Sun reached through the windows of the bar. It filled the room with a silvery light that you get there in late afternoons in May. The walls of Bad Joe's were draped with old trawler nets to give the place a salty feel that the owner, a man named Biagio, who had never set foot on a working boat, hoped would attract tourists.

To Suleika and me and the other boat crews who fished for a living out on Block Island Sound, seeing those nets all around gave us the feeling of being trapped in one. Some crews wouldn't come in here because of it. They remembered other fishermen who were only themselves when on the water, blind drunk and mean on the land, who had ridden out into storms, believing themselves indestructible, drowned in their own nets, and whose tattooed skin the crabs and lobsters plucked in shreds from their pale corpses.

Suleika inspected her hair. What she wanted to talk about was the fact that we had reached a breaking point. We had known each other for years and were as close as a couple in a good marriage, and yet we were not married. I never thought the time was right. My stalling had eaten away at us until suddenly, catching us both by surprise, everything we had together seemed to be falling apart.

I did love her. Do love her. No one more than Suleika. I couldn't chase her from my thoughts for more than ten or twenty minutes at a time. In the beginning, I had reasons why we should not be married. They were good reasons. Unarguable, even with her. When they stopped being good, I invented new reasons, and these were solid, too. In time, they also faded. After that, when I came up with fresh excuses, they were only excuses and we both knew it. Still I clung to my invented logic. It was only recently, only this day in fact, that I realized I had neither reasons nor excuses left. The only way I could think to explain my hesitation was to say I did not feel permanent. There was a great fragility to the life I had made for myself here. I could not bear the thought of dragging her down with me if something went wrong. It seemed to me an act of greater love to keep that one last thing apart from her. This was our great unfinished business.

She could have had anyone. Half the men on the dock would have dropped their wives and girlfriends to be with her and not looked back. It was not for some mythic beauty she possessed, because she did not, but for reasons they only half-understood. The proof of their attraction to her was precisely that they made no comments about their desire, as if to do so would reveal more than they cared to show. It was not rare to find a woman working on the dock, but it was more unusual to see one on a trawler. Because of this, she was respected by men who had spent most of their lives beyond the sight of land and who respected almost nothing in the world.

It used to be our favorite part of the day, just after quitting time, when we were tired in our bodies but not yet in our minds, and the sun off the water was bright but not blinding, changing from gold to brass to copper into bronze. The warmth of it still tight against our faces. It used to be the time of day when she and I could talk, but I thought better of it now. I would not have spoken clearly, anyway. Too many things were going through my head. I felt locked inside myself. If I said anything now, it would only make matters worse.

I pushed away my coffee, the milk gone chalky as it cooled.

"Are you leaving?" she asked, glancing at me through the mesh of her inspected hair.

"I'll be right back." I smiled weakly. I got up and went over to the jukebox. It was a Wurlitzer left over from the fifties. On its hazed plastic dome and dented metal sides were the imprints of fights among those same land-mean fishermen whose ships had gone down decades earlier. I rummaged in the pockets of my jeans until I found a nickel. Then I put it in the slot. Biagio hadn't figured out how to make the machine charge any more, so we still got music at the fifties price. But we also got music so out-of-date, some of it as old as the forties, that few us of had heard of even half the singers in the selection. As I scanned the names of songs, I caught sight of Suleika's reflection in the mirror behind the bar. She had stopped examining her hair and was looking at me. She couldn't tell I saw her. I lowered my head and pretended to study the songs. When I turned to walk back to the table, Suleika looked down again, not wanting me to know she had been watching. I stepped through the webbed shadows that the nets threw on the floor.

Biagio stood behind the bar with his arms folded. He dressed like a man who'd just arrived at Ellis Island at the turn of the century—a waistcoat and collarless shirt and sometimes a pair of suspenders with the half-gone elastic stretched over his shoulders. With his scrub-brush gray mustache and little bubble of a chin, he looked like he didn't speak English, but then he'd talk and you'd hear the generations-old Rhode Island Yankee twang in his voice. Newport became *Noo-poh-what.* Car became *cah.* He was one of those people who lived by the water but was not a part of it. He had no envy of those of us who made a living from it. He inhabited the middle ground of slate roofs wet with salt mist in the mornings, the sad crying of the gulls, seaweed wrapped around television aerials after the storms, and the talking drumbeat of sail lines against masts out in the harbor.

Biagio's name was pronounced *Bee-aj-ee-oh,* which the locals had abbreviated to Bad Joe. So many people would come into his bar asking who Bad Joe was that Biagio made up a story about Bad Joe being a notorious fisherman who died at sea with all his crew and whose ghost still haunted the dock. That was why Biagio liked to keep the fisherman's theme to his bar, with nets strung out across the walls.

Biagio bobbed his eyebrows at me and jerked his head toward Suleika. He knew what we were going through. He thought he did, anyway. Everyone on the dock had given me advice about Suleika. They gave her advice about me, too. They couldn't understand why she hadn't moved on to someplace else. She seemed too good for this hard and dirty work. They also thought she was too good for the likes of me. With us, people didn't see the whole picture. There was more to this unfinished business of ours, more than anyone knew except Suleika and me, which was why she had not left yet, as the dough-faced, fish-smelling women on the dock had often advised her to do.

She and I were usually the only ones in Bad Joe's at that time of day. We had just finished repairing our nets. All afternoon we sat on the great piles of nylon, weaving the tears closed with twine and large steel needles about a foot long and as thick as a man's thumb. They were more blunt than regular needles, but they still came to a nasty point at the end. If you let one drop from waist height, it would stick into the dock planks. We repaired nets every Saturday and they were patched with green, yellow, and orange.

Sometimes Biagio would sit down with us. He would talk about new plans he had to renovate the bar, which involved ideas as foreign to these surroundings as wicker, fake bronze tables with glass tops, and lunchtime specials like curry and falafel. You might get that stuff up on Bellevue, but not down here by the docks. More precisely, he came to talk to Suleika. He had convinced himself that she would know what to do. Suleika took this burden seriously, so as not to let him down. Privately, she admitted to me that she didn't have any idea what could draw in the herds of Day-Glo people who trooped down Thames Street all summer, their hands and faces and hair all sticky with ice cream and Dell's lemonade and homemade fudge from the Fudge Factory a few doors down. She and I didn't actually want them at Bad Joe's, but still we played along with Biagio's dreams. While the two of them talked, he would echo her thoughts by shaping the air with his scarred hands. The scars came from blue crabs that had pinched him while he was digging oysters down at Mackerel Cove in Jamestown. Biagio sold the oysters at the bar. When the dagger-shelled crabs lunged from the mud and clamped onto his skin, Biagio would take a pencil from his pocket and let the crab's other claw pinch that. This would release the pressure on the claw that was pinching his hand. He would hold the crab behind its legs, set it back in the water, and watch the beautiful swimmer sidestep away, claws raised, until it vanished in the rippling shadows. He could never seem to figure out why it was so often just the three of us. "Maybe if I sold fudge with booze in it," he would say. Then he would be back to square one.

I sat down at the table just as the Wurlitzer started to play the wrong damned song, as usual—"When the Swallows Come Back from Capistrano." The jukebox decided for itself, like a crotchety old man, just what it wanted to hear. It seemed to like the Capistrano song, and played it all the time. The worn-down record hissed and hummed. "Look," I said to Suleika while both of us ignored the record, "don't get how you get." I lowered my head almost to the level of the table, trying to stare up into her face. If I could get a smile out of her, we would be all right for another day. "We can talk," I said.

"No, we can't," she said, and did not smile. "That's the trouble."

You don't mean it, I thought. I saw you looking at me. I know you haven't given up on us yet, even if you want to make it seem as if you have. "I was thinking," I told her at last, when my thoughts had grown quiet enough for me to speak. What I wanted to say was that I had been crazy before. I would put away the past. I would ask her to marry me. I would tell her I was sorry for the waiting. I had been meaning to say this for so long now that I even had the pattern of my breathing figured out for when I spoke, except I never got any of the words out of my mouth. It was as if every time I came close, a hand clamped onto my throat, choking back the words.

"What did you want to talk about?" she asked. Her fingers worked masochistically through the brassy strands. She would focus and focus, blinding herself like an old lacemaker lost in the minute details of each thread, until she was exhausted.

The bell over the door clanged and a man walked in. Suleika and I raised our heads. We stared at the stranger, not to make him feel unwelcome, but because we weren't expecting to see anyone. There were times of day when almost nobody walked into Bad Joe's, in the afternoon limbo when it was too late for lunch and too early to be drinking except for the drunks. For a moment, we both forgot the fact that we might be breaking up.

The first thing I noticed about the man was that he was bald, and not bald because his hair had fallen out, but because he shaved his head. His skull was finely sculpted beneath the polished skin. His strong hands might have been fisherman's hands, except he was wearing a suit and his face was not weathered the way the skin of fishermen is like saddle leather after decades of riding the waves off Nantucket.

The man ordered a plate of Biagio's famous oysters.

"Who is that guy?" asked Suleika.

"I don't know," I answered. "Why should I?"

"You're staring at him."

I hadn't realized I was staring. I wanted to ask the man how he had found out about Biagio's famous oysters. They weren't on the menu. Biagio didn't even have a menu. Then I remembered that it was painted on the side of the building in letters so faded that I saw them every day but had forgotten they were there.

Biagio hoisted a bucket of oysters onto the bar. It was an old tin bucket and the oysters were resting in seawater with ice cubes floating in it. Biagio seemed eager to please. I imagined it going through his head that this might be the first of a whole new type of customer, one who had held out on him until now. He dug his hand into the bucket and fished up a gnarly-shelled oyster. "These are the best you'll ever eat," he said confidently. He held it out for the man to see, twisting it back and forth in the soft light as if it were a mighty diamond. Water dripped from the oyster onto the bar. "I choose each one and they are the best." Then, becoming flustered at the man's unchanged expression, Biagio said again, "The best!"

The bald man took out a large handkerchief. It was red and white, with a pattern. He began to mop up the spilled water on the bartop.

"You don't have to do that," said Biagio. He pulled his own, less impressive handkerchief out of his pocket.

The bald man still mopped up the water. "I'm going to wipe it up before it stains."

He made me nervous. I didn't know why. I was suddenly uncomfortable sitting there at that flimsy table. I felt sweat on my forehead. I looked at Suleika, as much as if to ask, You see why I was staring?

She nodded at me. She felt this strange man's trespass as much as if he had laid his hand on the small of her naked back.

Biagio stuck out his hand to the man. "Biagio," he said. It really did sound like Bad Joe.

The bald man nodded. He looked at his own hands for a moment, as if to check that they were clean enough for shaking. Then he seemed to decide that they were not and he laid his palms flat on the counter. "My name is Mudge," he said.

"Mudge?" Biagio raised his eyebrows. "I never heard that name before."

"Yes. Mudge," said the man, in a way that made me think he had gotten into fights over people making fun of his name. I figured, looking at him, that he won most of those fights. "Samuel Mudge."

S. Mudge, I thought. Smudge. That man's name is Smudge. I would make a joke about it later to Suleika.

"Where are you from?" asked Biagio.

"I'm not from here," he said. "That's for damn sure." His voice was deep and scratchy, as if his lungs were filled with smoke.

"It's too hot in here, Biagio," I announced. It was at this precise moment that the jukebox stopped playing, so my voice sounded idiotically loud. As soon as I had spoken, there was complete silence in the room. Biagio and Suleika turned to look at me.

Suleika was embarrassed. I could hear it in the way the air caught for a second in her throat.

"It's hot," I said again, but softly.

"No, it's not," said Biagio. "Is anyone else hot?"

The bald man Mudge was watching me now, as if he had not seen me before. Slowly he turned back to his oysters.

I slumped back in my chair. The cream from the coffee was a bitter slickness in my throat. "Well, it just seems stuffy to me," I said quietly to Suleika.

"You're out of your mind," she said. She never did let me off the hook.

"I'm with the trade commission conference up in Providence," Mudge said to Biagio. "I'm taking a break for the day. Thought I'd come down here and see the sights."

There was some international trade commission thing at the state conference center. It was a big deal and had been in the papers for a while. The Rhode Island Chamber of Commerce had campaigned for the commission to be held here as much as if they'd been campaigning to host the Olympic Games. It was all about opening up new trade routes between America and the former East Bloc countries: East Germany, Hungary, Romania, Bosnia, and so on. I hadn't paid much attention to it.

The bald man and Suleika and I watched in silence as Biagio shucked the oysters with a little blunt-tipped knife. Salty juice poured down his wrists. He lined up the half shells on the bar. "You want hot sauce?" asked Biagio.

"Not at all," said Mudge. "Lemon instead."

Suleika leaned across to me. "That's got to be the first person in months who's come in here and ordered oysters who actually knows how to eat them."

It made me jealous that she was praising this man who had so obviously snubbed me just because I thought it was too warm in the room.

Mudge raised the cup of shell to his nose, closed his eyes, and sniffed the oyster. Then he squeezed a drop of lemon juice into the shell, slid the oyster into his mouth, chewed once only with a sliding, grinding revolution of his jaw, and then swallowed.

I could taste those oysters going down his throat. The faint sweet saltiness of them, as if I knew even the particular texture of the water in Narragansett Bay, a connoisseur not only of oysters but of the oceans in which they lived. I tasted the cringe of lemon at the corners of my tongue. Saliva welled up in my throat.

Mudge turned away from the bar and walked over to a table. He sat down and, with his big-knuckled hands, he smoothed out the red-and-white-checked tablecloth. "I'll eat the rest here."

Biagio set the remaining oysters on a big white plate and brought them over.

Suleika clicked her tongue. "A man of the old school, I'd say."

"Oh, shut up," I muttered. "Now you're doing it on purpose."

Mudge turned his head toward us. He knew we were speaking about him.

We nodded back, clumsily. Then we looked away. "Well, I think," said Suleika, "that he should be allowed to eat in peace."

"Fine with me." I bounced the heels of my palms on the table. I was thinking that perhaps the man bothered me because he looked rested and well fed and as if he didn't do hard physical work for a living. I was thinking that if my life had gone the way I'd thought it would, I might be more like him than I was now. I knew what he would be thinking of me, in my work clothes and my heavy rubber boots with the heels worn down. Being out-of-doors all through the year had rubbed creases into my skin. I looked older than my age, which was thirty-two. I wanted to tell him that I had an engineering degree, that I spoke a couple of languages, that I wasn't who I seemed to be. But then I would have looked even crazier. "I'm good to go," I said to Suleika, trying to sound jolly, but all I could think about was that fact that we were only getting a reprieve. Nothing had been solved.

I was getting ready to stand up when someone else walked into the bar. It was a man. With him came a peculiar but unmistakable static, as when the air seems to crackle before a bolt of lightning strikes nearby. I knew this without having seen anything, because my back was to the door. A second later, when he walked by, I noticed that he was tall and heavy-shouldered, with short dull black hair. The man wore a brand-new blue-jean jacket. I didn't catch sight of his face, but I smelled a familiar smell. Musk. Cedar. Leather. Some crush of these together in a cologne or a soap. At first I couldn't place it. All I felt was a reeling in my head as my mind searched for the source.

The man in the too-blue jacket walked over to Mudge, who had seen him the moment he came in and had stopped eating his oysters. Mudge sat back slowly and set his hands flat on the table. "Now what?" he asked impatiently.

11

The man spoke to Mudge in a low voice.

Slowly, Mudge folded his arms. A calm and measured gesture of defiance. "That's right," he said. "So?"

If my instincts had been working, I would have taken Suleika by the hand and led her fast and quietly out of the bar, out into the street, and then we would have run for it. But I was so pre-occupied with the business of Suleika and me that I just sat there.

Mudge talked to the man in the jean jacket, jerking his chin upward to make a point. Whatever they were talking about irritated Mudge. I still couldn't hear exactly what they were saying. If they had been shouting, I might have felt a little safer. But they were both saving their energy. It looked like the beginning of a fight, but not the pointless bar punch-ups I had seen here before.

Suddenly, the man in the blue-jean jacket snapped his fist in the air.

I felt myself stop breathing. I thought for a moment that he was going to take a swing at Mudge. Then I noticed that there was a knife blade in his hand. Shock surrounded me. It muffled my nerves. I could barely register what I was seeing.

The man smashed the blade down through the top of Mudge's head, and only when he let go did I see that the knife was in fact one of the heavy spikes Suleika and I had been using to repair our nets.

Mudge tried to stand, but instead he slid sideways out of his chair. He tipped onto the floor and then tried to stand again, his legs thrashing on the tiles. The top of the spike stuck from his head. The rest of it was buried in his skull. His face was splattered with blood. It arced in crazy lines across the smoothness of his skin, as if his flesh had cracked like broken pottery. Mudge set one hand on the table and tried to raise himself up, but the table pitched over on top of him. Oyster shells crashed on the floor and skittered away.

Biagio was still standing behind the bar, a roll of white receipt tape in his hands. It unraveled slowly down to the skid-proof matting where he stood.

Mudge was on his hands and knees. His eyes were wide and dazed. His head hung down. Blood tapped the floor in a fast Morse code of droplets. He breathed in sucking rasps. He seemed to be trying to hawk something out of his throat.

The man reached down, hooked his fingers deep into the flesh around Mudge's jaw, as if he meant to break the bones of Mudge's face. Mudge's mouth was open and bloody, the teeth outlined in scarlet. The man held up Mudge's head until the tendons stretched in his neck. He grunted deeply, then let go. Mudge's face smacked against the floor among the shells.

I had no sense of how long this had lasted. Ten seconds, maybe less. I waited for the man to turn on us. It seemed inevitable. I felt powerless to prevent it.

Instead, the man walked unhurriedly toward the rear door, the jacket still shop-creased down his arms. He stepped out into the parking lot that separated the dockyard from Bad Joe's. As he swung the door open, sounds of the docks flooded into the bar—the groan of machinery and the whirring crunch of the chipping machine that loaded ice onto the trawlers. It was then that he swung his head around and stared straight at me. His eyes were the color of cigar smoke—gray and bottomless, the way smoke baffles depth. I knew those eyes. A prickling, burning sensation spread out from the center of my chest, like a sweep of fire across my ribs, curving around until it reached my spine. Then he was gone.

Suleika breathed in sharply.

Biagio was still holding the receipt tape. Tears were running down his face.

Adrenaline cascaded through my body. I ran out into the parking lot and dodged among the empty freight trucks. I didn't see anybody. The man had disappeared. Even if I had caught up with him, I would not have known what to do next. I just had to

13

be sure it was him. For a long time, I stood out in the lot, not knowing what to do next. I was sweating as if I had a fever. Then I heard Suleika call my name and I ran back into the restaurant.

Suleika knelt beside the body, her knees stained with blood. She had two fingers pressed against the artery in Mudge's neck, checking for a heartbeat. The dead man's eyes were wide-open, domed red and shiny.

I went behind the bar and dialed 911. I reported the killing, repeating it several times. The operator didn't seem to understand what I was saying. "Are you sure?" she kept asking. Biagio sat at my feet, coiled in his tape of receipts, weeping in sharply exhaled breaths. People out in the street still had no idea what had happened. They continued to shuffle past in a procession of pale legs, brightly colored T-shirts, and baseball hats. I shut the door, flipped the sign to CLOSED, and pulled down the blinds. In the milky, gloomy light, the nets that spanned the wall seemed to close even tighter around us.

I went out and slumped down on the pile of nets that Suleika and I had spent the afternoon repairing. A minute later, Suleika came out and sat beside me. Wind off the bright water blew her hair across her face.

I reached over and touched her bare arm.

Suleika recoiled, as if my fingers had been freezing against the warmth of her skin. She stared at me as if she had never seen me before. It lasted only a moment. Then she took hold of my hand.

I heard police car sirens. With them, I felt chaos riding toward me, swirling through the streets like water from a broken dam. I cannot place inside the scaffolding of words how it felt to recognize those eyes. They belonged to a man I thought had died in my arms years before, at the start of the journey that had brought me to the place where I am now, with a different name and a different life, on the other side of the world.

Two

I was born Paul Wedekind, in the city of Dresden in the former East Germany, on February 23, 1964.

At the age of twenty-four, I was taken from my studies in engineering at the Senior Technical College of East Berlin and was drafted into the East German army. This was part of my compulsory national service. I was sent to Afghanistan. Before I left, I was recruited by the Stasi, the East German secret police, to file reports on a childhood friend of mine named Ingo Budde. He was suspected of drug trafficking and had also been posted to Afghanistan. The Stasi believed he had been supplied through contacts in the Russian military and that he would continue to operate his business in Afghanistan. The Stasi had had no luck tracking his operation in Berlin. They believed that military intelligence, the GRU, would have a better chance in Afghanistan.

Filing those reports on Ingo Budde was the most shameful thing I ever did. At the time, however, I was won over by talk of duty and patriotism and the threat that my life would be ruined if I didn't do my part.

Several months after our arrival in Afghanistan, Ingo and I were taken prisoner by the mujahideen when we were driving through the hills outside the city of Kabul. I was released a few days later in a prisoner exchange. Ingo was left behind in the Afghan camp. I got sent home, but the Stasi wasn't finished with me yet.

I had officially been listed as killed in action. Taking advantage of this mistake, the Stasi transferred me to GRU/KGB, which set me up as an operative in the United States. It was either that, they told me, or be sent back to Afghanistan. To me, that was no choice at all. I was not allowed to contact my friends and few remaining family members. They attended my memorial service at the same time I began training twenty miles down the road at the Tatianawald military installation.

At Tatianawald, I was given a course in marine diesel engineering. I was told that I would travel to America posing as a West German. I would be working for a man named Mathias Hanhart. He and his wife ran a small shipping business. I wasn't told exactly what work I would be doing once I arrived. When I traveled, I carried on me papers and correspondence confirming that the job had been arranged through mutual friends.

I would be what the KGB call an "illegal resident." It meant that I was to be without the cover of diplomatic immunity. Diplomatic staff, even if they are KGB or Stasi, can claim immunity if they are officially attached to an embassy. They can be moved out of the country without prosecution. However, if the task is not one that can be performed by an embassy employee, the operative must take on the more dangerous role of an illegal.

Whatever the job, I believed that my time in America would be brief. I was classified as a short-term operative. At one point, my case officer at Tataniawald mentioned that he didn't expect it to last more than six months. I would do the work, whatever it was, return home after the killed-in-action "mistake" had been acknowledged, and get on with my studies. Until then, I felt lodged somewhere between life and death, living a rented existence in the shell of an invented man.

WHAT I DIDN'T understand, as I walked out of U.S. Customs and into the high-ceilinged, flag-draped hallway of Logan Airport in Boston, was that I could never go back to the way I'd lived before. All that remained of my old self were the hauntings I would soon experience. I thought I had come to terms with the things that had happened to me in Afghanistan. Since I so rarely returned there in my thoughts, I assumed it was because I had put it all behind me. I was wrong about that too. The nightmares were still out there, working their slow path toward me.

The arrivals hall echoed with talk and the rumble of jets leaving overhead. The brightly colored flags wafted in the air-conditioned breeze. I reached into my pocket and pulled out my photo of the Hanharts, Mathias and Suleika, who I had been told would be there to meet me. In the photo, the couple seemed so cheerful and harmless that I couldn't imagine what covert work they might be doing. I looked down at the photo, then up at the crowd, struggling to refocus. Faces around me started to muddle. God, I thought, there's no one here to meet me. I had the number of an Aeroflot office in New York City to call in case of emergency. I was supposed to ask for Sacha. How is it going to look, I wondered, if I make a panic call only half an hour after I've arrived in the country?

A short while later, I found Suleika. I first noticed her by the way she stood. Just like in the photo I had seen, she kept her hands folded across her chest and her back straight, conscious of her posture, as if she had been taught to walk with a book balanced on her head. Suleika was standing near a telephone booth, away from the cluster of people outside the customs exit. Despite the confident way she carried herself, Suleika looked lost. I wondered whether I was the one supposed to guide her through this unfamiliar place, instead of the other way around. I walked over, said my name, and shook her hand. "I almost didn't recognize you," I said. I was nervous. Afraid my English would fail me.

She looked at me as if she didn't understand.

"The picture." I held up the snapshot. "You. In the picture. I almost didn't . . ." My voice trailed off.

"It's an old picture," she told me.

We walked through the veil of air-conditioning and out into the summer heat. It billowed from the car roofs, merging brown and dirty with skyscrapers on the horizon. I had never felt heat like this before. It was the same as when you open an oven and your head is too close to the door. It sucked the breath out of my lungs. Sun peeled away layers of cool among my clothes until it reached my body. Then it tapped sweat from me until I was soaked.

I expected to meet her husband, Mathias, at the car. I had it in my head that one of them would have had to stay with the machine because this was America and if they didn't stand guard, someone would steal it. When I saw the parking lot, it took away my breath even more than the heat had done. Thousands of cars fanned out across the asphalt. Long before I got to engineering school, I had spent hours studying magazine pictures of automobiles available only in the West. This was the first time I had actually seen any. I wanted to go around to each car and pop the hood and take a look at the engine. It was the first of hundreds of things I would later take for granted but which at the time amazed me. In my first five minutes in America, I ran out of superlatives to describe what I was seeing.

We found her rusted blue Chevrolet Camaro. I touched the roof and burned the tips of my fingers. Mathias wasn't there. I figured he was still at work.

Suleika reached into her jeans to find her keys. "I have to tell you something," she said.

"Yes?" I asked. I gritted my teeth in the heat.

"My husband is dead." She continued to search through the jangling keys, as if unsure which one would start the car.

I felt dazed. It was not so much out of sympathy, because these people were still strangers, as from wondering what would happen to me now. "I'm very sorry," I told her.

Her eyes flicked up at my face and then quickly down again. She explained in a mechanical fashion, as if she had pared down events into the skeletal language of a telegram, that Mathias had died of a heart attack the week before while working on his fishing boat. Then she started to tell me things she thought I already knew. Their cover was running a trawler out of Newport, while their operative function was to rendezvous with Russian submarines and ferry people back and forth from the mainland. These were people who, if they went through standard commercial routes, would be picked up by American authorities, or who were carrying material too bulky or sensitive to be smuggled through ordinary channels.

I had thought they ran a whole shipping company. A small one, sure, but not this small. I had imagined tankers, freighters, a fleet of fishing boats perhaps, not just one little trawler. I wondered if the reason I had not been given a complete picture about the job was because I might have refused to go.

While Suleika talked, I saw her misery. Sadness hovered around her like the heat rising off the cars. She looked down at her dirty tennis shoes. "I didn't inform anyone about his death," she said.

"Why not?" I asked. Only now did I really begin to feel sorry for her.

"What will happen to the boat? The whole operation?" she asked without looking up.

"I don't know," I said. "Who are the other crew? Can't they do his job?"

"I'm the other crew!" She squinted at me, head tilted to one side. "It was just the two of us. Didn't they tell you anything?"

I shook my head. "Not enough, I guess."

"It should have been three people working the boat, but we weren't allowed to take on another crewman without approval. Mathias kept making requests for someone to help. Particularly with the engine. He'd been trying to get someone to take my place. I wasn't trained to work these boats, you see. Not like him. He fished on one of the big Polish factory ships. Mathias told me about how he used to come in sight of the American coast when he was on the factory boat. And he always wanted to run his own boat. It didn't matter how small. The chances of it over there"— she shrugged—"it would just never have happened. And then he gets this offer. Go to America. Get his own boat. Work for them every once in a while, but mostly he'd be his own boss." She shook her head. "Can you even imagine?"

What about you? I wanted to ask. Did you want to come here? But she was talking too quickly for me to interrupt.

"I'd carry on by myself," she said, "but it's too much for one person. It's not safe. I can't tell you how many times I've almost gotten myself killed. The people on the dock thought we were crazy having just two people."

I stood there, simmering in the cheap suit I had been given when I left East Germany. The cloth smelled of another man's sweat. A fishing boat, I was thinking. Jesus.

"We've been running the boat for several years now," said Suleika. "Now that you're here, there's no need to cancel the operation."

"I don't understand." I raised my voice to a shout as a jumbo jet howled through the sky above the airport, climbing steeply into the shimmering blue. "I don't see how."

"I can continue to work on the boat. I know how to run it now. I'll train you, if you aren't trained already."

"Just in engines," I said. She wants to stay here, I thought. This is her chance to leave and she's not taking it.

"In fact, we have to leave port tonight. We have a pickup in a couple of days. You can train on the job."

"You know," I said cautiously, "it's not my decision what happens to the boat. Or to you."

She sighed. Her eyes were glassy with fatigue. "No," she said, "I don't suppose it is."

I watched a group of people emerging from the arrivals terminal. Their family clustered around them, smiling and talking quickly. They squabbled cheerfully about who should carry the suitcases. I remembered what I had been taught, about not getting too comfortable here and about remembering that I was the enemy. But when you think about being the enemy, you imagine people coming at you, like the Afghans had come for me, their faces smoked with war. But how can you see them as the enemy when they are just getting on with their lives? How can you bring yourself to be an enemy to them?

We were still standing there in the heat.

"I'll do as much as I can," I said, "to keep things running."

"Will you?" she asked. Her voice was suddenly hopeful. "Have you ever been out on a fishing boat before?"

"No." The vinyl duffel bag slipped out of my sweating hand. It thumped onto the tarmac. Even then, I felt drawn to this woman. Already we shared secrets as profound and dangerous as if we had been having an affair. "Perhaps there's no need to say anything," I said, "at least not right away. There are reasons we could give. Maybe they don't care how it gets done as long as it does get done."

She reached across and tapped me on the arm and smiled. Then she picked up my duffel and threw it into the trunk, on top of a collection of musty-smelling clothes, odd shoes, welding rods, and crumpled paper balls that had once been hamburger wrappers. "This was his car," she said.

We drove south on Route 95 with the windows down, passing through the suburbs of Boston and along the wide, straight, fast-traveling road toward the city of Providence.

"So," she asked. "How did you get involved in all this?"

I glanced at her.

"Don't tell me if you don't want to," she said, "but I'll know if you're feeding me some bullshit cover story."

It was risky to say too much, but I also knew she was no Party member. Her husband might have been, but she wasn't. So I told her the truth—how I had first been recruited into the Stasi by a tutor at my university. The man was named Markus Knaf. He helped me with my physics. It was a subject in which I had never showed much promise, but without it, I couldn't get my degree. Markus was a popular figure at the university, with a kind of roving commission to help teachers and students. He was in his fifties, with thinning curly gray hair and a gentle voice. Even though he was not overweight, everything about him seemed somehow rounded. I got the impression that he had never exerted himself physically. He wore a tattered tweed jacket and was always polishing his thick glasses on his tie. I was slightly embarrassed at needing a tutor, but I couldn't help liking the time I spent with him.

Markus and I met each week in his cubicle office in the Physics Department. It had bare wood floors and rippled glass windows. Figures seen through them looked half-formed, like dreams of people. Around the time we started meeting, an old friend of mine named Johann Bader was found dead of a heroin overdose in a local bar called the Cyclone. The needle was still in his arm. A strip of rubber cut from a tire inner tube was knotted around his bicep. I heard his face was blue by the time someone found him. Bader had been doing drugs for a while, although I didn't know it at the time. He dropped out of classes and got thin. He didn't hang around with me anymore. I didn't know the signs of addiction. Everybody went through phases of being antisocial. I was just waiting for Bader to snap out of it. His death shook me up. I felt as if I had abandoned him, as if I might bear some of the responsibility for his dying. I had never even seen drugs before, although people often talked about them. The question around the campus was where he had gotten the stuff. The police came in with sniffer dogs to go through the locker rooms, but nothing turned up.

"It's a terrible shame about Bader," said Markus. He had a low murmuring voice, which you only heard if he was talking directly to you.

I had my notebooks laid out, ready to get down to work. At the mention of Bader, a picture of him popped rudely into my mind, as if someone had just shoved a Polaroid shot in front of my eyes. I imagined him dead, with stiffened blood tinting his skin and bulging in his veins.

"Doesn't anybody know who sold him the drugs?" asked Markus.

"I haven't heard anything," I answered.

"A person who sells drugs"—Markus shook his head—"can bring down a whole community. They prey upon the weak. Wouldn't you like to see a person like that taken away?" He scanned me with his watery eyes.

"Of course," I said. I had no idea where to start looking for a drug dealer.

Markus lifted a packet of Russian cigarettes from his pocket. They were the Papirossi type, with maybe an inch of tobacco at the end and a cardboard tube instead of a filter. A lot of the older people smoked them, a habit acquired in the days when Russian cigarettes were the only kind available. On top of the box he set an old brass lighter. His study was always thick with clouds of smoke, each quick movement stirring the blue haze. "You know," he said.

"Know what?" I asked.

"Well . . ." He rolled his shoulders as if his bones were aching. "Well, you know there are some of us who have our suspicions about who it could have been."

Slowly, one after the other, I closed my notebooks. Who was "us"? I wondered. I never thought of Markus as being part of an "us." It was always just Markus. Just "him."

In his low voice, Markus went on to accuse Ingo Budde, who was my best friend at the engineering school.

"What makes you sure it's Ingo?" I asked. I was astonished, less by the accusation than by the fact that Markus should take this kind of interest. The reason people regarded him so highly was that he never spoke badly of others; besides which, he was from an older, harder generation, which kept him apart from us in other ways.

"Look," he said, "it would take a long time to explain. But I have good reason to believe this is the truth."

"What are you going to do?" Even as I asked this, the whole idea seemed absurd to me. Ingo was a strange boy, and he did sell a few things on the black market, but he was friends with Bader.

"Actually . . ." said Markus, "actually, I want to talk about what *you* can do."

And here was where I started to understand. Markus was about to show his true face. He was with the Stasi. The more I thought about it, the more sense it made to believe so. He was mobile. He had no ties. Everybody liked him. The Stasi was a fact of life. They were not always seen as bogeymen, the way people remember them now. Even if they were vigilant to the point of paranoia, they were, after all, looking after the security of the state, whose enemies were no less vigilant. It was only luck that would keep a person from any kind of contact with them, and nobody had any luck. The Stasi were so completely woven into our society that they left us with the same feelings as people who have

24

cancer in their families—it seems foolish to hope you can avoid contamination.

But still I wasn't sure. You can't just ask a member of the Stasi if he is a member. You have to be more careful. And if you are asked to work for them, you can't refuse straight away. You have to think of what the Stasi has on you, where your family is, if any of them have done anything wrong, or if you have done anything wrong that the Stasi might know about. You have to see in an instant where you fit into the entire matrix. Do you care about getting a good job? Do you want to live the life of an outcast? All these things. My mind began to race.

"I happen to know," said Markus, "that Ingo is about to be called up for military service."

This did not come as a surprise. Eighteen months of military service was mandatory for all men and the postponement granted for advanced studies was not entirely effective. If you were called up, you could plead your case, but I never knew of a single instance where it worked and, anyway, the pleading would go on your record and you'd find yourself being sent to a nuclear-waste disposal site or some other lousy place.

"As it turns out, you are also being called up." Markus settled back into his blanket-draped chair and tucked his hands into the pockets of his tweed jacket. "Your grades are good, but not good enough to prevent it. Sometimes, if a student has maintained a truly brilliant average in classes, some argument can be made to detain him. But with you . . ." Even though his voice was gentle, I could feel the cruelty in what he said. I knew it was deliberate.

Slowly, I lowered my head. Unless I managed to get an engineering post in the army, I'd never be able to make up for the lost time. All the years I'd put into my training as an engineer would be pretty much useless.

"It's not so bad," said Markus. "You'll get an engineering post."

"How do you know?" Those were privileged positions in the army. Hard to come by.

"It's almost certain, Paul. It is arranged."

I turned to him. "Why?" I asked. "What have I done to deserve this?"

"You are both being sent to Afghanistan," he said, by way of answer.

I raised my hands to my face. "Oh Christ," I mumbled. It was bad enough to get posted over to the Russians, but the absolute worst was to get mailed down to a war zone and fight for the Reds.

Markus got up and walked behind me. He rested his too-soft hand on my shoulder. "You should be pleased about the engineering post. Pleased and, I should say"—he slapped my shoulder—"grateful."

"I am grateful," I said quickly, feeling uncomfortable with the way he was standing behind me. "It's just that this is all very sudden."

"In terms of your gratitude," he continued, drawing out the word, "you are fortunate in that you have an opportunity to help."

"Help whom?" My muscles were tense where his hand continued to rest.

Finally, Markus let go of my shoulder. He walked around to face me. "Your country," he said. "Yourself. And if it turns out that your old friend Ingo is innocent, you will help him, too."

I stared at Markus. I understood completely now. I would inform on Ingo. I would become a small-time agent, like thousands of others who never thought it would happen to them but who found themselves suddenly and hopelessly tangled in the great Stasi web. The alternative to doing as he asked was so obvious that neither of us needed to mention it—I would not get the engineering post. I would be sent to some chemical weapons battalion using experimental weapons, and if I survived that without

26

dying of a mysterious illness, I would return home to find myself without any hope of decent employment. The Stasi could screw up your whole life with the snap of a finger.

His pinprick irises showed no hesitation. "You see me differently now," he said quietly.

"What did you expect?" I asked him. I stood and fetched my coat from its hook. I began loading my books into my little briefcase. "Why not send someone else?" I threw this out in one last useless gesture. "There have to be others better qualified."

"You are one of the few people he trusts. Perhaps his only friend. That makes you qualified."

"And you expect me to betray this trust?"

"You're a sensible boy," said Markus. "Besides, what kind of trust are we talking about here? The trust of a murderer? What strange values you have, Paul! Weren't you friends with Bader?"

"Yes," I said.

"What would Bader think of you now, if he were still alive? What would his parents think? That you would protect the drug dealer who murdered their son? Is it that you approve? Do you condone what Ingo does?"

"Of course not," I stammered. I was frozen by the harshness of his words. "But Ingo is also my friend."

Markus exploded. "Your friendship with Ingo is canceled!" He spent his breath in a shout and gasped before shouting again. "Are you now going to deny help to the system that has cared for you and kept you safe your entire sniveling life?" He whipped off his glasses and began to polish them nervously with the end of his tie. He kept his chin tucked down into his neck while he tried to calm himself. His whole body was shaking. Eventually, he stopped twitching. His fingers stopped rubbing the silk against the lenses. "Are you going to help me or not?" he asked quietly.

Suddenly, he had gone back to just being Markus again. He was asking me to help him, not Bader or Bader's parents or the state. He and I both knew that there was little point in his asking

27

me again. I would go, and he had known all along that I would go because I had always been too obedient for my own good.

I think about the way I was back then, so serious about everything, in my clunky shoes and my father's old submarine coat made of heavy gray leather, running everywhere with my books in a black plastic briefcase with a fake crocodile grain. I didn't know how to relax. I never slept. Each task I did, I thought of not in terms of the individual job but in terms of my whole life. It seemed to me I woke each day and stared in the face of my own mortality. I worked so hard that about once a year I would fall apart and would have to sit in my room with a blanket pulled over my head for a couple of days, just breathing. As soon as I was rested, I would run straight back to my classes and keep on running. I always did what I was told. I didn't know how to get around rules, and I had been taught by my father that it was shameful even to try.

A few months after that meeting with Markus, I was on my way to Afghanistan.

AFTER I HAD finished telling the story to Suleika, she was quiet. I wondered whether I had said more than she wanted to hear. But then I saw her smiling.

"You remind me of myself," she said. "I had one of those plastic briefcases."

"From a plastic crocodile," I said. I looked out at the billboards filing past. There was the Marlboro man, sitting on a white horse and lighting up a cigarette in the middle of a prairie at sunset. "I'm sorry about your husband," I told her again. I meant it more this time.

Now she looked across. "We were happy. It was no marriage of convenience to make our cover more believable."

"An operational fictive marriage," I said, the terminology still fresh in my head from Tatianawald.

"Well, whatever they call it, that's not what it was."

We stopped at a rest area somewhere on the Rhode Island–Massachusetts border. She parked and cut the engine. Then Suleika and I went back to the trunk, which she popped open. She shifted my suitcase to one side, revealing the dirty, flattened clothes that I had seen before. They must have belonged to Mathias. "Take your pick," she said. "We have to get you into some different gear." She rubbed the cloth of my lapel between her thumb and first two fingers. "Pretty tacky stuff. You'll draw attention to yourself in this."

"They gave me these to wear. I wouldn't normally . . ." I smelled again the stranger's sweat sunk into the material of my coat and diesel exhaust from trucks plowing past on the highway.

She nodded at the bubbling tangle of undergrowth. "Go in there and take these clothes with you. Change into them and we can get rid of the others."

I picked out a pair of old jeans, some white socks, a pair of old work boots with the toes curled up at the ends, and a blue sweatshirt with YALE printed in white letters on the heavy cotton. In the months that lay ahead, I would wear the sweatshirt so often that a rumor went around the docks that I had actually gone to Yale. I walked into the bushes, smelling the heavy moisture of the undergrowth. Birds ranted in the leaves above me. When I looked up, I couldn't see them. I stripped and pulled on the rust-stained clothes. They were pocked with holes from welding sparks. The cold dampness of the cotton made the skin crawl on my ribs. The clothes had a certain smell to them. Later, I would know it as the smell of the boat. Diesel, salt water, fish, the piercing metallic freezer-burn reek of ice, and the smell of the nets. Before long, this smell would be so much a part of my life that I would barely notice it. It would work its way into my pores and my hair and into every piece of clothing I possessed. To me, this would become a comfortable smell, but just then it churned my stomach.

29

Before I stepped out into the parking lot again, I stayed still for a moment, eyes shut, sweat trickling down my face. Everything had been such a rush for so long that I just needed to be still for a moment, to make the world stop spinning around me.

"There you go," said Suleika when I reappeared again from the bushes, the cheap suit tucked under my arm. The crumpled jeans and sweatshirt draped awkwardly on my body. She leaned against the car door, hands tucked behind her back. "Now you look like you belong."

"I belong!" I shouted jokingly, and raised my arms over my head. I dumped the bundle of my old clothes in an orange wire garbage can. "And that's where those belong."

"Really," said Suleika.

That evening, I stood at the end of Gunther's dock in Newport. My feet shifted on the rough planking of the dock boards. I smelled the oil-scummed water at low tide, mixed with a breeze coming in off the ocean. Mooring ropes grumbled against their pilings. There was no one else around. The fish house and the loading ramps stood empty. The place is so familiar to me now that I can hardly recall what it felt like to be there for the first time. But just then, I felt as if I had come to the end of the known world.

Behind me, Suleika loaded supplies onto the deck of the trawler. She said I wouldn't be much help because I didn't know where everything went and that she could do the loading more quickly by herself. While she finished the job, I sat on the dock and watched the sun go down through the girders of the Newport bridge. The sky was a banner of orange and purple and pink, sliced through by the chevrons of gulls and held up by the sticks of sailboat masts in the harbor. Waves slapped at the barnacle-crusted pilings.

The boat was called *The Baby Blue.* It had a coat of sky blue paint on its hull, with a white trim around the edge. I had not yet seen the engine, not yet set foot on the boat, but what I saw of it

30

seemed hard and unforgiving. Everything was made of steel, except the net, whose nylon web seemed to have a harshness of its own. The other boats were the same—iron slabs with porthole windows like the beady eyes of the fish they caught, and no visible signs of comfort for the crew. Already I had a growing respect for Suleika, because she had not only survived in this world but was also prepared to go out into it with someone as inexperienced as myself.

The Baby Blue left port on the midnight tide. I stood beside Suleika as she steered past moored boats and the stone hulk of a place I later came to know was Fort Getty, past the Newport mansions, their crystal chandeliers lit and visible through arching windows that looked out over the water. We slid by the Brenton Reef light, a strange boxlike structure built up on stilts. I heard the warning buoys clang their bells in the rocking waves thrown by our wake. Soon the last pinprick lights of land seemed to tip into the water. We were left alone with the hammer of the engine. All around us, the blue horizon merged with the blue-gray of the sea. Suleika and I stayed silent. Darkness crowded the boat. I understood how a person could go mad out here alone. I wondered how she had managed to stand it for so long.

"Are we picking someone up or are we fishing?" I asked to break the silence.

"Both," she answered. "We have to come back with some catch or people will wonder what we've been doing."

"How about the engine?"

Suleika turned the ship's wheel. Its wooden pin handles were greased black from years of use. "That engine is a piece of junk," she said, "and if you can keep it running, you will be more of a magician than an engineer."

"Can we buy another?"

"Not unless they gave you the money to pay for it."

"But what if it breaks down? Don't they see the value in making sure you have decent equipment? If we miss the rendezvous because of a faulty engine, it would cost them more than just money."

"They don't think that way. Don't ask me how they do think, but I can tell you how they don't."

That was the end of the conversation. There was only one thing to do next. I went down into the engine room, feeling heat latch onto me as I swung open the iron door and descended the ladder from the deck. The engine looked like a giant beetle trying to shake itself loose from its mountings. Even the sound, a persistent angry drone, was like the song of a cicada. It seemed to be running all right, but I spotted oil leaking from several of the gaskets and there was the sweet smell of antifreeze. The bilge water glimmered with rainbows of oil and the greenish yellow glow of the antifreeze. I thought about the engines on their concrete blocks back at Tatianawald and regretted my contempt for their dilapidated state. They looked new compared with this rumbling monster. In fact, the whole boat seemed so precariously put together that it seemed safest just to leave everything the way it was. Wait for something to break before fixing it.

Sweat stuck my trouser legs to my calves and my shirt against my shoulder blades. I began to feel nauseous from the fumes, so I climbed up onto the deck and sat on the ice hatch, watching the stern of the boat bob and pitch into the waves. I felt seasick. It was as if my stomach had been filled with oil. I went inside the cabin, thinking this would help, but closing around me in that cramped space was the reek of diesel, cooked meat, and old cigarette smoke from Mathias. The dead man's smell was sunk into the wood and the ratty Hudson Bay blankets in my bunk. A while later, I threw up. I kept throwing up all night, holding on to the cables and heaving over the side into the waves. I would feel better for a few minutes and then I would go back to feeling sick. By morning, I was all right again.

Suleika cooked me breakfast. She said I had my sea legs now.

It felt so good to be released from this constant violent clenching of my guts that it was almost worth having been sick.

"You've never been to sea before, have you?" she asked.

"I always wanted to," I said.

She laughed. "You don't have to be polite."

"I'm not just being polite," I insisted. "It's in my family. It's in my blood." I explained how my father, who died when I was ten, had been a U-boat captain in World War II. During the war, he ranged across the North and South Atlantic, up into the Arctic Ocean, and along the Mediterranean coast, where I imagined him to be like Odysseus, cruising the wine-dark sea. One story he told me had remained more vividly in my thoughts than all the others, and normally I kept it to myself, but I felt the need to offer up some part of myself to Suleika so that she could see I trusted her.

I told her that my father's U-boat had been on patrol in the Gulf of Mexico in the summer of 1942. One evening, when his submarine surfaced, he looked through binoculars at a white strip of beach and some low-lying scrub jungle. It was the Yucatán peninsula. As he looked along the coast, he caught sight of a huge ruined fortress made of white stone. It perched at the edge of the rocks, overlooking the sea. Later, he searched his charts and discovered that it was in fact the remains of a thousand-year-old Mayan temple called Tulum. He used to talk about going back one day, but he never did. For him, it remained always beyond the horizon, as it was meant to be, always just the memory of a place he had seen long ago in the sunset.

I wished I knew a place like Tulum. I carried the image of it like a talisman inside me. It held the promise of something that was not clear to me, something miraculous, which I might never be allowed to see and which might remain, as it had for my father, always a mystery, always out of reach.

At school, I was taught that my father and all men like him who fought on that side were savages. Their names were not used,

33

of course, but their role in the war, my teachers said, made clear the line between civilization and the beast. I thought a lot about the savage who was my father.

I used to have nightmares about him down in the submarine. It seemed too much like a coffin. When I asked him how he could stand it, at first he did not have an answer. It was as if he'd never thought about it. But then, after a moment's reflection, he said, "In the beginning, it was easy for us. We were unstoppable. We called it the 'happy time.' We called ourselves the 'Glory Boys.' This was before convoys and sonar. When those things came along, it all went bad for us. Sometimes, when the depth charges were exploding all around us, we would start singing. We would sing at the tops of our lungs. Those songs were what kept me going through the worst of it."

"Which songs?" I wanted to know.

"Love songs," he told me, "always love songs."

I knew one of them because he often sang it to himself. The name of it was "Erika." I thought of the U-boat men, the Glory Boys in their leather coats and white turtleneck sweaters, singing with the trancelike rhythm in their chests. I imagined their voices, echoing like whale song miles across the ocean and up into the lonely blue-black sky of a North Atlantic winter twilight, the only proof that they were still alive.

"That's why the sea is in my blood," I told Suleika when I was done.

She made no comment. Later, when I knew her better, I would know that this was a sign of her approval. But, at the time, I was embarrassed to have confided so much.

Early the next morning, half-blinded by the sunrise off the water, we sent down the net. It unraveled clumsily into the waves. Soon there were only the two lead cables, coiled rusty iron as thick as my wrist, shuddering as they marked the path of the net. When we hauled it back an hour later, Suleika clicked her tongue at the poor catch, but I had never seen so many fish in one place.

They tumbled across the deck, slapping and wriggling, all brown backs and white underbellies. We gathered them into different baskets and then I handed them down to Suleika, who laid them out on beds of ice.

I took off my shirt as the sun warmed my back. The closeness of the night disappeared now and the vastness of the ocean was not threatening. When Suleika sent the net down again, we took a break. We sat on the ice hatch, squinting in the sun. I could tell she was glad to have company, but it was a thing that could not be mentioned without some awkwardness.

Over the next few days, as I walked the deck and fussed over the temperamental engine of *The Baby Blue,* I was not filled with any great desire to push forward a political cause. All I had was a feeling of being involved in something far larger than I was able to understand, perhaps even larger than the people who had sent me here could grasp. I was wrapped up in events that had a life of their own, created by people but no longer controlled by them. I was not afraid of being caught. I felt brilliantly camouflaged by the strange clothes I wore and the papers that I carried. I didn't know enough then about how operations are really compromised, and what happens to those who are discovered. Agents aren't usually unmasked by faulty disguises. More often, they are betrayed by people they might never have met but who know of them and of the operation. Who sell what they know or give it away to save their skins when they are themselves betrayed. If I'd known then how things worked, I would have been terrified. Instead, I felt a sense of freedom—the greatest of my life so far.

I slid into the rhythm of the boat. The rust began to disappear as the net dragged across its deck and I was no longer plastered with the fine orangy powder that reminded me of dried blood. *The Baby Blue* seemed somehow gentler out on the waves, like a penned animal released into its natural habitat. I was no longer afraid of every sharp edge and corner. The engine's rumble became constant and reassuring.

"Did you leave a lot of people behind?" Suleika asked me late one afternoon. She had just finished explaining to me how her Russian father and German mother had split up shortly after she was born. She showed no sign of regret at being separated from them. Instead, she seemed more saddened by the fact that she did not miss them at all. She was lying on the deck in between haul-backs, cooling herself in a puddle of seawater that had gathered in the dented plates of the deck. The puddle soaked her T-shirt and her back. "Did you?" she asked again.

"I was thinking about that." I sat on the ice hatch, looking down at her.

She twisted her neck around until she was staring right up at me. "And what's the answer?"

"I did leave people behind, but it doesn't matter." I thought about Ingo then. I missed him, but being here or being there did nothing to change that. I smiled down at Suleika. I was smiling at her pretty eyes. Everything else was out of focus. I realized I was in trouble with this woman.

I wondered how it might have been if Mathias were there. Living so closely together on the boat might have brought jealousy skulking from the corners of the little bunkroom where we slept. Another man would have sensed how I felt about Suleika, even if Suleika herself didn't know. It was not something I could hide. It seemed to me as if each of my thoughts were projected on the bunkroom walls like some old movie. I could not help looking at Suleika as she pulled off her clothes before climbing into her bunk. I saw the pale smoothness of her legs and the muscles of her calves flexing as she balanced while she took off her jeans. The arches of her feet as she climbed into her bunk. The narrows of her wrists as she shook her fingers through her hair before lying down on the pillow. Her hair. Her hair was killing me. On rainy days, she would tuck it back into her oiler jacket. Then, when we were back inside, she would take off the jacket and wring the water from her hair over the sink, because the rain would go down her collar. She wound it into a cable of twisted, shining wheat and brass and she squeezed the drops from it, showing her fragile neck, not reddened by the wind and sun. And when she let it go and shook it out, I watched the sweep of it across her shoulders. If instinct ever made her look in my direction, my eyes were staring someplace else by the time she had her focus.

I didn't think about anything happening between us. Soon, I thought, I will be gone. It would only hurt the both of us to be together and then to be apart. She was just my fascination. I enjoyed her company and she was beautiful, and it warmed me to see her beauty in among the steel and rust and the sinewy splatters of fish blood that made up the boat. I didn't try to reason it all out. There was no time for double-meaning conversations. Out on the water, I discovered, everything is what it is. The life is too hard and too dangerous for it to be any different. That is why people who go to sea fall in love with it. Because what you do is who you are. And what you think becomes known, whether you say the words or not.

Suleika was not the only reason I found it so difficult to fall asleep in the tilting, rocking bunk. The sound of *The Baby Blue*'s engines reminded me too much of being in a plane. Each night as I sank down into sleep, I tried to purge it from my thoughts. But again and again I returned to the image of myself on a Soviet military transport aircraft as I flew out to Afghanistan.

AFGHANISTAN. I USED to say the word to myself over and over, until it was no longer a word but part of an incantation. For me, it became as much a place in the mind as on a map.

The first I saw of the country was the mountains of the Hindu Kush as we flew over them at twenty thousand feet. It occurred to me that nobody, neither the Russians nor anyone else, was going to be able to chase an enemy out of those hills. I looked at the other passengers, strapped into their seats so that they couldn't lean forward more than a few inches. From the creases on their foreheads, I knew they were trying to digest that slick feeling in the guts of leaving safety and coming to a place where nothing was safe. Nothing. Not safe even to imagine safety.

Only Ingo Budde managed to look calm. While the rest of us were just thinking about staying alive, Ingo had plans. To Ingo, the hills and snow-cup valleys that filed away beneath us were the greatest opportunity of his life. Having disobeyed orders to keep his straps tight, he slouched down in his seat with his legs splayed. He waved his heavy-booted feet back and forth as if he were taking part in some bizarre sit-down cabaret. He looked around with slightly jerky movements, the way a baby looks around, but his gaze always returned to me. Then he would smile and clap his hands together and shout, "Well, Paulie!" over the constant thunder of the engines. That was his name for me. He never called me anything else. "Well, Paulie!" he shouted again.

"Well what?" I wanted to ask.

Ingo was a tall, ungainly man. If you only knew him from his speech and went to find him in a crowd, his breathless, high-pitched voice would have you looking for a nervous little person, frail and sickly. But Ingo was six foot five, heavy-boned and powerful. His shoulders and ribs jutted out awkwardly, as if his skeleton didn't match the frame of his body. His black hair had no shine to it and the skin was smudged dark under his eyes. He was not handsome, but that never seemed to bother him. Romance was not on Ingo Budde's mind. He was a man of different opportunity.

Everybody knows someone like Ingo Budde. From an early age, he bought and sold everything from Western clothing to cigarettes to alcohol. Ingo was the man you saw if you needed something you couldn't find in the shops, which amounted to most things. With Ingo, it was always business first. If you knew that and accepted it, he could be good company. There were a lot of people who despised Ingo, but there was no one, not even among those who gossiped most fiercely about him, who had not at one time drunk liquor bought from Ingo or coveted the Nike high-tops that he produced miraculously, as if he had in his grasp a genie's lamp and an unlimited number of wishes.

I wished Ingo had been a stranger. It was my bad luck that I had known him so long. But it didn't really matter. Everyone remembered Ingo. He carried in him, like a static glow, the stubborn faith that his luck would always hold. Built into this philosophy was the idea that nothing came free. He would ask a favor and be sure to pay it back, even if you didn't want him to. But when he did something for you, there was always a bill to be paid. Debt and payment. Ingo kept a tally and enforced it. He could not stand to have someone take advantage of him. He treated his own life, reputation, and wealth as if they were something to be laid down like a card and gambled upon. The fact that he was prepared to do this at a moment's notice set him apart from almost everyone else. He would risk everything. It was his weapon, this disregard of the basic instinct to keep safe.

"Well, Paulie!"

There he went again. Why the hell was Ingo so happy? Didn't he sense what kind of trouble he was in? It made me sick to watch his lips split open and to catch sight of his tobacco-stained teeth.

I couldn't bring myself to return his smile. I was ashamed that the Stasi had picked me to keep an eye on Ingo. As much as I resented Ingo for getting me sent down to Afghanistan, I couldn't help feeling some sense of obligation to our friendship. It wasn't because of any one moment in the years we had spent growing up together. It was the years themselves, the fact of so much time. I tried to remind myself that there was still no concrete proof of drug trafficking against him. If it turned out he was guilty, that might be different, but for now I hoped that I would one day look back on this as an unpleasant but necessary job I once did a long time ago for my country. Perhaps I could even help Ingo. I had the opportunity to judge him fairly, which others might not do.

My job was simply to keep an eye on him and to make weekly written reports, which I would then hand in to the camp commander, Col. Alexander Volkov. Other than Volkov, I had no case officer or contact with any intelligence service while I was in Afghanistan. I wanted to dispense with all the secrecy. I just wanted Ingo to admit what he had done, if anything, and get this over with. I didn't think I had the patience to go through with it. The fact that it was secret did strange things to my head, compartmentalized my world into secrets and nonsecrets, until after a while I realized that these two worlds were not separate at all. Once I had a reservoir of lies, they seeped into everything, until my whole existence became a kind of lie.

I told this to Suleika, not the whole thing at once, but soon she knew it all. I was confessing things to her that I had never told anyone else. It helped me to talk about them, and the fact that our acquaintance seemed so temporary made this easier.

We fished for two more days. Then it was time to meet the submarine. We had a respectable catch and Suleika said there would be no questions asked at the dock if we came home with half our hold full. We made one final drag of the net before sunset. When the fish were basketed and iced below, I climbed out of the ice room and found Suleika sitting on the sun-warmed deck. She sat cross-legged, as if she were meditating. Her hands rested in her lap. She looked out of the gap at the stern where the net usually payed out into the water.

"Damn," she was saying. "Damn. Damn."

I sat down next to her. The breeze tousled my hair. I didn't ask her what she meant. She would tell me if she wanted to.

"I hate this part," she said. "It never seems to go right. There isn't one time it has gone smoothly. I can fish. I can run this boat. But I just don't seem to have the knack for picking people up off submarines in the middle of the goddamned ocean."

I said nothing. I followed her gaze out across the unbroken

plain of waves. Somewhere below it was the submarine, prowling the deep like the biggest shark in the world.

As if in gratitude for my silence, Suleika slowly put one arm around me.

For the first time, I felt the warmth of her body. I didn't put my arm around her in return, although I wanted to. I didn't push her gesture past what it was meant to be. Besides, I was afraid that holding her even in one arm would take from me what little self-control I still possessed.

Suleika steered the boat toward our rendezvous coordinates, which she measured on the red digital letters of our loran location finder. The sun went down. A clear burn of purple filled the sky. The water turned black. Again I felt a sense of things closing in around us. With the lights on inside the cabin, the night seemed to press itself against the glass. It slithered under the door and coiled under the bunks and the grime-spotted stove with its cross-bars over the burners to keep the pots from tipping with the motion of the waves.

"Let me show you something," said Suleika.

We went down to the engine room. Just behind the steel-runged ladder was a toolbox. She moved the box aside and lifted a trapdoor. She had to use a screwdriver to pry up the lid because the door was flush with the rest of the deck. Under the trapdoor was a radio with Soviet navy markings and a date of 1980. I knew immediately what it was. I had seen these things in training. It was a burst transmitter, with a fixed frequency and a short range. In order to prevent messages from being picked up by anyone listening in, you first typed out your message on the little keypad, fed it into the transmitter, then pressed the send button, which transmitted the message in a single burst, too fast for anyone to decode it, or track its source and destination. The radio was fitted into a waterproof tublike container whose lid was rimmed with grooved rubber strips. We crouched over the radio. Slowly, with ceremony, Suleika reached down and switched it on. The transmitter made a swishing sound as the static came to life. The red battery switch blinked at us slowly, like the eye of a tiny, patient dragon.

"I have to stay down here," she said. "Starting at"—she looked at her watch—"seven P.M., we transmit every five minutes until we make contact."

"What if they don't show?" I asked.

"They'll show. They may be cheap, but they're punctual."

I left Suleika sitting before the little altar of her transmitter. She held her fish scale–flecked Swatch in her hand, waiting for the time to make contact.

I stayed in the cabin, running the boat around in circles to keep us in the designated area. The loran coordinates were two rows of four numbers, one on top of the other. The last of the four digits changed and changed back with each shift of our position. I sat in the captain's chair, which was upholstered in red vinyl.

When the electric clock above the cabin entrance nudged against seven o'clock, I turned off the cabin lights and looked out into the dark. The wind had picked up. More than once, I mistook the black crests of waves for the conning tower of the sub. I didn't know how big it would be. I had never seen a real submarine before.

Seven-thirty. Nothing.

At eight o'clock, Suleika stuck her head into the cabin. The ends of her hair were damp with sweat from the heat of the engine room. She didn't look at me. She just looked at the loran.

I had the coordinates right.

"Shit!" she shouted, and disappeared again.

After a few minutes, I hooked the wheel into its retaining ropes, which were two greasy braided loops. Then I set the engine at idle and walked out of the cabin. I crouched at the entrance to the engine room door and looked down the ladder to where

Suleika sat. She had taken off her shirt because of the heat. The cloth lay in a soaked and crumpled heap beside her, looking like one of the rags we used to wipe blood off the fish knives. Her bare back was streaked with sweat. I saw the bumps of her spine and a birthmark under her left arm. She typed out her message and then pressed the send button, which fed the message to the machine. At the correct moment, she hit the transmit button and the red light on the keyboard flashed from red to green and then back to red. Just then, she sensed that someone was watching her. She looked up and saw me. Her fingers slipped off the little keyboard on the transmitter. "You know how it is," she shouted over the rattle and hum of the engine, "when you're working for someone and they don't think they're getting their money's worth, so they jerk you around and make you sweat for no good reason? I bet that Russian sub captain is just sitting there with a Papirossi stuck in his mouth and waiting until he gets me really pissed off. I bet it's because I'm a woman." It was only then that she became aware of her nakedness. She bent back down over the radio. "Go away, you!" she shouted.

I went back to the cabin, unhooked the braids, and took hold of the wheel. The ocean currents tugged at my forearms as I maneuvered us back on course. I thought about the bumps of her backbone, about how it would feel to run my finger down them.

It was nine o'clock. I was starting to get nervous, remembering one of the rules that I had been taught at Tatianawald: Never wait for a contact who doesn't come on time. But I wasn't in charge, so it wasn't my choice what we did. It took off some of the pressure, but didn't make me any less edgy. I settled back into the familiar numbness of doing exactly what I was told.

At 9:15, Suleika walked into the cabin. Her hair hung in straggles down her face. She had her clothes back on, the shirt buttoned up to the throat, as if to compensate for the way she had been earlier. "They sent me a message. They haven't surfaced yet. They're going to send up a flare so we can locate them."

43

"Can't they just locate us with their sonar?"

"Mathias told me that these subs have two kinds of sonar. One of them is passive, which means that they just pick up sounds that are out in the ocean. The other is active, which means they send out a ping and the sound bounces back off whatever's there. They could probably find us if they sent out a ping, but they say it's too risky because those sounds can be heard for miles. So they're sending up a flare. It's risky, because these flares are pretty huge and any surface vessel in the area would see it, but it's less risky than anything else. They're sending up the flare through one of their vertical tubes and as soon as they do that, they're going to surface, so go out on deck and watch for it. I'll stay down with the transmitter. If you see the flare, get back to the wheel and head toward it." Then she was gone again, cursing her way down the ladder.

I walked out to the bow. The boat rolled lazily in the waves. With my seasickness gone, I wondered how I would ever get used to the solidity of land again. I held on to the rail and breathed in the salt breeze, which filled my lungs with a strange emptiness.

I heard a noise. It sounded like someone slamming a heavy door under the deck where I stood. My first thought was that Suleika had gone looking for something in the bow compartment, which was a mess of broken tools and rope and things to be fixed.

Then I saw something strange in the water. It was as if I had stood up too quickly. Wierd flickering lights seemed to dance all around me. Then this flickering took shape. I looked over the side and the water was filled with streaking pale green-yellow sparks. Some of these sparks broke the surface. They rode off across the water, hissing and trailing thick white smoke. The sparks twisted around under the water, leaving phosphorescent paths down into the black. It was all so beautiful and unexpected that at first I couldn't understand what I was seeing. By the time I figured out that this was the flare and that it had slammed against the underside of the boat, the sparks had already extinguished, leaving only a cordite-smelling fog to drift past my face and vanish out across the waves.

The next thought through my head spun me around as if I had been struck. The sub was surfacing directly below us.

I lunged for the wheelhouse door and jumped inside. I jammed the heel of my palm against the engine throttle. The motor howled and the whole ship groaned as we lurched forward. I didn't bother to remove the straps from the wheel. I grabbed the two puffed orange life jackets from the peg next to the wheelhouse door and ran out to the engine room ladder.

Suleika had tipped facedown on top of her radio. She picked herself up, more confused than angry. The engines thundered around her. Then she saw me. When she noticed the life jackets in my hand, she jerked her head around as if to look for water pouring in through the hull. She grabbed the greasy rungs of the ladder and began to climb.

I turned to face the deck and saw the white boil of our wake make a ragged tear through the waves. As I watched, the bulbous nose of the sub rose from the water. Then came the conning tower with its black-and-white zigzag-painted periscope tube. In the darkness, it was hard to make out what I was looking at. If I hadn't known the sub was surfacing where we had been only a few seconds before, I would have perceived the huge machine not as something solid but instead as a huge absence of light. I had no idea the sub would be this large. I heard no sound over the drone of our own engines. It looked primitive and dangerous and alive, like something that should have become extinct a million years before. Nothing on earth could have persuaded me to climb down inside that creature.

Suleika jumped from the engine room as if she had been catapulted up the ladder. She landed on the deck on her hands and knees. She was gasping for breath. Then she looked up and caught sight of the submarine. "Oh my Lord," she said.

I ran back into the wheelhouse, wrenched off the wheel ropes, and spun the boat around. We tilted hard into a wave, which struck our side and sprayed across our deck. Suleika took over the controls. She had a bloody nose, which she wiped on her wrist. The blood smeared through the fine blond hair on her forearm, matting it down.

"I'm sorry," I told her. "As soon as I saw the flare—"

Suleika laughed. "I'd rather have this than end up marooned on that fat slab of steel." She brought the boat to an idle and we both went out on deck. *The Baby Blue* lay alongside the sub at a distance of about three hundred feet. From where we stood, we could see the whole length of the submarine. Both ends of it trailed off into the night. From the conning tower, a bolt of light punched into the misty air. The light flickered as people climbed up on deck. Their silhouettes were the same blind man's black as the rest of the machine. They shone a searchlight at us.

I turned away from the brightness that scratched at my eyes. As I turned, I caught sight of Suleika. She was frozen in its glare. Her skin looked almost blue, as if she were a statue chipped from old glacier ice. The light swung the length of the boat, then returned to where Suleika and I stood, holding us in a blinding cone in which everything seemed to be melting away. Then the light went out. Orders were barked from the conning tower down into the sub.

Two men climbed from the conning tower down onto the deck. They carried a large bundle, which they laid out like a blanket. Then they both stood back and the blanket inflated into a rubber dinghy. Now a third man climbed from the conning tower. He moved clumsily down onto the deck. From his silhouette, I could tell he was overweight. His shirt had come untucked and a noose of a tie hung from his throat. He carried a small suitcase with him down into the life raft, which by now had been lowered over the side with one of the crew. The fat man babbled and the other man told him to shut up. He sat in the dinghy, clutching the suitcase while he was rowed toward us. The dinghy slid in and out of the waves, tilting back dangerously with the weight of the fat man.

"Here's our boy," said Suleika.

"You know him?" I asked.

"Oh yes." She nodded without looking at me. "A regular customer."

After what seemed like a long time, the rubber dinghy nudged up against the side of *The Baby Blue*. The fat man tried to stand, but the Russian crewman knocked him back down with the flat of his boot. "Stay put!" he snapped at him.

It took all the combined strength of Suleika and me to heave the fat man onto our deck. As I hooked my elbow underneath the man's armpit and strained to lift him, I caught sight of the crewman. He wore a black turtleneck sweater and a black wool cap. The only flesh I could see was his face and his hands, which gripped the little dinghy oars. These parts of his body seemed to drift around in the darkness.

"You're new," he said to me.

"Just got here," I replied, and nodded hello.

"Hell of a job." He dipped the oars in the water, keeping himself steady as he bobbed beside our boat.

"I'd rather do this than go down in that thing over there." I jerked my chin at the sub.

"When you're down there," he said, "it's not like you're under the water."

"Well, what is it like, then?" I asked him.

"It's like you're traveling through space."

A voice yelled at him from the sub, calling him away. Without another word or a gesture of good-bye, he set out across the waves.

The fat man gave Suleika an enormous sweaty hug. "My darling, I am your knight in shining armor!" Then he spun around to me. "You're the new man!"

47

"Yes," I said, "I'm—" I was holding out my hand to greet him, when he started talking again.

"A coffin!" he said. "Three weeks in that coffin!" He rolled his neck like a man gone out of his mind. "I have waited a long time to breathe good air again!" He raised his arms. The bulbous sag of his stomach hung down, the belly button only a smile in the flesh.

"What did you think of it?" Suleika asked me. "The submarine."

I turned to look at the black machine. "It's like riding through space," I said. It didn't matter if she heard me. I was thinking about what the crewman had said. This thing, which first seemed like a monster, now possessed for me a kind of beauty. The light from the conning tower dipped and vanished. The sub moved slowly forward. It slid beneath the water. I thought of the fish and the hungry sharks and then of the great sub swimming down among them, and the crewman with his vision of the galaxy far below, inside the pressured dark.

The fat man was Jeremiah Liedke. He had gone this sub-to-trawler route many times and seemed like an old family friend to Suleika, who fixed him a two-pound can of Dinty Moore stew in the galley. Liedke didn't pay much attention to me, as if I was not yet worthy of acknowledgment. He concentrated on spooning up the stew, too quickly to taste anything but the warm saltiness it left in his mouth. He was old enough to be my father, tall, bald on top, and with graying hair cut short like the spines of a hedgehog on the sides. His eyes were a handsome brown and he laughed with them in the soft light of the galley. He spoke English with an American accent, and what he seemed to have learned fluently was the American of someone who didn't speak the language properly himself.

While he ate and caught up on news with Suleika, I went down into the engine room to check up on the engine. Revving it hard and suddenly, the way I had done, could have blown out some of the oil seals. When I came up again, Liedke was sitting on the ice hatch. He was wheezing a little, since the food was still working its way down. He pulled a flask out of his coat pocket. The coat had ripped under his armpit. The sleeve lining puffed out and made him look like an enormous burst cushion. He looked at the tear, then looked across at me. "Can you sew?" he asked.

"No, sir," I lied as I shut the engine room door. I could have sewn that rip up nicely. I'd learned to sew and darn and patch so well in Afghanistan that I could have made a business out of it in civilian life. But this man was testing me.

"What a pity," he drawled, looking away, as if there might be someone else on deck that he could ask. "I would have been grateful."

I sat down next to Liedke, on what little space remained on the ice hatch once he had established his rump. "I'll try and earn your gratitude some other way," I said.

He held up a flask. "I filled this in a bar in Leningrad twenty-four days ago. I've been saving it for the moment I arrived here safely." He offered me the flask. *"Davai,"* he said. "Go ahead." The screw top dangled on a tiny chain, tap-tapping against the silver sides of the flask.

I drank some of the vodka. It was warm from the heat of his body. "You're not safe yet," I told him, and handed back the flask.

He sighed noisily as the vodka burned his mouth. "That may be."

"I take it you heard about Mathias."

He nodded but stayed looking straight ahead. His eyes looked unfocused. The vodka purred in his brain. "He was a strange one. He had not learned civility." He wiped sweat off his forehead with the side of the flask. Drops ran down the silver. "But I suppose that's not a thing you need out here. He was a savvy man, though. You'd have to be savvy to keep a wife that pretty, don't you think?" He didn't look at me as he said that last part, but he was testing me again. He had already measured up my situation and all its possibilities.

I gave him no reply, which was probably what he expected. For a long time, we sat on the ice hatch while Liedke finished his flask and got a little drunk because it was a large flask, and he did not share more than one sip. He kept his suitcase on the deck, tucked between his ankles. It was a ratty leather case with two combination locks. His shoes were city loafers, which squelched because they were filled with salt water. I saw how easily he would have blended into the crowd at Boston airport, vanished among the other overweight, pasty-faced businessmen who look as if they have eaten too much meat in their lives.

"Suleika says you died in Afghanistan," he said. "At least, in a manner of speaking."

"Yes," I told him. "I had a very nice memorial service." I made a joke of it, but the mention of Afghanistan dropped me back into that place as hard as if I had been pushed from a great height and landed on my hands and knees in the mud of Diaghilev transit camp.

INGO AND I had not been in the camp more than an hour before he began laying the groundwork for his black-market business. Diaghilev, on the outskirts of Kabul, was a city of tents in a dried-out riverbed, entirely surrounded by razor wire and mines. Helicopters were airborne above the camp twenty-four hours a day. At night, their searchlights staggered up and down the wire. Red-brown cyclones of dust were stirred up by the prop wash, thrashing any tent flaps that had not been tied down.

As soon as we were shown our tent, Ingo immediately disappeared across the compound. I stayed behind and unpacked my things. It was dark in the tent, except for sharp stabs of the bright khaki light that shone through cracks in the canvas. Carefully, I lifted out my socks and trousers, smelling the last scents of home as they sifted out of my duffel bag and into the hot air. Just as I was beginning to wonder what had happened to Ingo, the tent flap was flung open and he stepped in with another man. Or rather, the other man seemed to have been shoved unwillingly into the cramped and musty-smelling space.

"Say hello to Colonel Volkov!" boomed Ingo. He turned on a small battery-powered lamp that he had just procured from somewhere and revealed the thin face of a Russian officer in a neatly tailored uniform. On his face was a mixture of bewilderment and annoyance.

Volkov was my contact down here. I wondered if Ingo had found out somehow. But over the next few minutes, I realized that Ingo was only trying to ingratiate himself as quickly as possible with the rulers of the camp. I stood up sharply and saluted. "Sir, I am Lieutenant Wedekind," I said in a loud and respectful voice.

Volkov returned the salute without enthusiasm. He watched me carefully. He was also wondering.

Ingo laughed as if we had just shared a joke. "This is my old friend Paulie. You won't get much talk out of him. Paulie is a thinker." Now Ingo turned to me. "And Colonel Volkov here runs the camp. He's top dog."

Volkov and I stared at each other, barely an arm's length apart. We were both aware of the barrier that our ranks made between us. I understood it from one glance at Volkov's face. He would endure it this one time only, and then only because I was with GRU. He was probably afraid that I had been sent here to file reports on him, as well.

Ingo didn't like the quiet. He fished in his duffel bag and brought out a dark green red-labeled bottle of Danish aquavit. He held it out to Volkov. "A present for you," he said.

Volkov peered at the bottle. "Aquavit?"

Ingo tipped the bottle one way and then the other. "It's yours," he said.

"I cannot," Volkov mumbled, glancing at me. "I regret I cannot . . ." He could probably imagine me typing out the word in my report: *a-q-u-a-v-i-t*.

"No such word as *cannot*!" Ingo stuffed the bottle into his hands. Then from the folds of his combat jacket, he produced a red-and-white carton of Marlboro cigarettes. He set them on top of the bottle, which Volkov now cradled like a baby, unable to release it even in his fear. Volkov stared at the carton. Then he stared at me, as if I might at any second pull out a gun and arrest him.

I shrugged. I started to sweat, trails of it raking my back. How was I supposed to know what he should do? I wasn't writing any reports about him, after all. The only person I was supposed to watch was Ingo. I was hardly going to hand damaging reports to the same person I was incriminating.

Volkov seemed to make the same equation in his head. "Are those Marlboros?" he asked, a faint smile twitching on his upper lip.

"Absolutely," said Budde.

Volkov stood there for a moment, looking down at his shoes as if searching for a place within the confines of his close-cut uniform to stash the bottle and the cigarettes. He departed from the tent five minutes later, carrying the loot and squinting worriedly into the blinding dusty light. Ingo grinned and watched him go. Then he pulled back the tent flap and enclosed us in the weak glow of our battery lamp.

"Damn, that was a risk, Ingo," I said quietly, hanging my head with exhaustion at everything that had been said and even more at what had not been said these past few minutes.

"A risk. Maybe. But that man will remember me now. He owes me." Ingo sat down and put his arm around my shoulders. "This is a great time for us, my friend. It is the test of who we are. It's like your father used to say, Paulie. Now we get to be the Glory Boys."

The next thing Ingo did was something only he would have done. He went to the quartermaster, who handled all the supplies for Diaghilev, and he bought the uniform he had been issued. Normally, you didn't have to pay for your own equipment unless you lost it. You could wear it out or break it, but as long as you returned the article, it didn't cost you. Ingo bought it, anyway— the boots, the trousers, shirts, quilted winter combat jacket, helmet. And when he was done paying for that, he bought the tent in which we were staying. He bought the footlocker, the lamp. He got receipts. So that when he returned to this place we would call home, for God knows how long into the future, it was his. It wasn't that he liked the stuff. He just needed to own it. He told me it gave him a strange feeling to walk around in borrowed clothes and sleep in a borrowed bed. He couldn't quite explain it. The whole idea just bothered him.

"Doesn't it bother you, Paulie?" he asked, plucking at the dappled camouflage of my jacket. "That it's not yours?"

I pulled a face. "Well, Ingo . . ." I said cautiously. The truth was, I hadn't even considered it, but I didn't want to tell him that. I felt as if I ought to have a reason all worked out. "It won't be any use to me when I get home. I mean . . . camouflage?"

"But what about now? You're alive now, aren't you? You're living out your life. Do you think you are in some kind of suspended animation when you're here? Because you're not! Time is going by."

"But what does that have to do with whoever owns my clothes?"

He looked blank-faced at me for a long time. Then he slowly shook his head. "You don't get it, do you, Paulie? They will never own a piece of me, not even"—he glanced down—"the bed I'm sleeping in." He had forgotten to buy the cot. He went back to the quartermaster and paid for that, too, and got a receipt.

Over the next few weeks, while I set about organizing the repair of an endless stream of vehicles that made their way out of the hills of Afghanistan, Ingo began the task of networking himself into the Russian population. Within days, he had established what goods were wanted, who would buy them and for how much, and he set about bringing them in. How he arranged this, I never found out, but soon he began receiving crates labeled "Automotive Parts," the contents of which he kept secret. Markus had been right about one thing: Ingo's contacts were military and most likely Russian. There was no other way he could have set himself up in business as quickly as he did. Ingo rarely came around the motor pool except to pick up these shipments when they arrived. When he did show up, he wore his overalls out of deference to the dust rather than to his membership in the army. They were by now *his* overalls, and they must have been the cleanest ones in the country. He checked over the shipping manifests and made off with whatever was addressed to him. He was polite to everyone. He handed out cigarettes. Nobody got in his way. He never offered me a word of explanation or apology for his absence from the labor pool. Any work that might originally have been assigned to him had long ago been transferred to someone else. And because I knew Ingo, I knew better than to call him on it. To expect manual labor out of the man was an idea bordering on the absurd.

Volkov did remember Ingo, just as Ingo said he would. He remembered Ingo as "that caviar- and vodka-dealing pig who has turned my camp into a fucking bootleg supermarket." But by then, Ingo did have Volkov in his pocket. Or at least he had Volkov too nervous to do anything about the various deals that were going on. Volkov looked to me like the caricatured White Russians that I had seen in history books, the corrupt hedonists of imperial days. With his thin legs, narrow face, and pale, reedlike fingers, I could imagine him at some tsarist ball—one-hundred-candle crystal chandeliers and a chamber orchestra and the clip-clop of boots and dainty shoes across the marble floor of the Winter Palace. I saw him in a blood-red tunic, brushing a dab of sour cream from his mustache after eating a salmon-caviar blini and laughing at some joke told to him in French. Volkov seemed to know what images he conjured up in other people's minds, so to hide his family's real or imagined past, he surrounded himself with the trappings of a Soviet fanatic. He had a bookshelf crammed with volumes of speeches given by the great Communist leaders. He hung propaganda posters on the wall of his office hut, instead of more sensible maps of the region. Most often, I could hardly see these posters through the haze of his tobacco smoke. Nothing but Marlboros now, of course, all compliments of Mr. Budde.

The vodka that had previously circulated in the camp, most of it homemade, became so worthless that I actually used it as windshield washer fluid for the trucks. We had run out of the correct fluid and there was no point using water, because it froze up in the hills. The vodka worked well as a substitute, except that it smelled up the trucks.

Corruption at Diaghilev was a psychological necessity. It was, for most of us, the only escape. The simple fact that it was illegal made it important. People had to rebel against being sent to a place that, before they arrived, most could not have found on a map. Volkov and I never discussed this, but we both understood it. I simply handed him a report at the end of the first week, in which I wrote that Ingo had begun a small black-market operation within the camp, and then I listed the kinds of things he was selling, which did not include the drugs that GRU was looking for. I feigned ignorance of everything else. I did not give the names of anyone he dealt with or where the goods came from. I figured that if I proved to be a bad informant, they could always fire me and I wouldn't mind that. I even left the envelope unsealed so that Volkov could read what I'd written and see I'd said nothing about him.

He did read it.

The following week when I dropped off my letter, he looked

up from his desk with such a smile on his thin face that he appeared a decade younger. He offered me a cigarette. Then he offered me some vodka, which he had chilling in a bucket of ice. The ice came from the morgue refrigerator at the far end of camp. You had to scrape it off the walls. The morgue was the coldest place at Diaghilev and its generator made a steady hum night and day, so that on the few occasions when it shut down, the silence it left behind became unnerving. I smoked the cigarette, the first of hundreds I would puff away over the coming weeks, and drank the vodka, green-tinted steppe grass–flavored vodka from Soviet Georgia called Tarkhuna. We didn't mention my reports or the unspoken understanding we had reached. But Volkov made it clear to me in other ways that I would have no trouble from him.

"If you ever need a break," he said, "from all that out there"—he waved his hand to take in the camp outside the flimsy walls of his office—"you should feel free to come in. Sit. Read a book. Have a smoke. No one will bother you here. I will tell my secretary. If I am gone, this place is yours. I give this privilege to very few people." He glanced at me.

"I am grateful," I said stiffly, as befit the occasion. "And I will continue to be grateful."

Volkov's attitude toward Ingo was a completely different matter. He and Ingo made an uneasy peace. Volkov had been here long enough to know the difference between what people were expected to withstand and what they really could endure. He had agreed not to interfere with Ingo's dealings, not for huge bribes, but, as I learned from rumors in the camp, in exchange for Ingo's promise that Diaghilev would stay free of drugs. Drugs were where Volkov drew the line. This meant not only that Ingo couldn't sell drugs but also that he had to keep others from selling them, too. It was a strange logic, but one they held to absolutely. A man could smoke his lungs into porridge and be drunk as long as he could still function, and he was not punished for it. But with drugs, they would haul you off in chains and break your shins with a hammer. As a result of the diligence with which Ingo kept up his end of the bargain, I never saw any drugs at Diaghilev. Other camps were infested with hashish and heroin. To accomplish his bargain, Ingo made powerful allies of people in the camp who had no respect for rank and among whom seniority was earned only through the willingness to make threats and carry them out. It was another of Ingo's fine talents.

This left me in an awkward position. I knew for certain that Ingo was not dealing drugs. He dealt in almost everything else, which would certainly have been enough to get him locked up in a basement in the KGB's Lubianka jail in Moscow and tortured until the KGB had whatever confessions they needed. But my job, as I saw it, was only to report on his drug activity. This gave me some control over my own conscience.

There were times when I actually enjoyed myself, which is hard when you are living in a tent in the middle of Afghanistan. I had my space and often that was all I needed. My space was the motor pool, where I fixed the temperamental leviathan engines of the T72 tank and fiddled with the poorly designed fuse boxes of the Poltawec armored car. As was the nature of places like Diaghilev, too much was going on for anyone to care what anybody else was doing as long as they got their job done. I struggled to find a little time each day in which I could relax and just think. There were moments of great contentment, when I raised my head from the tangle of wires and pipes on some engine and spent a few minutes watching the sun set over the snowy mountains in the distance.

It was two months before I received any mail, and then the only letter I got was from my uncle. He rambled on enthusiastically about his latest love affairs, which were as similar and doomed as all his others. I could have written it myself. The letter made me realize how little I had left behind, especially when I spoke to Volkov, whose wife wrote to him almost daily. He even let me see some of her writing, which was so painful and exquisite in its sadness, that I did not know whether to envy him for having the love of such a woman or pity him for being separated from it.

"Memory is not enough," said Volkov one afternoon when we were alone and drunk. "I see my wife now only in broken pictures. I see her in midstride across the front room of our apartment. I see her raise her head and smile. I find myself thinking of her hands. Just her hands, with their long fingers and shallow palms and her cut-short nails. I tell you, Lieutenant Wedekind, my memory is going blind."

No wonder he drank so much.

I started drinking, too, and smoking—heavily. I felt the burden of my secret life.

Ingo, on the other hand, never received mail and didn't seem to care. He was too caught up in his enterprise, oblivious to the fact that the Russians disliked him, even though they bought his goods and payed his outrageous prices largely without quarrel. He was providing a service that eclipsed the petty dealings that had taken place in Diaghilev before Ingo arrived. Everyone seemed to be making use of it. In Ingo's mind, his world stood in perfect harmony. His dealings flourished in this muddy in-between place. Men spent wages, which should have been sent home, on the clear medicinal burn of Stolichnaya vodka, or the sea-glass green and honeyed aftertaste of Tarkhuna, the blue-and-silver jars of Beluga caviar or the red-and-silver jars of the smaller-beaded Sevruga caviar, the black-and-green boxes of Papirossi cigarettes, the red white and blue of Sputnik cigarettes. There were balls of Gouda cheese wrapped in bright yellow wax, which was then melted down into candles by the Russians, using lengths of shoelace for the wicks. Ingo even sold the wood from the automotive supply's packing crates. Once a week, he would stack the crates in a corner of the maintainance compound and would pay someone to smash them to bits with a sledgehammer. He then sold the pieces as kindling, which the Russians used in their little fires, called "stewpot fires," which they liked to start up outside their tents in the evenings. He could have sold almost anything, and the Russians, just to break the monotony, would have bought whatever he had to sell.

Meanwhile, I was turning into a Russian. I bought a goatskin vest with thick, straggled, and stinking-when-wet fur and wore it under my quilted winter jacket. I looked like a tramp. That didn't matter. I was warm and I felt privileged. It made life more interesting, knowing there was luxury to be found. I never enjoyed these luxuries more than when they were so hard to find and set against the oversalted slop of Diaghilev camp food.

I accepted Volkov's offer to rest in his office while he was away on other business. I was hesitant at first about approaching Volkov's thug of a secretary and expected to be thrown out. But whatever Volkov had told him brought the secretary to his feet when I appeared, and I received such a sharp snap of a salute that it looked more like the man was trying to karate-chop himself into unconsciousness. After that, alone in the room, I would sit and smoke or even read the political manifestos that were the only books in Volkov's office. I did not read them out of curiosity. I was no student of politics, after all. I read them simply so that I could be transported away from the camp by the words, to imagine a place other than Diaghilev. It was in that office that I learned to smoke Papirossi cigarettes. You pinched the tube one way and then another, allowing the smoke to collect and cool before you breathed it in. I understood the gift that Volkov had made in allowing me to use this tiny room: the gift of mindlessness and solitude and warmth, even if only for a while.

Something else was happening to me, as well. For a while, I tried to ignore it, saying to myself that this was just the result of living in a new environment. I no longer recognized myself. I became obsessed with the idea that my father would have been outraged if he knew I had agreed to inform on Ingo. To my father, the bond of friendship would have outweighed any loyalty to the state. With him, it was always a question of honor, and that had been the source of the first real argument I remember having with him, back when I was only six or seven.

It began when I asked him about a neighbor of ours, a man named Hanno Spey. He was tall and dignified. His gray hair was combed straight back on his head and his eyes were clear and focused. When he left his house each day to drink a cup of coffee at the local café, he moved with great deliberation, as if any failure to carry out his mission might somehow set the world off balance. He wore heavy clothes, even in summer—wool coats and whipcord trousers and shoes with thick soles, as if they were meant for walking across continents and not just down to town. From the way I saw people treat him, including my own parents, he seemed to me to be the most despised man on the planet.

People did not talk to Mr. Spey more than they had to. He sat by himself at the coffee shop, staring into space, drinking the black liquid with precise and regular slips. Seven to a cup, I counted, from my spying place up at the bar, where I often stopped to buy cocoa on my way home from school. He seemed as oblivious to me as he did to the rest of the world. I wanted to shake him out of it. Say something. Make a loud noise. Shake him by the shoulders. Because I wasn't worth his time. I wanted to tell him I was there and I was important. But I was too well behaved for that. Or perhaps I was only afraid.

When I asked my father why Spey kept to himself, I wasn't ready for what he told me. At the time, we were on our way to see a soccer match at the local playing field. It was late in the spring. The air was filled with the tiny parachutes of dandelion seeds. Mr. Spey walked past us on the other side of the street, heading for the coffee shop. My father and I knew that the coffee shop was closed. The owner had gone to see the game. My father didn't say anything to Mr. Spey, and I figured if he didn't, then I shouldn't either.

He waited until Spey was out of earshot. Then he started talking. "There was a group of men," he said, "who tried to assassinate Adolf Hitler in July of 1944."

I knew about this. The Hitler bomb plot. Many of the conspirators had been members of the German high command, including Erwin Rommel, the hero of North Africa. The conspirators were hanged or shot or handed a loaded pistol and given a moment alone to shoot themselves. I had learned all about it in school. To the Communists who taught us, these men were considered to be martyrs. They were all heroes. They had died to put right the crimes they had committed earlier and to free the world of tyranny in the great patriotic war. I had thought all the conspirators were dead. I didn't understand how Mr. Spey could still be alive. I asked my father about it.

"He was taken prisoner by the Americans before the Gestapo could get to him. He was driving around in France somewhere and his driver got lost and he ended up being stopped by an enemy patrol. When the war was over, he came back to live in our town." My father stuck to the details. He pared it all down to the bones.

"Are you friends with him?" I asked.

"No," said my father, "I am not."

"Is anybody?" I heard the soccer crowd in the distance. They were singing.

"He is not well liked." My father quickened his pace. He didn't want to talk about it anymore.

But I wanted to know. I couldn't let it rest. If I had never asked the question, I might have been able to let myself believe whatever invented story popped into my mind. Now that I had asked for the truth, I had to know it. "Why?" I asked. "Isn't he a hero? The other people who tried to kill . . ." and I didn't say the word Hitler. Instead, I said a word that I knew was a nickname for Hitler, "Grofass." I didn't know what it meant. I had heard my father use it to his friends.

"It's easy to call people heroes when they are dead," my father told me. "And the way you are taught in school now, of course these people are going to be called heroes."

"But it was good that they tried to kill him. Everybody says so." The soccer game had started. I heard a cheer as the two teams ran out onto the pitch. Just then, I didn't care about the game, even though I had been looking forward to it for over a month.

"I'm not saying he shouldn't have been killed, Paul. If he had been killed, the war might have been shortened and tens of thousands of lives might have been saved. You won't find many people who disagree with that."

"So why do people hate him?"

"I didn't say they hated him."

"They don't like him."

Now my father stopped. We were alone in the street. I didn't like how empty the place seemed, the same way I didn't like the stillness of Sundays. I liked the bustle of the working day. Everything seemed to be holding its breath. My father sat down on a bench that was painted dull green, the paint dusted with yellowy pollen. He slapped his hand on the bench slats next to him to make me sit, as well.

I sat. I looked up and down the street and felt the loneliness of it. The soccer match raged in the distance. All the life of the town was there and we were here, trapped in the in-between place, me, my father, and Mr. Spey with the seven sips of coffee that he was not going to get.

"The reason Spey is not liked," my father said, still unwilling to use the word *hate,* "is not because people disagree with the fact that . . . that Grofass deserved to die. It is a different thing entirely. It is a complicated issue." Then he just fell silent.

I waited for the explanation. I put my hands on my knees and felt the warmth of the sun on my corduroy trousers. I waited a long time.

"The thing is," he said at last, "that Spey took an oath. It was

62

an oath of loyalty, loyalty until death. And Spey broke this oath. He broke his word. And what good are you if you cannot keep your word?"

"But he was right to try to kill Hitler." I said the name. It seemed to boom around the street and off the closed doors and the empty shop windows and it snaked along the power lines.

"He was wrong to break his oath. If he didn't believe it, he shouldn't have made the oath. You can't just take an oath and change your mind about it later. An oath is a sacred thing. It is you saying to the world that you have decided what is important and that you will stand by it no matter what. Do you see? He didn't keep the faith. And millions did keep the faith and they are dead and Spey is still here breathing the air that better people should be breathing."

I heard the rising anger in his voice, but I could not contain myself. "But it was Hitler!" I shouted.

"I don't give a damn about Hitler!" my father yelled back. "Your word is who we are!"

That last sentence changed my life. If he had said, "Your word is who you are," it would not have struck me the same way. But he said "we." Suddenly and for the rest of my life, I would feel the burden of this. Not merely the threat of letting down myself. I could live with that. But letting down my whole family, the whole history of my family, the history of my people. The weight of that burden was almost more than I could bear.

Now, all these years later, the argument still raged back and forth inside my head. I imagined that I could feel my father's anger in every frozen gust of wind that barreled down out of the mountains. He bellowed at me in the thunder, and sometimes, during the vicious lightning storms that stalked up and down the valley, when everybody else was running for cover, I would just stand there in the open, in the middle of the motor-pool yard, the mud turning into a frothing brown lake. The lightning walked toward me on its giant spider's legs. I refused to get out of its way.

The lightning was my father. I would not give in to him. The lightning came down all around. I could hear the shouts as men called to me from the shelter of the garage, but I did not move. I heard the sucking hiss of the thunder booming simultaneously with the lightning strikes, and still I held my ground, beyond all sanity or will to live.

I could hardly recall who I had been before I arrived in Afghanistan, when my life was not governed by the black and white of oaths and absolutes. I think back now to those thunderstorms. I failed to understand that my father was trying to warn me, not to fight against me. Instead of realizing it, I felt as if someone else was living in my body, my thoughts entwined with his, like a parasite ruling my mind. I heard the gibbering of insanity from the dark corners of my brain. I longed to be myself again.

I LOOKED ACROSS at Liedke. He was lying on his back, asleep. His huge chest rose and fell. I went in and fetched him a blanket.

By morning, we were in sight of Block Island. Its reddish khaki cliffs rose from the water and breaking waves rode foaming up the beaches.

"Why don't you just fly to the States?" I asked Liedke. He and I were sitting at the galley table. Our caginess from the night before was gone. Now I would have done that sewing if he'd asked me, but because we were friends, he would never ask.

"I used to fly in," said Liedke, "but then I got flagged by customs. Flagged for what's in here." He tapped the suitcase that never left his side. "Believe me, if there was a way to avoid spending all that time on the submarine, I would do it. But there's too much at stake."

"Why don't they just send someone else?"

"Because I'm the only one they trust, and no one else can do it." He didn't say what was in the suitcase. Instead, he muttered,

"I bring back cash, you see. Currency. Untraceable." He jabbed the index finger of one hand into the palm of the other to emphasize each word.

The sky had lost the colors of the dawn by the time we saw a boat heading toward us. It was a sportfishing boat, with two large antennalike rods rising high above the wheelhouse and trailing back in the wind.

Suleika came out on deck with a pair of binoculars. "Prepare to send the nets down," she said to me, "in case it's not who we think."

"Do you have anything else to eat?" asked Liedke.

He had already cleared out our fridge.

Suleika didn't answer him. Her face was grim and serious. When she and I were out on deck, she said, "By lunchtime, Liedke will be stuffing his face at the Plaza."

"What's in that suitcase?" I asked.

"Diamonds. That's a case full of diamonds, which he sells in New York City. Sells them for cash, and he takes those dollars back to Russia. That's one of the ways they get hold of foreign currency, to bribe people, pay off agents, you name it."

"Where do the diamonds come from?"

"Siberia, mostly. That's what I hear." As she spoke, she raised the binoculars to her eyes again and studied the approaching boat.

I couldn't tell whether she was nervous or not. She always seemed a little on edge. She took her life so seriously.

"I guess they must trust him a lot to let him loose with all those stones."

"They don't trust him at all," said Suleika, "but he's got a big old family back home and he knows what would happen to them if he made a run for it." She adjusted the focus on the binoculars. "One day it's not going to be the right people. One day it'll be the Coast Guard with their fifty-caliber machine guns."

"Could you ever hide someone on this boat?"

"Not so the Coast Guard wouldn't find him. You see, sometimes we drop off the people by ourselves and sometimes we have to rendezvous with another boat. It all depends on the orders. The best way to hide him is not to hide him at all." Suleika had lowered the binoculars and waved to the approaching boat. "It's okay," she said. "I see who they are now. We're all right this time."

They pulled up stern-to-stern against us. The boat was named *Miss Behavin,* painted in bright blue on the white fiberglass. Underneath the name was MONTAUK L.I. There were two men in the crew, and they looked happy to see Liedke again.

"What'd you bring us, Liedke?" shouted a man who wore a T-shirt cut off just below his nipples. The muscles of his stomach were hard cables under the skin.

"Yeah, did you bring us any presents for our girlfriends this time?" This man wore a bandanna on his head like a pirate.

Both men had Slavic acccents.

Liedke showed them a fat smile. He held up the suitcase. "Well, it's all for sale, boys. All's you need is a fistful of those Yankee dollars."

I wondered if they knew what was in that suitcase.

"How about a tuna? I'll trade you." The man with the bandanna reached down into a cooler and hauled up a big fish, his hand buried deep under its gill plates. Its silver sides were smudged with blood and its fins were streaked lemon yellow.

Liedke boomed a laugh.

"We're going to tell people you caught this on your fishing trip today," he said.

"I am such a good fisherman." Liedke grinned at each of us in turn. "I am a fat and talented man." He shook our hands and boarded the boat. There was the same clumsiness in his departure, the same coming-untucked of his shirt. Liedke broke out in a fresh and cheerful sweat. The tear under his armpit grew a few

66

more inches. The boat gunned its engines to back away from us. Liedke waved good-bye. Then the boat kicked into forward and wheeled around hard. The stern dipped close to the waves and it sped away.

Then it was just Suleika and me again, out on the water, the way it would be many times in the months and years to come.

Three

THE NEWPORT DOCK WAS BUSY.

Trawlermen and fish packers shuffled around in their rubber boots. The accents of many nationalities, all giving their own version of English, echoed around the steel rafters of the packing-house. There was Italian, Portuguese, Vietnamese, Spanish, Irish, Quebecois. Suleika spoke English fluently and her foreign accent had almost disappeared, but my own English was made stranger here by the fact that the English I had learned at school was from an Englishman. My teacher had been a member of a British Communist cell group and had gone to Eton and Oxford in the 1930s before defecting to the East. He told me he spoke the King's English. This merging of nationalities made me feel less of a foreigner. All of us here were strangers, more or less.

I looked around at the seagulls, who stood guard on the tar-topped pilings or squabbled on the planks for scraps of rotten fish. A large black-and-red container truck beeped as it reversed off the loading ramp. My ears were filled with the rumbling crash of the ice-chipper machine as it loaded up a trawler that was preparing to head out. Its crew stood out back of Bad Joe's, toasting themselves with one last heavy shot glass full of mescal before they put to sea. I promised myself that in the future I would also drink a toast before I headed out to sea—a toast to Suleika and me and the clapped-out *Baby Blue.*

But that would be next time. Suleika and I were home now. Not thinking about going out on the water. Thinking about a bed that stayed still. The smell of the land. The sound of cars in the street. A fine, warm rain was falling. We hid under the hoods of our Helly Hansen raingear, muffled from the outside world and smelling the rubberized cloth. We hoisted the baskets of fish, crusted with ice, up onto the dock, where they were sorted and weighed on a conveyor belt by men and women with cigarettes dangling from their mouths. They talked in sarcastic voices about a baseball game that had taken place while Suleika and I were gone.

The dock was owned by a man named Gunther. He also ran a small trap boat that rode out each morning at sunrise to haul up huge permanent nets anchored in the shallow water off Narragansett Beach. Suleika had told me that the trap boats were a last-ditch job for fishermen who were down on their luck and that Gunther was a fabulously wealthy man who dressed in rags, fired people for no reason, and other times would hand out hundred-dollar bills to his crew. He had almost been put out of business the year before when one of his huge cargo trucks loaded with fish for the Boston market had been pulled over by an unmarked police car. The officer, who in fact was no policeman at all, made the driver get out of the truck, then shot him dead on the side of the road. The body was never recovered. All they found at the crime scene was some blood and a 9-mm pistol cartridge. "And they won't ever find that body, either," said Suleika. "He's probably scattered around a hundred different lobster pots out there in the bay."

Gunther was a tall, gaunt man. His thin legs were plated in heavy rubber boots, in which he shuffled across the concrete floor of the fish-packing area. As he moved from the warmth of his office into the chill of the packing area, his small round glasses fogged up and he wiped them clean with his sleeve.

When the work was done, Suleika went to settle up with Gunther.

I sat on the concrete rim of the loading ramp. Beyond the dock, Newport hummed with color and movement—green, red, colors I had missed out on the water.

"I don't suppose they've given you a place to live," Suleika said when she returned from Gunther's office with the money from our catch.

"No," I said. "I'll stay at the YMCA until I can get an apartment."

She handed me a wad of bills.

I put them straight into my pocket without looking.

She watched me for a moment, unsure what to make of this gesture. Then she said, "You can stay at my house." A second later, she added, "Until you get your own place."

Suleika's house was over the Newport bridge on the island of Jamestown. She lived on South Main Road in an old house set back from the road, with a large windmill at the back. The windmill was built in the Dutch fashion, dark-tiled and steep-sided. At night, the breeze blew through its still sails, changing pitch as the wind changed direction. It seemed as if the windmill were singing in a deep and wordless voice.

That night, I slept on the couch in the living room. I didn't feel unwelcome, but I could tell it would be better if I got my own apartment very soon. Now that we were back on land, we seemed to know each other differently. I was frightened that if I told

Suleika how I felt about her, things would be ruined. I was pre-pared to live in this half-painful, half-beautiful in-between place, rather than risk losing everything.

In the house, there were still many signs of Suleika's husband. Part of Mathias was still here. I could smell his soap and his sweat and his cologne. It rankled me to see a picture of him on the mantelpiece, his winter boots in the back hall, a Morris chair draped with a Navajo rug, which looked out over the bay and in which she never sat because it had been his. Suleika wasn't ready yet to say their last good-bye. To clear away his things seemed dis-respectful, even to me, who wished them gone. I said nothing about it. I waited for her to bring up the subject if she wanted to, but she didn't. So we let it be, and how she dealt with her grief, I do not know exactly.

The next day, I just kept her company. I listened to her while she talked about boat repair, big storms, the crazy people on the dock. She didn't talk about her life back in Europe. Even though I was curious, I knew better than to question her. We drank strong tea without milk at the kitchen table, Russian tea, with its peculiar smoky dry taste. It felt good to drink the wet heat on a rainy day and know that tomorrow there would be no work to do.

After dinner, when the rain had stopped, we walked down the hill toward a saltwater marsh. White egrets stood on their stick legs in the tall grass, waiting and waiting in the sunset. It was strange to be taking big strides down the hill, instead of the short, drunken shuffle that I had grown used to on the boat. We strolled with our hands wedged into the pockets of our jeans.

At night, I lay again on the couch, wrapped in the Navajo blanket. The swaying of the waves still barged from one end of my head to the other. Upstairs, I heard Suleika's steady breathing. Around me was the stillness of the land, the way it never is on the ocean. Wind coiled around the huge blades of the windmill sails, making music. Making words. Talking to me. I didn't sleep. I just lay there and listened to the wind and Suleika breathing upstairs.

While I let my thoughts wander, I asked myself why so much of what had happened in Afghanistan remained locked away inside my head. Originally, I thought it was because so little here could remind me of that time and place. Now I worried that the reason might be different. The things that I had lived through, terrible things, were still out there somewhere on the tundra of my mind—patient, but always moving closer. I dreaded their arrival. Before that night was over, the first of them had reached me.

INGO HAD BEEN running his business out of our tent. At first, he was cautious. The only time people could buy anything from him was at night. But that precaution soon faded away. He was too strong in his connections for anyone to object. Before long, he kept regular shop hours and even ran sales when he had overstocked. Already he had a reputation for never allowing credit. All debts had to be paid at once. Anyone who tried to get around this soon regretted it.

One October night, as I was lying on my cot with my right arm hooked over my eyes to block out the magnesium light of a hissing propane lamp, I heard someone sweep back the tent flap and walk in. Cold air shocked the tiny space. I groaned and wriggled deeper into my sleeping bag. It was a Wednesday, which meant that Ingo was staying open late. He had a sale on caviar that week. It was 10:00 P.M. and Ingo was just counting receipts, getting ready to close for the night. I pulled back my arm to see who had come in so late. It was a Russian sergeant named Ilyushin. He was in charge of stocktaking at Diaghilev. It was his job to order more tents, more fuel, more "automotive parts," all of which were shipped direct from an airfield near Odessa. Clearly, he had a role in Ingo's business. How much of a role, I never knew and was careful not to inquire.

Ilyushin demanded two pounds of Sevruga. He said he and some friends were going to stay up and drink and they wanted some caviar to go with it. Ingo stacked four jars on the table and slid them across to Ilyushin. Then he quoted a price. Ilyushin laughed. Said something about working too cheaply as it was. He picked up the cans and turned to leave.

"Don't joke," said Ingo. "You have to pay for those like everybody else. You are well compensated for your trouble. Don't ask for more than you deserve."

Ilyushin turned around. In a quiet, measured voice, he said, "You are still alive because I allow you to go on breathing. Now I'm taking this and I'm taking whatever else I want the next time I come around."

I stayed very still, lying on my bunk, wishing I could melt through the tiny crossed strands of the canvas tent and slip away into the dark. Ilyushin was no coward. Neither was Ingo. Now the two of them had insulted each other in a way that could not go unchallenged.

When Ingo pulled a gun from a pocket in his combat jacket, he seemed to move so slowly that I felt sure Ilyushin would rush him, or pull out some concealed weapon of his own. But Ilyushin only watched with surprise growing on his face until, after what seemed like many seconds, the barrel of Ingo's almost-antique Tokarev pistol was aimed squarely at Ilyushin's stomach.

I wondered where he had gotten the gun. He had not been issued one, and if he had, it wouldn't have been something as old as a Tokarev. But it was still a gun, and I had no doubt that it worked.

"You want that caviar?" asked Ingo.

Ilyushin said nothing. He had become as much of a spectator as I was. All reason had now been thrown aside. Ingo would shoot him and not care about the consequences. That was the one lesson you had to learn about Ingo: not to call his bluff, even over a few jars of caviar. To Ingo, the caviar was irrelevant. All debts were to be paid.

"Sit down," said Ingo. Without taking his eyes off Ilyushin even for a second, he nodded toward the corner, where there was a collapsible wooden chair, over which he folded his clothes at night.

"What are you going to do?" asked Ilyushin. His courage was gone now. "What's going to happen?"

"You're going to sit down," said Ingo.

"But the clothes," whispered Ilyushin. "Your clothes are on the chair."

"Tip them on the floor."

Ilyushin put down the jars of caviar and began to lift the clothes gently from the chair. He held them while he searched for a place to set them down. That was when he saw me. From the look on my face, he understood the trouble he was in.

"On the floor. Drop them," said Ingo.

Ilyushin dropped the clothes. He winced as they landed with a soft rustle in the dirt.

"Now pick up the caviar."

Ilyushin did what he was told.

"Eat it."

Ilyushin looked up. "What?"

"Eat the caviar. Eat it all now or I'll put a bullet in you."

"There're two pounds of it here! I can't—"

"Two and a half pounds, actually. You have four minutes to eat all of it."

Ilyushin just stood there. The jars of caviar were precariously balanced in his hands.

I was afraid he would drop them. Ingo would shoot the man before the first jar hit the ground.

"Do you think I'm joking?" asked Ingo.

"I don't believe you are," said Ilyushin.

"Four minutes," said Ingo. "Eat."

Ilyushin hesitated for a moment, perhaps waiting for Ingo to smile or for some act of God to stop this. But when no smile came and no God, either, Ilyushin pried off the lid of the first jar of caviar, tearing his fingernails on the sharp metal. He scooped his first two fingers into the black beads and packed them into his mouth. The heavy, oily, fishy smell of the caviar billowed out into the tent. Ilyushin chewed and swallowed, breathing in snorts through his nose. Before he had even half-finished, Ingo told him that one minute was up.

When Ilyushin heard this, he grunted in panic and began to shovel the caviar more quickly into his mouth. He tipped back the jar and shook the beads down his throat. Dots of caviar stuck to his chin and his tunic. He swallowed it now without chewing, and when the jar was empty, he threw it away and tore the lid off another.

All this time, the Tokarev stayed pointed at Ilyushin.

In about four minutes, Ilyushin swallowed a delicacy that might have cost a month's pay for the average sergeant, without anything to drink, cramming into his gullet the rare Sevruga, normally eaten half a teaspoon at a time with bread and sour cream and maybe a little chopped onion, transporting the taster for a flicker of time beyond the barbed-wire entanglements of the camp and away to some region of pleasure.

Ilyushin sat gasping in the chair. His fingers were bloody. The empty jars lay at his feet and the twisted-off lids reflected the light in the tent. His face was smeared with caviar. The stench of it filled the tent, mixing rudely with the propane of the lamp.

Now Ingo lifted a bottle of Stolichnaya onto the table. "Drink this," he said.

Ilyushin got out of his chair and edged nervously forward to the table. With a gentle grasp, he took the bottle by its neck and stepped back away from the table. He began to drink. Ilyushin drank it all, three-quarters of a liter, before Ingo told him he could go. Ilyushin staggered out into the dark. When the cold night air barged into him, he fell in the mud, and climbed to his feet and stumbled off again.

Then Ingo turned to me. The blood had left his face. "What good is my business and what good am I," he asked, "if I don't keep my word?"

"Ingo," I said quietly, "it was a couple of jars of caviar."

"And vodka," he added patiently.

"All right. And some lousy vodka."

"It was," he said, "my reputation."

After I'd thought about it for a while, I understood why Ingo pulled the gun. Everything that he had built for himself in Diaghilev had been at stake these past few minutes. If Ilyushin had been allowed to walk away unchallenged, then everyone else could do the same. Ilyushin had been the first to flex his muscles. He also had to be the last, if Ingo hoped to survive, not just with his business but with his life, as well. If his illegal trade had collapsed, then people like Volkov who had turned a blind eye until now would close on him. Then it would be all over for Ingo Budde.

I was at the motor pool the next afternoon when the Russian Special Forces military police, Speznas, came looking for Ingo. The fact that it was Speznas who came for Ingo and not the regular military police meant that, whatever his crime, he had already been found guilty. No one had told the Speznas boys that Ingo never showed up for work at the motor pool. After a few minutes of searching, they found him in our tent, where everyone else knew he spent his days, sitting behind a stock of contraband. He was arrested and driven out of the camp in the back of a truck, having first been chained by the feet to a rail that ran under the wooden seats and was designed for that purpose. As the truck drove away, Ingo peered from the back. He didn't look afraid. He was concentrating. He scanned the faces of the soldiers who had come out of their tents to see what was happening. Ingo hoped to catch a glimpse of the ones who had turned him in. He would know from their expressions who was guilty and he would come for them later, if he ever made it back.

It turned out that Ilyushin had almost died of a combination of alcohol poisoning and hypothermia. He had passed out within ten feet of his tent and lay there all night, and when he was found by his friends the next morning, his hair had frozen into tiny icy spikes. I wondered whether anything would have happened if Ilyushin had made it back to his tent and slept it off. Maybe he would have learned his lesson and contemplated nothing more than curses against Ingo. But it didn't go that way. All the alliances that Ingo had cultivated since he arrived in Afghanistan now suddenly ceased to exist.

Ingo never told me what happened to him while he was gone, or even where he went. I heard a rumor that he had been reported as a drug dealer to the Speznas and that two pounds of hashish had been planted in a shipment of cheese that he was due to pick up. If it had been anything but drugs, Ingo could have bribed his way out of it. Whoever shopped him to the Speznas knew exactly what they were doing.

A strange thing happened while Ingo was gone. I was tidying up the tent one day when I found, stashed behind his locker, half a dozen letters to a woman. I read them. They were love letters. I saw a tenderness in those letters that I didn't know Ingo had in him. My first thought was that he had a woman I didn't know about back home. I knew for certain that he had no woman at Diaghilev. Nobody did. I didn't believe he had a girlfriend anywhere else, either. Also, these letters had never been mailed. They seemed to be some kind of experiment. Ingo was trying to imagine how it might be if his life was governed by forces different from the ones that ruled him now. He observed the rest of the world, myself included, with a mixture of curiosity and contempt. There seemed to be some inefficiency in all the rest of us that Ingo simply could not comprehend. And yet he was curious. He was willing to give it a try. Carefully, I packed away the letters and never mentioned them to Ingo.

Another thing that happened was that I saw a Russian helicopter get shot down by an American-made Stinger missile. The missiles were being smuggled through Pakistan into Afghanistan by the CIA. I didn't actually see the helicopter before it was hit. I was taking inventory in the motor pool when it happened. I heard the helicopter over in the next valley. I could hear from the deep-pitched *doom-whop, doom-whop* of the engine that it was one of the big Zemlya-type gunships. I had grown used to the sound of them. At least a dozen flew by every day, usually at high altitude, so that you could see them only if the sun reflected off their sides. The first unusual noise I heard was the faint hiss of flares being launched from the helicopter. This was done if a plane or a helicopter ever came under fire from a heat-seeking missile. The flares burned at a very high temperature and were designed to lead the missile off course. The helicopter's alarm system must have registered the launch of the Stinger, but by then it was too late. I turned to look out of the warehouse door and could see the bright path of the flares high in the distance. Then I saw the white smoking arc of the Stinger. I didn't see the helicopter itself until the Stinger found its mark. I saw the explosion several seconds before the sound of the impact reached me. There was an orange flash and then the flash seemed to break into several large pieces, each of them falling to earth in what seemed like slow and lazy arcs. I made out the blades of the rotors, twisting and flickering away from the main bulk of the wreckage. The sky popped silver and gold with exploding ammunition and flares. By then, all of Diaghilev had stopped what it was doing and stared up into the sky to watch the death of the Zemlya. At the time, I gave no thought to the crew or the passengers the Zemlya might have been carrying. There was an erratic beauty to the falling wreckage. It tumbled away into the next valley, which was an uninhabited mass of stones and dried-out riverbeds and scrub trees with black thorns like fire-hardened needles.

When Ingo returned, he had been badly beaten. He was thin.

The rings under his eyes had turned a darker shade, as if he had touched his finger in a pot of ink and smeared it on his lower eyelids. He wouldn't speak more than a few words, and nothing about what had happened. All he wanted, he said, was to get some sleep. As Ingo was undressing that night, I noticed bruises on his ribs and the back of his neck and on his groin. The wounds were purple-yellow, deep beneath the surface. When he lay down, I saw he had been beaten on the soles of his feet.

By that time, all of Ingo's "automotive parts" had been confiscated, but not before they were raided by various members of the camp, including Ilyushin. I watched them from the garage where I worked. They went into the parts shed, carrying empty laundry bags, and came out with the sacks weighed down and slung over their shoulders.

It was days before Ingo and I even had a conversation. "I thought they were going to kill me," he said one night, sitting on the edge of his cot. He dabbed at his bruises with rubbing alcohol. It had become a nightly ritual since he returned. "One of the Speznas people whispered in my ear, 'Anyone can commit a murder, but it takes a real artist to commit a suicide.' That was when I thought they were going to finish me. They'd say I killed myself. And I thought, The only person who won't believe them is my friend Paul. He'll know what really happened."

"You're still alive, Ingo," I said. It seemed that he was not completely sure. "That counts for a lot after what you've been through."

"But I have nothing." He held out his empty hands, as if to prove his point. "They took it all."

"Yes," I said. "Yes, they did."

"Someone had to make life a little more bearable here." He was suddenly defiant. "A little Beluga. A little Sevruga. A little Stolichnaya to forget the day. I did everything I could to make it a good business. And, I mean, look what I was up against! Look how far I had to bring that stuff. How much red tape I had to bypass. In the end, it was the people who profited most who brought me down. And who could have done a better job than I did?" he asked.

"No one," I said truthfully.

"No one," he echoed me. "Not Volkov. Not that brute Ilyushin. Not you, my friend. You least of all."

"Why's that?" I asked.

He shrugged, as if it was too obvious for explanation. "You're too much by the book. That's why I like you. You make no sense to me." He managed to smile. "Now that this has happened, you'll still stick by me, won't you?"

I had to remind myself that the normal give-and-take of a friendship did not apply to Ingo. The way he saw it, now that he could no longer sell me cut-rate vodka, he couldn't be as good a friend to me as he had been before. "Don't be crazy, Ingo," I said.

"Crazy," he mumbled. "Sometimes I think the whole world's crazy except for you and me, and even you are a little crazy." He thought for a moment and then added, "You know, we may have nothing, but we are still friends, you and I."

At that moment, I realized I could not continue writing reports about Ingo. I had been worrying about it all along, and now I knew I was finished. Ingo deserved better treatment than this. He was right that everything stopped making sense at Diaghilev. Everything was crazy here.

IT GOT SO that I couldn't sleep at Suleika's. I was too restless. I wanted to stay, but the worst thing I could do was crowd Suleika. She had to make up her own mind.

I found myself an apartment over in Newport. It was a one-bedroom place above a pasta shop called DiRenzo's at the far end of Thames Street, about a five-minute walk from the dock. I woke up to the smell of the pasta, the quiet whir of the pasta machine, the owners talking Sicilian, and an Italian-language radio station playing corny Italian music.

When we were on land, I would meet Suleika on the docks each morning and we would get the boat ready to head out to sea. As before, we kept our distance from each other. Over the weeks that followed, especially out on the water, the distance grew smaller. The first time she ever let slip that she cared for me was when one of our net cables snapped with a huge gunshot crack. It lashed out of the water like an iron snake and hovered, cobra-necked, over the deck before it crashed down onto the wheel-house. It smashed the revolving arm of our loran location finder into chips of white plastic. Suleika had been inside steering the boat. I was just climbing out of the ice hatch when the cable broke.

By the time Suleika came running out on deck, having thrown the engines into neutral, I was standing by the ice hatch.

"Are you all right?" she shouted.

I was still too shocked to speak, realizing I had almost been killed. The flying cable could have cut me in half.

"Oh my God," she said, and stepped toward me, hands held out. "Oh my God, what happened to you?" She took hold of my bare arms. "Oh, Paul, are you hurt?" She smoothed the hair from my eyes, her hand passing over my forehead.

"I'm fine," I said.

"Are you sure? Are you completely sure?"

"I'm fine," I said again. "It didn't come anywhere near me."

Her arms dropped. "Oh," she said.

I grinned at her. The cold from the ice room peeled from my body like the layers of an onion.

"What are you smiling at?"

"You."

"Well you can just stop!" she commanded. She strode the three paces to the stern of the boat, where the one remaining cable shot down through the powdery green. "If that other cable breaks, we'll lose the whole net. Do you have any idea how much it would cost to replace? And we might not even be able to haul it back. Then we're stuck!" She bawled all this out in one breath.

"It's very serious," I said, but I couldn't stop grinning. I had caught her out and she knew it. She with the stony face and locked-away heart.

"You think I pretend not to care about you?" she asked. "Is that it? Well, to hell with you!" she shouted. "It's none of your damn business if I care."

"I can't read your mind all the time, Suleika. I try, but I can't."

"All right." She looked down at her boots, hands on hips. "I do care about you." She couldn't even look at me when she said it. "I just don't feel as if I should. You'll be leaving soon. Isn't that what you said? Isn't it true?"

"Suleika," I said. I closed the distance between us and kissed her very gently. She did not turn away. Her lips were slightly chapped. Then, so as not to bring awkwardness, I went straight over to the cable drum, set the motor on low, and began to haul back the net. We both watched the remaining good cable twist out of the water. Its rusted sinews creaked with the strain.

I knew then that even if she did fall in love with me, as I was falling for her, she might never tell me so. She might never say the words—at least not the great declarations of love, without which I had once believed it was impossible. Partly, I think, this was because of the life she'd had with Mathias. From all that I'd learned about him, he would not have talked much about love, because it wouldn't have occurred to him to do so. The reasons for Suleika's silence about what she felt inside came from a different source. She had lived too long among lies. Each friendship that she made here was bracketed with these lies. Each thought was filtered through the lies she'd told before. She'd had to find some other currency than words, even if I was the only person to whom she could tell the truth. She might prove she loved me, but she would have to show it, and in her own way. The clues of her devotion would be clear once I learned how to see them.

But I would tell her, if and when I reached the point where I no longer cared what her reaction would be. I would tell her I loved her, because I would no longer be able to help myself.

We brought in the net. It took us the rest of the day. A blue shark had become tangled in the nylon, probably after it went in to feed on the fish that had been trapped. Normally, the net is moving too fast for the bigger fish to get in and out with our catch. The shark was about six feet long. Its back was cobalt blue and its belly was cream white. Suleika went to the tool chest and came back with a fish club. It was made from an old baseball bat that had been sawn in half. The grip had been wrapped in coarse-finish electrical tape and the end was studded with carpeting nails that had been hammered down until they were almost flush with the wood. She was getting ready to finish off the shark. But then we just stood there, looking at the huge fish. It was a pretty thing. Suleika set down the club. We took the fish by its half-moon tail, dragged it to the gap in the stern where the net payed in and out, and heaved it back into the sea. Suleika and I watched it gliding gently down with the movements of a falling leaf.

"We should go home," said Suleika.

When she said that, it occurred to me we were already home. The boat was our home. Back on land, we were separate. Out here, circumstances forced us together in ways that we didn't have to feel confused about. I still felt a sudden lightening in my chest at the mention of returning to land. I loved the first sight of it on the horizon, the cliffs of Block Island, the green of the mansion lawns in Newport, and finally the bustle of the port, the sound of voices apart from our own, land beneath my feet. I loved the sea, but when I saw the earth rise steadily from the water, I felt a stirring in my blood. Out on the water, we were all only dreamers.

"I'll take you out to dinner at the Black Pearl," I said.

We both laughed at the idea. We couldn't afford that. We

would probably talk ourselves out of it and have pizza instead. We laughed because we knew each other well enough to know we wouldn't really go.

We did have pizza that night. We bought a ready-made pizza crust and baked it at her house.

I liked to watch her in her kitchen. Washing dishes. Wiping the counter. Liked to see the way she tied her hair back from her eyes with a piece of blue ribbon. I told her so. She said I was a pervert, but she was laughing. I said it was because she cleaned up so rarely. She was not the tidiest woman. She had a study, in which she kept all her paperwork from the boat—receipts for gasoline, receipts for the fish we sold to Gunther. It looked like a bird's nest. I called it "the Pit of Despair." Now even she called it that.

Suleika was not a good cook. Actually, it was worse than that. Everything was boiled and too salty or too sweet, or both, if I was really unlucky. Of all the things she could not do, she was worst at making coffee. When she would ask if I wanted a cup, I would say, all bright and cheerful, "Oh, no thanks. Not right now." Then I would wait fifteen minutes and make one for myself.

Out of self-preservation, I did most of the cooking. I learned to cook when I was living with my uncle, who had the strange habit of not eating anything that looked the way it had done before it reached his plate. If I served him fish, for example, it had to be cut into neat geometric shapes. Even beans were hacked almost into vapor before my uncle would touch them. I told Suleika that she would have gotten along well with my uncle.

"I don't get along well with anybody," she said. "At least I never have before."

I was surprised that she would say this. She never said a bad word about Mathias. She rarely talked of him at all. I assumed they'd had a perfect marriage. If they hadn't, I knew she would never tell me outright. It would be up to me to guess from clues that she would leave along the way. I used to believe that she kept her distance from me because she was still mourning for Mathias. I knew she felt a loyalty to him, even though Mathias was past caring about loyalty now. But she also didn't want me to think that she was leaving Mathias behind too quickly. If she did, she was afraid I would think less of her. By keeping me at arm's length, she was, at least for now, showing me greater affection than if she had been close.

"I do love you," I said.

After a moment of silence, she answered. "Don't tell me that. It will only make things harder when you leave."

I didn't know anymore what she thought of me. I was beginning to think I would never know, but then on our next trip out to sea, I got my first glimpse inside the oyster of her mind.

We pulled up the shredded remains of a balloon in our nets. Attached to the balloon was a note written on a piece of plastic in waterproof pen. The note said that the balloon had been from a Hebrew kindergarten in Far Rockaway, New York, that each student from the kindergarten had released a note, and please to write and say where we had found it.

We hosed down the fish, left them on the deck, and went inside to the galley. Suleika laid the piece of plastic out on a paper towel. Carefully, she wiped away the slime that it had gathered on the ocean floor. We found the name of a boy, Josh Neufeld, faint but legible, in one corner.

"The boy will be so happy," I said. "I bet he went to the mailbox every day for months to see if his balloon had been found." I was thinking to myself how I would have been and smiling to myself, recalling the click of the mail slot when it shut and the sound of the postman's steel-shod boots as he walked down the garden path. Then suddenly, I noticed that Suleika was crying. "Jesus," I said. "What's the matter?" Her tears caught me completely by surprise.

She looked up, eyes shot red. She had the piece of plastic pressed against the galley table with its pieces of glitter embedded in the white surface. She framed the message with the web of her thumb and index finger. "You have no idea, do you?" she asked.

"None," I said.

"You see yourself running to see what's in the mail, don't you? As a young boy, you see yourself, don't you?"

"Yes," I answered slowly, wondering if I should feel guilty about that. "That's who I see."

"I see our child," she said. "Not myself or you or some moment in our childhoods that reminds us of ourselves. *Our* child."

The words broke hard against my face. She had never said she loved me, or even liked me. She just never said things like that. Now, for her to tell me this, leapfrogging all the smaller measures of devotion that lay between us and a child of our own, stunned me.

"That's the way it is with us," she said.

"How? What way?" I demanded.

"How did you imagine it would be when you got here? What pictures did you paint of how your life would be?"

"I . . ." I stumbled around in my brain, hunting for an image.

"You didn't have any image of it, did you? You don't worry about things like that. You can't change how it will be. You see no point in trying to predict. It is how it is. That's the way you think, isn't it?"

"Yes," I said hoarsely. That was exactly how I thought. I wanted to offer up as an excuse the fact that my case officer at Tatianawald hadn't told me enough even to imagine how it might be, but I saw Suleika's point. Mine was too practical an answer. This was no time to disagree.

"I imagined everything," she told me, her eyes fixed on nothing. "The house we would get. The boat. The people we would meet. You always look to the past," she explained. "It's safer there. It's the place where everything gets to make sense, even when you know it didn't at the time. I envy you, the way you cast your thoughts. I'm the one who always ends up looking into the future and being dissatisfied with the present. Sometimes I see such huge gaps between the way things could be and the way they probably will be that I can't stand to think about it. But then something like this comes along—she held up the disintegrating message from the balloon—"and I am forced to see the failings of our life. Why should I set myself up to be miserable again once you are gone? Why shouldn't I try not to love you?"

"Failings? But everything is fine for now."

"No, it isn't." Her voice echoed around the galley. "Because the future is connected to now. I want something permanent in my life. Mathias is gone. If the KGB decides it, this boat will be gone. My life in America will be gone. Sometimes I feel as if everything around me is made up of nothing more solid than clouds. I expect to wake up one morning and find it all vanished."

"Clouds?" I asked. "But this is real." I set my hand on the galley table. "Everything around us is real."

"No." She was crying hard, hands pressed against her face.

When she got like this, there was nothing I could do to snap her out of it. Sadness encased her.

"You love your life too much," I said.

She looked up, outraged that I would say such a thing. "Damn you!" she shouted.

It was the cruelest thing I'd ever said to her, but I had to say it. We both knew it was the truth. She had become so frightened of losing what she had that she deliberately searched out things that might be going wrong, like the fact that she had no children yet, the fact that I might be leaving. So when her luck eventually faded, as she was sure it would, she could say she had known it was coming. Suleika was the kind of person who needed to know a thing like that. She might even cause it to happen. She would destroy what she loved rather than lose it. And because things can always be lost, she would destroy them before their loss could hurt her. "Suleika," I said, "if you want to ruin this, then ruin it. Only do the job quickly and get it over with."

We barely spoke for the rest of the trip. When we made it back to shore, we went away to our separate places, with no plans to meet or even a day when we would head out to sea again.

We didn't talk for a week. During that time, I stayed mostly in my apartment. I drank too much coffee. Sometimes I went over to Bad Joe's and ate oysters with Biagio. He didn't mention Suleika. He was smarter than that. Then I'd go back to my place and drink more coffee and try to do crossword puzzles, which I was never any good at, and I would piss myself off more than I already was.

A STORM WAS riding up from the southwest. New Englanders call them nor'easters because they blow toward the northeast. They are more dangerous than the rainy sou'westers or the cold, dry winds that blow straight down from the north. "Nor'easters turn into hurricanes," said the old-time fishermen with their elephant-hide faces, drawing people around them with stories of ships riding under the waves. The dock was crowded with boats that had cut short their fishing trips in order not to be caught in the rising seas. Even the crazy scallop fishermen had come in. The sky closed around us. It was a vault of pasty gray. Thunder rumbled in the distance. Gusts kicked old tin cans back and forth among Gunther's refrigeration trucks.

I was sitting in the one chair in my apartment, glad to be inside and warm. I was reading a book about a boy who used to work the Newport docks. Gunther had given it to me. His name was mentioned inside.

"I'm famous now," he told me. He tapped his grubby-nailed index finger against the blue-and-white cover of the paperback. "Fucking famous," he said, rolling his lips around the words.

I asked him if he ever saw the boy who wrote the book.

"Not these days," he said, his voice gone soft. "Sometimes I think I see him sitting by himself up at the Ocean Coffee Roasters place, but I don't know for sure. He was here for a while and then he left. That's the way it is around the docks."

The phone rang and I put down the book. My phone didn't work too well. It was ugly sea-foam green, with huge push-button numbers, as if the machine had been made for a child or a blind person. I bought it in a Salvation Army store, and sometimes I had to whack the receiver on the wall to get any sound out of it. "Hello?" I shouted. "My phone's busted. Hello?"

It was Suleika. "Liedke's back," she said. "He needs a ride."

"What about the storm?" I asked. Even with news like this, I was glad to hear her voice, the click and purr of it.

"It's not the first time he's made me go out in a storm. He doesn't want to go any more than we do. But the orders have come through. The sub will be there."

"Can't argue with the sub," I said. I looked out the window. The air was heavy with approaching thunder. It was insanity to leave the land on a night like this, with nothing but the ghosts of the sea and the static on our radio to keep us company. There was no point arguing with her. I couldn't force her to stay. She would go without me rather than fail to meet the sub. "I missed you," I said. "I drank too much coffee."

"So did I." Her voice was soft.

"I'll see you on the dock," I told her. Then I hung up the phone.

A drunk scalloper stopped us in the echoing shed of the fish house as we passed through to *The Baby Blue.* He had the place to himself and was running from one wall to the other, barging into the corrugated steel and laughing and stumbling back until he hit the other wall. Wind howled through the rafters. At the next dock over, sail cables thrashed urgent and metallic against the masts of sailboats. "Where you out to?" he asked. I could tell from his accent that he was a southerner, maybe one of the men up from Wanchese, North Carolina, the wildest of them all.

"Out fishing," Suleika told him. In the orange glimmer of the dock lights, the danger of leaving land now was clear in the hardened muscles of her face.

"Woo!" The man spun around. He climbed up on the fish weigher and rolled himself across the wet concrete floor on the little fish scale–crusted wheels attached to the bottom of the trolley. "You guys are going to die." Behind the scalloper, through the opening that led to the other side of the dock, Liedke's crow black silhouette slipped past.

"Nobody's going to die," Suleika told him. "Don't wish bad luck on us." She talked like the fishermen talked, their intonation and their phrases—old swamp Yankee drawl, southern white, black, Italian, a little Portuguese, all merged into the language of the deep-sea crews.

"I ain't making a wish on yourself." The scalloper rolled up to us on the squeaking wheels. "It's just that you don't mess with a nor'easter. It's like messing with God. He'll swallow you up and leave no trace behind." He was drunk, and loud with his righteousness and prophecy.

In a couple of hours, I thought as I looked at him, you'll be passed out and stupid again. Then, over the sound of the wind, I heard shouting up on Thames Street. It was the kind of noise people make when they have been watching a sports game in a bar and their team has won. From where I stood, I couldn't tell what the fuss was about.

"Come on," Suleika told me. She tugged at my arm.

I walked up to the drunken scalloper. I was getting ready to knock him down for the things that he had said.

"I'm sorry," he mumbled, realizing even through his drunkenness how serious it was to call down disaster on a crew heading out on the water. "I take it all back," said the Wanchese man.

"You can't," I said.

"I know it." He rolled away, sad, and hammered into the shadows on his squeaking fish-scale scooter.

We fired up the clanking engine of *The Baby Blue*. It was no less stubborn than the jukebox up at Bad Joe's. Sometimes I wondered if they were related. Liedke had sneaked into the wheelhouse. He sat on a bunk in the dark, carrying two small suitcases now instead of one. By the docklights, I saw that he looked miserable. "I don't like this one bit," he said. "I should be safe in bed now and not going out on this crate. And there's something else going on."

Before I had a chance to ask him what, I had to go out on deck and untie us from the dock pilings. After that, I coiled the heavy mooring ropes on the bow. We headed out toward the open water.

"Why look so grim, Liedke?" asked Suleika, turning from the wheel but keeping her hands locked on the greasy pins. "Didn't you sell all your rocks?"

"Oh, I sold them. I always do."

I watched the gusts racing across the water, illuminated by the lights of Newport. Out beyond the shelter of the bay, I could see the white tops of churned waves. If *The Baby Blue* had been a sailboat, we would have run with the wind, tacking back and forth. That might have made it easier to ride out the storm. But *The Baby Blue* was a tub, and there was nothing to do but stick to our course.

Out to sea, the storm closed in around us. Hours passed. With each pitch of the bow, the floor dropped away from under my feet. Then it smashed back up into my knees. The muscles of my legs stayed permanently clenched. Waves sprayed so often across the wheelhouse that I could see nothing but the trickle of water on glass. Suleika and I took turns steering the boat. Sometimes Liedke made his way up to the wheel. He had nothing to say. He set his hand on my shoulder, either out of comradeship or because he was losing his balance. Liedke was sick from the motion of the boat. Now and then, he staggered out on deck. His monstrous gurgling wretch reached me even over the moan of wind through our iron-cable rigging. Then he'd totter back inside, wiping his mouth on his sleeve, but still managing to smile.

"Liedke," I called to him. The jars of catsup and mustard swung clinking in their rack.

"Tovarisch Kapiten, I am yours to command." In the brief moments before his nausea returned, he found his sense of humor again.

We stood together at the wheel, staring grimly at the rain-crazed windows.

"Liedke," I said as softly as I could. I didn't want my voice to wake Suleika, who had strapped herself into her bunk to get some sleep. Her head rose from the pillow and fell back with each cresting wave and still she managed to sleep. "Liedke," I asked, "what is all this about something going on?"

He was quiet for a moment. There was only the sucking hiss as our bow cleared the water and the thump as we slammed onto the crest of the next wave. Eventually, he spoke. "I guess it doesn't hurt to tell you now." But then he said nothing. He just stared into space.

"What?" I asked him again.

He snapped out of it. "Some of my contacts were gone, people who have been there for years."

"Like Sacha at Aeroflot?" I wanted to show I knew something.

He laughed. "Bigger fish than Sacha. When I went to the rendezvous points, no one was there to meet me. The first time it happened, I thought it was strange, but by the fourth time, I knew something was wrong. Maybe a CIA roundup. You know I always have to scramble to meet all these contacts. They deliberately keep me off balance so I won't try to disappear. I'm never more than half a day out of their sight. I used to have these daydreams of going to Penn Station, getting on the first train that came along, and going wherever it took me. And then I'd do the same with another train, and the same with another and another, until even I didn't know where I was. But now, when the opportunity finally presented itself, I didn't go." He scratched his chins. "I don't understand myself sometimes."

We crested the waves so steeply that things began to fall off racks. I caught sight of Suleika, eyes open, lashed into her bed, trying to rest while her head lolled back and forth in the white trough of her pillow. The props squealed as they cleared the water. They spun madly before plunging below the surface again. Water swirled in a black-and-silver sheet across our deck. Then it gushed from the scupper holes.

"So, Liedke," I said. "So talk to me. How did you end up standing next to me on this shitty night?" I wanted to hear his voice. Hear him crack some jokes the way he did.

"You mean . . . "

"I mean right from the start. I'm not going anywhere."

"All right," he said. He was glad to take his mind off the storm. "Back in the late seventies, I ran a pawnshop in Minsk. A diamond ring here, a gold bracelet there. I never had enough money to buy the really good stuff. The only way a man like me had a hope of playing the game was to deal on the black market. At first, I was too nervous. How long is a fancy-clothes bum like me going to last in a Soviet jail? But after awhile, I got bolder. One or two items. Covering my tracks. Then a few more items. A little bolder still. Eventually, ninety percent of my business was in stolen goods. And of course I was caught. I was on my way to prison for twelve years when they made me this offer. Go to America. Sell stones for us. Bring back the Yankee dollar. And in the meantime, I can go on selling black-market goods as long as I do as I'm told. It was like the Americans say, an offer I couldn't refuse." Now from his pocket, Liedke pulled an old silver pillbox. On its lid was the two-headed imperial Russian eagle. The surface was burnished smooth, the metal shining darkly. He had jammed himself between the wheelman's chair and the dashboard. This freed him up to use his arms. He took from the box a pinch of brick red snuff. He pinched the dust from its box the way a person might pinch together the wings of a small butterfly that they are going to set free. He snorted it and rocked back, eyes shut and watering as the dust went up his nose. As the sneeze built inside him, I could see it on his face, which seemed to widen and flatten. His hand frantically gouged the bright blue handkerchief from his pocket. The sneeze was such an explosion that it made Suleika start. Afterward, Liedke smoothed the box with his thumb. He rubbed the silver as if it were a wishing stone. I wondered what nobleman's pocket the little box had lived in before the Russian Revolution, what grand days it had seen. Liedke saw me watching. He held out the box. "Try?" he asked.

I shook my head. "Trying to cut down." I changed the subject. "So why didn't you get on that train, the way you dreamed of doing? You're a smart man, Liedke. You could disappear."

Liedke's eyes seemed to go out of focus for a moment, he was so lost in thought. "Every time I came out here to meet the sub for that lousy trip home, I'd ask myself why I hadn't bolted. In the end, I was forced to admit"—he breathed in deeply, like a man stepping over the edge of a cliff— "that I like my life the way it is. I like my little shop in Minsk. I like my dirty little apartment and my dirty little family and friends. That's the difference between the dream and what is real. I don't care if they think they own me. I own what I want of my life. The rest they can have."

How different he was from Ingo Budde, I thought. Ingo, who needed to own everything he touched and wore and thought about. I missed Ingo.

The boat rode up, gasping from the water, the same as it had done hundreds of times that night. But instead of us crashing down onto the back of the next wave, something different happened. I still don't know exactly what caused it. I've heard stories of rogue waves, which form themselves in the havoc of storms. They don't follow the ribbed flow of other waves, but instead sweep across them perpendicularly. A boat caught by one of these can't roll and pitch at the same time, sideways and forward at once. Sometimes a ship will break its back on a rogue wave, spilling itself into the sea and sinking so fast that sailors drown in their bunks.

The Baby Blue jolted, shuddering, high to the right. I was knocked from the wheel and slammed my head against the CB radio. The blow spun me around. I ended up slumped in the corner. The boat was still shaking, as if we had run up on a rock and were scraping down its jagged sides.

Oh Christ, I was thinking. I'm going to die out here.

I couldn't see Liedke. In the cabin, pots and pans clanged inside their cupboard. I thought we were capsizing. The wheelhouse door flew open. The roar of the storm burst into the muggy warmth of the cabin. Out beyond the door I saw the white boil of the waves level with where I was standing. The boat struck another wave, this time in the stern. Water exploded across the steel plates of the deck, arcing over the wheelhouse and splashing down against the bow.

"The wheel!" screamed Suleika from her bunk.

Her shout brought me to my senses. In that moment, I was no longer afraid. I stood, feeling dizzy from the knock against the radio. The wheel was spinning on its own. I grabbed it and felt the sharp tug at my tendons as I brought it under control. The boat reared like a horse. I had to get us into the wind. I spun the wheel, feeling another blast against the hull. Silver spray flew past us. We tipped downward. I gripped the wheel to stop from being hurled back into the bunkroom.

Suleika stood beside me. She kicked the wheelhouse door shut. It was suddenly quieter in the cabin. "Did you let go of the wheel?" she yelled at me, her face close and angry and out of focus. "Did you fall asleep?"

"I was at the wheel!" I shouted back. "Liedke and I were talking. Something hit us from the side." I wiped what I thought was sweat from my forehead and my hand came away bloody. I realized I had cut my head against the radio. I dabbed my fingers against the wound. The skin was puffed and torn at my hairline. I wiped my hand against my shirt. "I wasn't sleeping, Suleika. I swear."

She knew she'd have to put her anger someplace else. "Where is Liedke, anyway?" she asked.

We looked around. There was a red splat on the cabin floor where the catsup bottle had exploded. Spoons and forks from an emptied drawer lay scattered in every corner. A blue-and-yellow cylinder of Morton salt rolled back and forth, scribbling grainy white lines.

"Liedke?" Suleika called cautiously into the tiny space of the cabin.

"Liedke?" I called, too.

There was no answer.

"He's been washed overboard," said Suleika.

"Bastards!"

I looked at Suleika. "What?"

"I didn't say anything," she replied.

"Damn bastards." It was Liedke.

At first, I couldn't see him. Then I saw Liedke crawl out from under Suleika's bunk. His nose was bleeding. "Where are my suitcases?" he asked frantically. "Those little bastards!" He scrabbled around the floor and then crawled back under the bunk. His rear stuck huge and awkwardly in the air. "Oh, here they are! Come here, my beauties." He collapsed in relief, still wedged under the bunk.

Suleika turned to me. "Watch the wheel, Paul." Her hand brushed my arm as she moved by.

Liedke crawled out from under the bunk. Then he sat against the galley table, puffing.

I faced the front, gripping the sweat-polished pins, blind again to what lay beyond the bow. I was hypnotized by the windblown mosaics of water across the windowpanes.

Three hours later, we neared our coordinates for the rendezvous. The storm was worse than ever. Suleika took over from me. I managed to sleep a little in my bunk, but it was a twisted sleep, in which Suleika's and Liedke's conversations and laughter, which were maybe theirs and maybe not, warped my dreams. Voices bled from the sea. In my half sleep, I saw the gray-white alabaster faces of the ocean ghosts. The drowned rose from the hulk graves of their ships to gape at me with their empty-socket eyes. They pressed their clammy hands against the porthole glass. I shook myself awake and rubbed the grit of dreaming from my eyes.

Suleika kept her eye on the loran's red digital letters. "Close," she said. "Close now."

Liedke checked his suitcases for the hundredth time. He unsnapped the locks on one and opened it. The case was filled with stacks of money tied with rubber bands. He saw me looking, then grinned and closed the case again. "This is for the bear," he said.

He meant the Russian bear.

I thought back to what Liedke had said about his contacts failing to appear. I wondered what was up. I had a sense that something had gone badly wrong.

We reached the coordinates at 11:45 P.M. I wondered if I would see the submariner again. I was going to ask him for a Papirossi and be for a minute like Volkov, drugged in the haze of fast-returning memory.

It was hard to keep the boat on track. We couldn't let the engines idle. If we did, the wind twisted us around and we took waves broadside, each strike like a battering ram, threatening to crack the hull apart. We had to move around in circles, downwind and upwind.

Suleika opened the cabin door. The damp howl of wind filled

the cabin, exhaling the warmth of our bodies. She pulled on her black rainproof coat and hid her face under the Grim Reaper hood. Then she ducked outside. A moment later came the iron-on-iron grinding sound of the engine-room door being opened. She was going down to signal the boat with the burst-transmitter radio.

I kept us turning. It was like being strapped to a vicious merry-go-round. When we got in from this trip, I promised myself a week of doing nothing but sitting in my room in my one comfortable chair and having pizzas delivered. This time, Suleika would be there, too. No coffee and no crossword puzzles.

Ten minutes later, she staggered back into the cabin.

"Did you reach them?" I asked.

"No." She pulled down her hood. Water trickled from her sleeves. "The bilge is flooded. We're taking on water."

A burning slashed across my stomach. If the boat was leaking from a seam below the bilge line, it could not be repaired out here on the ocean. Then it would only be a matter of time before we sank.

"Are we all right?" asked Liedke.

We didn't answer him. I fixed the ropes on the wheel. Suleika and I headed out of the cabin and hauled open the heavy engine room door. I climbed down the ladder first. The room was filled with its usual sauna heat, drawing painful threads of sweat from my back and face and hands. I crouched down next to the plywood sheets cut out around the engine. I hooked my finger into a gap and pulled up the board. "Jesus Christ," I gasped. Oily black wash tipped sluggishly back and forth only a few inches below the rusty engine block. Normally, the bilge was at least a foot and a half below the engine. I tried without success to calculate how much water we had taken on.

A motor started up behind me. It was a thin, rattling sound, and when I turned, I saw that Suleika had set the bilge pump going. It looked like the motor from a lawn mower, attached to a fat black rubber hose that snaked down under the floorboards of the engine. The motor shook on its hinges.

"Can you tell how fast it's coming in?" she shouted.

"Too fast for the pump." Heat fanned, prickling, across the tops of my shoulders. "We should head back now. Forget about the sub."

"No!" The urgency was clear in her voice, even above the sound of the engines. "Too much trouble if we let them down."

I looked at my watch. "They're already half an hour late!"

"We'll wait one hour," she said. "You work the radio." She told me to prepare a message, which I could feed through the burst transmitter at regular intervals. As soon as the sub replied, I was to switch the communication lever to talk and then I could use the microphone attached to the side of the set by a coiled rubber cable, like a telephone cord. She made me run through the procedure twice and very quickly, just like one of the instructors at Tatianawald. Then she was gone, climbing the ladder. The worn-out soles of her rubber boots disappeared up the rungs. When the door shut, I felt the change of pressure in my ears. Heat swelled inside the bottled space of the engine room. The air smelled greasy. The thump of waves against the bow reminded me of artillery firing in the distance, which I had heard so often at Diaghilev.

I tapped out the code, then squashed my thumb against the yellow button. I set the burst and triggered it. Then I began a countdown until the next burst would be sent. I turned the receiving volume up high and kept the headphones around my neck. I listened to the whispering static.

The bilgewater sloshed under the floorboards. When we caught a wave hard, the water splashed up and trickled over the duck-egg blue paint of the boards. I kept my eye on my watch. Twenty-five minutes until we headed back to Newport. The pump motor rattled. I tried not to move. The heat was more bearable if I kept still. Tapping out the code, I imagined the pulses of sound fanning out and fading away into the skull-cracking pressure below us. Somewhere out there, maybe, they reached the great black iron hide of the sub, where the submariner was sleeping soundly.

I kept shaking my watch. Couldn't understand how time could be passing so slowly. I sent another burst, then pressed both headphones to my ears. Nothing and nothing and nothing except static. I pulled the headphones down around my neck and wiped sweat and sticky blood off my face.

Three minutes. The engine whined as our props cleared the water yet again. The propeller shaft spun, screeching.

Two minutes. My legs cramped. I was choking in the heat.

I looked at my watch and seven minutes had gone by. I was confused. I must have blacked out. I had no sense of time. I tapped out the code again and then transmitted the message. No reply. Enough, I thought. I switched off the radio, dumped the headphone on top, and closed the waterproof case. I stood too quickly and chips of light whirled around my face. I watched a greasy slap of water belch up from the floorboards. The pump wasn't doing enough. I breathed in deeply, ready to howl out some obscenity. But I just stood stone-faced and silent. The breath trailed out of my lungs. In that moment, I realized we would not make it back to land.

Four

I OPENED THE ENGINE ROOM DOOR JUST AS THE GLASSY ARC of a wave jumped the deck. The force of it barged me back. I found myself swinging by one arm from the engine room ladder. Water poured past me onto the engine. The rest of the wave sucked back, gushing through the scuppers. I looked down the dripping ladder rungs. The engine was still working. The engine housing steamed and salt crusted white on the rusted brown metal as it evaporated.

The bilge pump was still working, but not well enough. I shut the engine room door and went into the cabin. In the wheelhouse, Suleika was yelling at Liedke. "You can stay with Paul, for God's sake! Spend some of that damn money, why don't you? They'll send another sub."

I sighed with relief. We were heading back.

"No, they won't send another!" Liedke's humor had gone.

He peered through the portholes, looking for the submarine. "Just wait a little longer," he begged.

"You don't get it, Liedke." Suleika took hold of Liedke's collar and heaved him away from the porthole. She slapped the flat of her hand against his forehead. "The boat is leaking! If we wait, we will die. How much good are your suitcases full of money if they're at the bottom of the sea?"

Liedke staggered around the cabin, red in the face and his shirt untucked. "Oh, I am in so much trouble."

Suleika was furious to have taken these risks for nothing. We would be the ones to pay for not waiting, even if we did make it back to land. "You sent the message?" she asked me.

"Of course."

"You listened?"

"Nothing." I held up my hands. "I would have said."

With a pin-blurring spin of the wheel, Suleika turned the boat around. She jammed the red-topped lever of the throttle as far forward as it would go and we headed west toward land. "Get the charts," she said to me.

I brought the rolled and rubber-banded maps down from the chart box.

Suleika fished through them until she found the one she was looking for. She spread it out flat. It was a map of Block Island Sound. I could see Nantucket and the tip of Long Island and Block Island and Narragansett Bay. The depths were marked all over the map: 100 ft., 300 ft., 330 ft. They looked like tiny insects. Suleika cross-checked the map with the readout on our loran. Her finger rustled across the chart. "Here."

I looked at the huge sweep of blank paper between Suleika's finger and the jagged edge of land.

"We'll head for Nantucket," she said. It was thirty miles away.

"What about me?" Liedke loomed behind us. "How are you going to explain me being on the boat?"

"I don't know," said Suleika. "We'll figure it out when we get there."

"Well, you'd better come up with something! What are you going to say, that you found a Russian in a business suit carrying half a million dollars in cash just bobbing around like a cork in the ocean?"

"Half a million dollars?" asked Suleika. Even in the middle of all this, her surprise was clear.

"Not a penny of which belongs to me!" barked Liedke.

The jabber of angry voices died away. We were left again with the constant rolling thunder of the storm. *The Baby Blue* ploughed on toward Nantucket. Liedke lay in my bunk, the suitcases stacked on his chest. He looked like someone laid out for a wake.

I don't know how long Suleika and I stood there. I had taken off my watch and stuffed it in a pocket rather than torture myself by looking at it every thirty seconds. I had no idea how much ground we were covering. There was nothing to do but pray to the engine, like praying to some primitive God whose effigy we had created out of grease and pipes and gasoline. I felt as if I were strapped to the wheel of a time machine, growing old too fast, gray-faced age rushing forward to meet me.

"What we all need now," said Liedke suddenly, "is some genuine pleasure."

"What?" Suleika and I said simultaneously.

"Ecstasy!" said Liedke. "Rapture!"

The lights went out.

Liedke gave a high-pitched panicking squeal.

Down below, the engine coughed. It stopped and started again and chugged and gave a lazy, dragging moan and then quit. The noise of the storm was suddenly deafening. The screech of the wind pierced my ears. As my eyes grew used to the night, I saw a purple bluish glow that rimmed the portholes.

Suleika fumbled behind the wheel. Then a flashlight beam jabbed out of the dark, illuminating Liedke's face. He looked like a ghoul. Suleika turned the boat's ignition key back and forth. A red light flickered on the control panel, but there was no response from the engine.

Liedke stood. He banged his head on the roof of the bunk.

Suleika and I made our way outside to the engine room door. We each grabbed one of the lever handles and released the clamps. As I was helping to swing open the door, I caught sight of Liedke's face in the rear porthole. His skin was pale like bone, haloed in the paint-chipped brass of the porthole, just like the ghosts I had dreamed of.

A smell of scorched oil wafted into our faces from the blackness of the engine room. I heard the heavy slop of water. When Suleika switched on the flashlight, we both let out a moan. There was no engine room. There was only water. The ladder vanished down into it. The yellow of the CAT engine glimmered under the oil-rainbowed surface, lying there like something once alive and now drowned. I had never felt such helplessness.

I didn't need Suleika to tell me what to do next. I went back into the cabin, switched on the CB radio, which, like the loran, had an auxiliary battery built into it. I switched to the emergency channel and began broadcasting an SOS.

Liedke stumped up behind me, groping from one handhold to another. "You think it's my fault, don't you?" he asked.

"Shut up, Liedke," I said quietly. The boat rocked heavily, wallowing. We rose sluggishly from the trough of each new wave. We were going under. Nothing could save the boat now.

"I can hardly swim, you know." His voice wavered with panic. "Oh, I knew we should never have come out."

He made me angry with his useless talk. I wondered whether a part of me did blame him for bringing us here. I thought about telling him the truth, which was that we didn't have expensive survival suits, only life jackets, and that this time of year a person only lasts about twenty minutes before his jaw locks and he goes under.

"What can I do?" Liedke asked suddenly. He had finally said something useful.

"You can see if Suleika needs help." I just wanted him out of my way. I wondered how far we were from Nantucket. I tried to imagine us all swimming up onto the beach, bodysurfing the waves, riding the white foam out of the dark until we hit the boil of tide-churned sand and would be safe and maybe I would never put to sea again, not even for Suleika.

A minute later, Liedke ran back inside. He slammed the door, boxing my ears with the pressure change. "She's gone! I looked into the engine room and called for her, but there was no reply. She's not out on the deck. I looked everywhere." Liedke's large, weak, fat-fingered hands took hold of me. His bloodless lips were like strips of candle wax. "She's gone, Paul! What are we going to do?"

I felt something drop away deep in my stomach. I rushed out on deck. I reached myself from cleat to cable, handhold to handhold. I found the flashlight wedged against the first rung of the engine room ladder. I switched it on and aimed it into the engine room. At first I saw nothing and then I saw a bubbling hiss rise from the base of the ladder. Suleika's face, seeming half-formed in the dirty water, rose, streaming bubbles from her nose until she burst to the surface. She gasped in air and clung to the ladder with one hand. With the other hand, she heaved up the yellow radio in its black waterproof carrier. "Help me with this!" she shouted.

A wave shoved me into the door, dousing Suleika and filling the engine room even more. As soon as it had passed, I crouched down and helped to lift the radio. It was heavy, like lifting a basket of fish with one hand. I raised it to the deck and then held on to it while Suleika clambered over me and up onto the top of the wheelhouse. In the gloom and thrashing rain, I saw her releasing the straps of the barrel-shaped life raft container. She untied a rope with a clamp at the end from around the cylinder and set the clamp on the mounting for the life raft. Then she brought the barrel down to the deck, paying out line as she went. "When we throw this overboard," Suleika shouted over the howl of the storm, "we have to throw it out as far as we can. The line has to be pulled taut for the life raft's inflation cylinders to engage. It will still be attached to the boat, so if we're low in the water by then, you have to cut us loose as fast as you can. Do you understand?"

The cabin door flew open, jarring its hinges. "There's someone on the radio!" bellowed Liedke. "I don't know how to make it work!"

Suleika and I lunged for the wheelhouse. Liedke followed, a suitcase under each arm.

Suleika talked into the CB mike, but there was no reply.

"There *was* someone out there," Liedke told us. "He told us to repeat the message."

I wondered if Liedke had imagined the voices.

Then the CB crackled. "This is Coast Guard station Nantucket Light. Repeat your message. Over."

Suleika set the mike to her mouth, the plastic still smelling of her dead husband's cigarette smoke. "This is fishing vessel *Baby Blue*. Our engine is out and we are shipping water. Pump has failed. Over."

"Fishing vessel *Baby Blue*, can you relay coordinates? Over."

Suleika glanced up at the loran. Then she gave our coordinates. She was shivering. Her skin looked blue. Her straggled hair glimmered with oil from the flooded bilge.

"Fishing vessel *Baby Blue*, we have your coordinates. We'll see if we can get a rescue vessel out to you. Stand by. Over."

All three of us heaved out a breath.

"We'll be all right, won't we?" asked Liedke.

I said nothing. There was no guarantee. This time of year, a lot of boats went down and their crews were never found, even though they had sent out distress calls that had been picked up by the Coast Guard. Even with all the available technology, finding a small ship in a storm is hard and sometimes impossible.

"Fishing vessel *Baby Blue,* we are in launch procedure at this time. Over. You will need to stay on the radio. Over."

"I'm on auxiliary power, Coast Guard. Over." Suleika released the speak button and wiped sweat from her forehead with the fist-shaped black plastic microphone. There was a long pause on the radio. The rush of static filled our ears.

"*Baby Blue,* we will need you to broadcast every couple of minutes. You are twelve miles out. We cannot afford to overshoot you in this weather. Is that clear? Over."

"Clear, Coast Guard. We will broadcast every two minutes. When you get close, I'll start sending up flares. What is your ETA? Over."

"Uncertain, *Baby Blue.* We'll be heading out within the next twenty minutes. You hang in there. Out."

"*Baby Blue* out." Suleika switched off the machine.

Liedke started up immediately. "How are you going to explain that I'm here? And what about the money? Are they going to search us?"

"Just give me a minute, Liedke." Suleika set her thumb knuckle between her teeth, thinking.

"Maybe we could dress him up as a crewman," I offered. "We could say he lost his wallet and all his ID. That is, if they check it at all."

"What about the money?" Liedke butted in.

"I don't think there's any way you can keep it," said Suleika. "They'll find it on you. You'd never be able to explain that."

"Then I might as well stay on the boat. I'm dead."

"You aren't dead, Liedke," I snapped. "You're making too much noise for a dead guy."

We broadcast our position again and the Coast Guard radioed us to say they were heading out. Meanwhile, our boat was foundering. Waves sloshed constantly across the deck. Our bow was starting to rise as the engine room swamped. We felt the change in angle, straining the muscles in our calves to remain steady.

We broadcast again. Again they called us back. Suleika explained to Liedke what we had to do to launch the life raft.

I felt strangely distant from *The Baby Blue*. Over the past weeks, I had begun to form an attachment to it. I was even a little proud of the fact it was the shabbiest boat at Gunther's dock. I had grown used to its failings. But already I could imagine it slumped at the bottom of the ocean, its angles softened by algae, and this dry, sweat-smelling room become a chamber of silt and weeds for the tiny, nibbling fish.

Broadcast. Their scratchy voices answered us. The first gray smears of dawn showed on the horizon. Patches of star-speckled blue showed among the tumbling clouds.

Liedke kept his face pressed to the window, watching for the lights of their approaching boat.

"Liedke," said Suleika, resting her fine-boned hand on the fat man's shoulder as if to calm him so he would hear what she had to say. "You're going to have to lose the money. If they find it on us, or if the boat fails to sink completely and they salvage it, they could find this stuff and then the whole game would be up."

"I can't just drop the cash. All you're thinking about is yourselves."

"All right, Liedke! What if I am thinking about us? What if they do castrate you when you don't show up with that money? I'd rather it was just you than all three of us spending the rest of our lives in an American prison."

None of us had noticed *The Baby Blue* turn broadside to the wind. The boat heaved abruptly to the side. Suleika flew backward, spread-eagle into the wheelhouse door, which flew open and left her clinging to the door frame. I wrapped myself around the wheelman's chair as the starboard side of the boat dipped underwater. A wave cascaded over the top of the boat. One of the porthole windows punched open, swinging back. The glass shattered into a spider's web. A bolt of water blasted through it and across the wheelhouse. I had lost sight of Liedke. I waited for the swing to the other side as we rode up the valley of the next wave, but it never came. We were swamped. There was too much water in the engine room. It was only a matter of time, perhaps even seconds, before *The Baby Blue* went down.

Water was pouring into the cabin. The floor was already shin-deep. The cold water knifed my legs as it poured in over the tops of my boots. I kicked off the boots, tore off my socks, and moved barefoot to where Suleika was on her hands and knees. I raised her up and she clung to me, coughing and spitting. "Where's Liedke?" she choked out.

"We have to get out on deck." I half-carried her, half-dragged her toward the door. Another wave smashed into the side of *The Baby Blue.*

"Find Liedke," she said.

I wanted to take care of her first. I led us out onto the sloping deck. *The Baby Blue* was going down stern-first. The bow rose high. The hatch had come off the ice room. Condensation from melting ice billowed out of it, as if there were a fire down below. When the waves tumbled over the deck, they poured down into the ice room. I left Suleika clinging to the ladder that led to the top of the wheelhouse. Then I scrambled around trying to find the hatch cover.

"Leave it!" Suleika shouted. "It'll just come off again. It's too late. We have to find Liedke."

I waded across what was left of the stern, my arms raised above my head and my fingers dug into the nylon mesh of the net to stop myself from being washed overboard. I turned to look back at Suleika. Then I saw him.

Liedke stood on top of the wheelhouse. His torn jacket flapped around his shoulders. He had hold of the life raft cylinder and was looking down at us, showing his teeth, his eyes gone wild. I knew without anything more than a glimpse of that face that he had no intention of waiting for us to climb aboard the raft. He was going to leave us to die on the sinking boat and let himself drift with his money, preferring to face the slim chance that he might float to shore or be the recipient of God knows what other miracle, rather than let go of his cash.

Liedke coiled his body and then with a grunt heaved the life raft barrel into the sky. It flew end over end, trailing the rope, and then the rope pulled tight. There was a pop and the barrel burst in two. A slithering sound reached us as the raft's inflation cylinders engaged. The raft hit the water like a huge yellow pancake. It swelled until its sides ballooned and the canopy raised like a tent.

I saw the rogue wave coming. It channeled along the crest of another wave, trailing foam and filling the air with a huge gasping hiss. The two crumbling bars of the waves came together like the zeroed-in sights of a gun on the crippled bow of *The Baby Blue.* Even with the weight of tons of water flooding belowdecks, the wave raised the bow. Jets of water shot from the portholes. Liedke was lifted into the air, a suitcase and one of his polished and now ruined shoes cartweeling after him. The enormous bulk of the man's belly flopped hard and painfully into the ankle-deep water on the deck. The bow rose high and higher, so high I thought it would flip us over. Liedke rolled onto his back and grabbed with his dough-soft hands at anything to stop him moving. Water was pouring in a sheet through the gap in the stern where the net normally payed out when we were fishing. Liedke was going with it and he knew. He saw his own death coming.

I still clung to the net, fingers locked among the strands, smelling the rancid fish. The water pulled at my body. Cold water rinsed around my feet and between my toes.

Liedke flailed his arms and howled, pitiful and wordless. The rogue wave broke around us. The bow fell and the stern began to rise and for a moment it looked as if he might stay on the deck. But the force of the water was carrying him. He swept past below me. My eyes met his eyes and even in the half-light I could see his terror. His mouth was an open, screaming hole. Liedke was carried from the boat, down below the brass fins of the unspinning props, polished by the sea. The rogue wave traveled on, closing the gap where it had met us. For a second, I heard Liedke cry out before the stern of *The Baby Blue* slammed down on top of him. The sound was shut out. I knew I would never see him again.

"Get out to the raft," Suleika shouted. She was fighting her way up to the roof of the wheelhouse. She checked that the launch cable was still fastened to the raft. Then I saw her lift up one of Liedke's suitcases that had been wedged under the holding rail.

"We'll swim out together!" I shouted.

"I'll be there. Just go." She kicked open the top hatch of the wheelhouse and dropped down inside.

The sky was lighter now. My face stung from the jabbing rain. I found my way to the side. By now the boat was almost level with the waves. Chunks of ice from the flooded ice room clunked around the deck and half-frozen fish slid out of the scuppers. I saw the life raft and jumped overboard without thinking of anything else.

I sank down and had to struggle to reach the surface again. My clothes were heavy, but I had no time to shuck them off because already I had begun to drift behind the boat. *The Baby Blue* loomed huge out of the waves. I thrashed forward through the foam to the raft, grabbed hold of a black nylon strap, and heaved myself inside. I slid onto the platform of the raft, which was flooded. I had to fight even to turn over so I could breathe. As I rolled, I saw *The Baby Blue*. Soon only the wheelhouse would be above water. My clawed fingers ached from gripping the net.

Suleika scrambled back onto the roof. She was wearing a life jacket and carrying the Russian radio she used to contact the sub.

In her other hand, she held Liedke's suitcase. "Catch this!" she yelled.

Water splashed in my face. I held out my arms for the suitcase. At that moment, out in the distance, far over the white-slicked crests, I caught sight of a strange and blazing light, as if the sun had broken through the night, but it was fragmented, flickering like embers in a gust of wind. My first thought was that it might be the Coast Guard boat, but the light was in the east, out to sea, away from the direction the cutter would be arriving. I stared, waiting until we rode up on another wave so that I might see it again. All this took only a second. The next thing I knew, the Russian radio in its heavy rubber case slugged against my chest and sent me to the other end of the raft. I couldn't breathe. My eyes fizzed. I felt myself blacking out. Blood poured out of my nose and down the back of my throat.

A moment later, Suleika flopped gasping into the raft. Immediately, she pulled a knife from her pocket, hooked out the blade with her thumbnail, and cut us loose from *The Baby Blue.*

I felt a sudden rush of movement as we slid over a wave, leaving the boat behind. I was doubled up with pain.

Suleika bailed out the water with her hands. Then she zipped the canopy shut. Gray light filtered through a clear section of the canopy. She unbuckled the radio case, under which the floor of the raft sagged down. She switched on the radio, moving as quickly as she could. "I hope this works," she said.

I rolled over and groaned. My face was pressed against her blue-jeaned knee. My soaked clothes were pasted to my body. Shivering fanned out across my back.

Suleika turned the frequency dial and then began to speak into the microphone. "Coast Guard, this is *The Baby Blue.* I am in the raft now. Do you still have us on radar?"

"*Baby Blue,* your signal is spotty. The waves are obscuring you. Right now we have you at three miles' distance. Try to stay in radio contact until you have us visual. Over."

"I'll broadcast every two minutes. As soon as I see you, I'll start sending up flares." She released her forefinger from the speak button and heaved the radio set up onto her crossed knees so that it would stay as dry as possible. Then she fell back, exhaustion catching up with her. "Are you all right?" she croaked at me.

I raised my head. "I thought you were going to throw the suitcase," I said. It hurt to talk. I felt a pinching sensation whenever I took a breath.

"They'll fix you up," she said. She was too preoccupied to show sympathy. "We have to stay in radio contact and the only way for us to do that is this thing. If I'd tried swimming with it, I'd have sunk like a rock."

I coughed up some water. The pain closed me off from all that had happened. I watched with detachment as she took the knife and opened up a seam of her orange life jacket. She unzipped the canopy about a foot. The storm howled in again, loud and angry. She began to empty the fluffy kapok stuffing from the life jacket over the side. When this was done, she opened up Liedke's suitcase and began to pack money inside the life jacket cushions. She crammed all of the money inside. Then she unzipped a panel in the side of the life raft and pulled out the survival pack. The contents—flares and Band-Aids and plastic packets of drinking water printed in several languages in blue on the clear packets—spilled out across the floor. Suleika used the sewing repair kit from the survival pack to restitch the life jacket. When she had done this, she strapped on the life jacket again. She buckled it tight and the money stuffing bunched around her throat. She looked as if she was in a neck brace. "Hell of a thing," she said quietly.

For the first time since I'd climbed on board the raft, I remembered Liedke. When all of this was over, I would miss the jolly fat man, who had been, however briefly, the only tangible link between my old life and my new. I looked out through the foggy plastic window of the life raft, which was streaked with water. The sky was almost light now. The foamy crests of waves sped by. I looked for *The Baby Blue,* but either we were facing the wrong way or she had sunk. I thought about the whirlpool that a sinking ship trails behind it as it sinks, pulling down everything close by. I pictured Liedke, eyes wide and dead, trapped in the swirling, bubbling vortex. I imagined the ship thudding down in a silt explosion on the seabed, the neatly coiled bow and stern ropes descending in a snake dance onto the upturned hull. I imagined the net, Christmas-bobbled with flotation buoys, in a huge patchwork fan around the boat. I saw it all so clearly, as if the cold and shock and pain of my ribs had let me see beyond what my eyes would let me glimpse.

I don't recall too much about the arrival of the Coast Guard and the trip to Nantucket. I passed out a couple of times. I remember Suleika shouting that she could see them and immediately heaving the Russian radio out over the side. It was too high-tech a piece to be found aboard a grubby trawler, and besides that, all the working instructions were in Russian. No lie in the world would have covered that track.

I remember leaning out of the raft and striking a red handheld flare and reaching up with its hissing scarlet blaze, whose flame burned my hair and filled my lungs with burnt hair's rancid smoke. I saw the Coast Guard cutter, a white sixty-footer with a blue-and-orange stripe across her bow. It signaled to us with a lamp. Windshield wipers seesawed on its wheelhouse windows.

I recall being wrapped in crackly silver blankets by one of the five-person crew, two of whom were women, and being handed some hot coffee without milk or sugar.

I remember the captain of the Coast Guard boat, a clean-cut man in a yellow rain slicker and blue baseball cap with USCG in yellow on the crown. He asked Suleika if there were any other crewmen onboard and Suleika said, "No. Only us."

"Don't ever go out in a storm like this again," he said, swaying back against a rack of bright orange life jackets. "Don't make me risk my life for something as stupid as a few more fish in your ice room."

"No, sir," I said, and was ashamed. He had every right to say what he was saying and to be angry. I wished I could have told him what had really been at stake. "I believe I am through with it now," I told him.

"We'll see about that," he said. "I bet you're out fishing on the next calm day we get. I know you guys. You can't stay away for long. You go land-crazy."

"Land-crazy," I said. "After this, I might just go regular crazy first."

I saw the first gray hump of land that was Nantucket. I had given up hope of seeing it. To have that hope back again unnerved me as much as losing it in the first place. Through the veils of rain, I saw the lightning flash so furiously that it actually turned the air over the island green, like bright sunlight through a summer leaf. As we pulled up to the dock, the storm grew even worse and the light became rosy red, like blood diluted in water. I don't know what caused it or even if it was possible, but I saw it with my own eyes.

There was an ambulance waiting for us at the dock. I said I didn't want to go to the hospital, but I ended up in the ambulance anyway, with Suleika lying beside me, hearing the squeeze and puff of a blood pressure monitor being inflated on my arm. When one of the ambulance men tried to get Suleika to take off her life jacket, she acted so crazy that they let her keep it on.

At the hospital, the examining doctor discovered that I had three cracked ribs. The police came to talk to us and then the Coast Guard came and asked us the same questions again. Suleika gave them some story about wanting to get a load of fish while the other boats were docked because she knew the price would be higher. This was not unheard of. Fishermen who needed the money or who were crazy would go out in almost anything. The Coast Guard were curious about a woman working on such a small boat. I could tell from the tone of the men's voices that they were impressed and trying to hide it. After the questioning, we were both taken to separate rooms. I was in too much pain to protest. Pain sparked across my chest. I took some kind of medication and slept, but not with a gentle drifting into the dark. The drugs slammed a black door in my face and I fell into a chasm without dreams or peace.

When I woke again, it was night. The storm was still blowing. At first, I didn't know where I was. The hospital was quiet. Feet in rubber-soled shoes padded by in the corridor. Somewhere I heard a TV and a newscaster talking about the weather. My clothes were slung over a chair beside my bed. They had been cleaned and dried. I felt embarrassed at how filthy they must have been. I had come ashore barefoot and someone had left me a pair of hospital shoes that looked like white tennis sneakers. I swung out of bed and put on the clothes and the shoes. Still buried in the crossed threads of the cotton was the smell of the boat—of oil and sweat and fish and salt. Even after what had happened, I felt comforted by the smell. It made more sense to me than the bleached tang of hospital disinfectant.

I went into the bathroom and splashed water on my face. My skin was rosy pink with sleep. I smoothed the hair back on my head because I didn't have a comb. Then I inspected the bandage that circled my torso. There was nothing for it, the doctor had said, but to wait until the ribs healed by themselves.

I wanted to get home. Once I got there, I would be safe—in my own bed, listening to the Sicilians downstairs in the pasta shop, and their violin-raked music from the worn-out radio. I went to the front desk and asked about Suleika, because I didn't know which room she was in.

The nurse told me she had checked out. She said Suleika had tried to wake me, but the painkillers had me so knocked out that

I wouldn't open my eyes. I asked where Suleika had gone and the nurse said she didn't know.

I wondered if I would ever see her again. I felt guilty even for thinking it, but the thought was there nonetheless. She had not left me a note, or stayed until I woke up. She had just disappeared. I knew she had left the island. Even in this storm, she would have found a way. *The Baby Blue* had held us together. Now that it was gone, I could not say for sure what we had left, especially after our fight. Besides, she had all that money now. She could go anywhere. There was nothing I could do about it, except to hope I was wrong.

I checked myself out of the hospital and walked outside, hearing the boom of the waves through the cobbled streets. Rain stabbed out of the dark. I moved past shops that were either closed for the night or closed for the season. Some lights were on in apartments above the shops and I could see the blue-reflected glow of television sets on the rain-spattered windows. I came to a road that ran beside the ocean. Waves bludgeoned the massive stones of the breakwater and fractured into spitting spray. For a long time, I just stood there. At that moment, even to breathe the watery air of the storm was a pleasure. I remembered what Liedke had said about wanting to feel genuine pleasure. I wondered what he was talking about.

There was a small restaurant still open on the corner, its sign rocking and creaking in the wind. The name of the place was the Toto Diner and its logo was a little black dog with a red tongue peeking out of a basket and winking. An old couple, still wearing their rainproofs, were sitting at a table in the corner. Two men sat up at the counter, drinking coffee and smoking cigarettes. They wore blue overalls that said NANTUCKET FERRY SERVICE.

Everyone looked up when I walked in. I sat down at one of the tables and a boy about eighteen years old brought me a menu from behind the counter. He wore a white T-shirt with a white apron. "The chef's gone home," he said. "He goes home about eleven and then we just have sandwiches." He said it all in one breath and with great seriousness.

"Good," I said. I could tell he hadn't been long on the job. Still proud to be in charge and not long enough at work to think about the lousy wage he was probably earning and the fact that he was working the graveyard shift.

"Well, what kind of sandwich would you like? If we got the fixings, I'll make it all right."

I looked up at him. "You go ahead and pick what you do best," I said. "I'm a little too tired to choose. You can bring me some coffee, please."

The ferrymen had their eye on me. There was no meanness in their gaze. They were just watching. Just for something to do. The same way I watched strangers coming into Bad Joe's bar. "Mother of a storm," said one, talking to me but not looking directly at me. He wore a greasy blue baseball cap with PHIL embroidered in red onto the crown.

"Not wrong about that," I told him. My neck muscles were tired. When I spoke, I didn't look at him either, letting him know I wasn't looking for conversation.

"They brought in some people off a boat that was sinking," said Phil, telling the world.

"I heard about it," I replied. I didn't say I was one of them. I wanted to be anonymous for now.

"One of them was a woman."

"Goddamn," said the other man. "A woman in a boat on a night like this."

Another man walked in and he was carrying a bundle of newspapers. "Evening to you," he said in a loud voice, as if he had been saying it to people in this diner for years and as if it was the only thing he ever said to them. He smiled unseeing at the congregation and made his way to a blue-and-white machine that held copies of *The New York Times*.

"How'd you get those papers in with the storm and all?" asked Phil.

"The miracle of flight, my friend." The man unlocked the blue machine with a stubby key and stacked the newspapers inside.

"It's a crazy thing," said Phil, "going anywhere on a night like this."

In the kitchen, the waiter was singing "Blue Moon." "You left me standing aloooone . . ."

"They're crazy all right," agreed the newspaper man, "those guys who fly the planes. I asked the men in the cockpit how they can do it and they said they just don't think about it. They have to fly and it don't make no difference about the weather. They say that keeps things simple. They just don't ask the question about whether it's safe to go up. Myself, I'm waiting here until it blows over. There was a lady who went back with them instead of me. She offered me a hundred dollars to take my place, but I let her have it for free. I tell you, I think it's a fifty-fifty thing that she ever makes it back."

I knew it had to be Suleika.

"Yeah, well in that case, you should have taken the money," said Phil. "I plan to grow old and die in my bed." The diner sign whacked against the side of the building, straining at its hinges in the wind. "This is some storm," said Phil. "I heard that someone saw the fire ship last night."

It went quiet in the room. Even though no one else was speaking, it still went quiet.

The old man in the corner, who until now had said nothing and who I thought had been asleep, chin tucked into his chest, suddenly raised his head. "Who saw it?"

"I just heard that a Coast Guard guy saw it when he was heading out to rescue those people."

"What's the fire ship?" I asked.

Phil glanced across at me. I was still a stranger in the room,

119

even on a night like this, and he seemed to resent me joining the conversation. Like I hadn't earned that yet. *"The Palatine,"* he said.

"Don't say the name!" The old man slammed his hand down on the table and the coffee cup and the spoons and knives and forks and the old lady all jumped at the same time. "I goddamn knew you'd say it and you know you ain't supposed to!"

"Not saying it don't mean it isn't out there, old man." Phil wiped his napkin against his forehead and the paper came apart on his face.

"You can't say the name," said the old man. "It's like any other piece of bad luck on the sea. You say its name and it will show its face." He spoke these last words slowly, marking time with the flat of his hand on the tabletop. "It . . . will . . . show . . . its face!"

"What is it?" I asked again.

"Back more than a hundred years, there was a ship by that name," the old man told me without turning around to see who I was, and he left me looking at the back of his gray-bristled head. He just stayed staring straight through his wife and through the side of the building and out toward the ocean. "And the people on Block Island used to lure ships by setting up lights on the rocky beaches and making it seem as if there was a harbor there. They would tie a lamp around a horse's neck and walk it up and down and the people out on the ships would think it was a port. And this ship, it got caught in a storm and then it saw the Block Island lights and headed for safety. But there was no safety, and this ship ran up on the rocks, just like the Block Islanders wanted it to. And the islanders, they looted the ship and killed every person who came off it and then they set the ship on fire and turned it around and sailed its leaking hull back out to sea. And they were thinking it would sink, because there isn't no land between Block Island and the coast of Africa, but instead of that, the ship come about, as if they had missed one of the crew on board and

120

now this crewman was sailing the boat. So it come about, like I said, and it starts sailing around the island, all blazing like. And it sails around the island for a day and a night, and burned itself to the waterline, and then the Block Islanders, all of them scared out of their thieving, crooked minds, they think that's the last they've seen of the boat. But now when the bad storms come, the really bad ones like this is tonight, you might see the ship, and then it's your bad luck, like it was for those fucking Block Islanders, because all of them died of scarlet fever that same year. Seems that it was on the boat when they grounded it, and they took the clothes off those dead people and then they caught the disease. And worse luck it is"—he raised his voice to Phil, the sweating ferryman, who wore flecks of his napkin like razor-cut Band-Aids, "if you are *dumb* enough to say the name! I ought to damn well know. I been working out on this ocean fifty years and I seen that boat. The time it came rearing up over the waves, all three of us on the boat, we were so shit-scared, it was like we forgot how to talk. Like we forgot the language of man. We just stood there on the deck and howled like wolves. We howled until blood was coming out of our noses and out of our split lips, split from howling. And the boat rode past, with its rigging all ablaze, and we could see the people on the decks, all of them burning and the captain at the wheel, his head a ball of fire and the wheel all spoked with flames. And they howled back at us, as if it was the only thing we understood between us, and I heard the crackle of the inferno and the water hissing and steaming in its wake and I felt the heat of it and I seen the boat's name on its charred stern. And the next thing I know, I'm waking up on the deck with blood clotted in my throat and my nose, and there's the other two crewmen lying there asleep or dead—at first I didn't know which. But it turns out we all must have fainted. It was years before we could even speak of what happened, even among us who had seen it. I tell you, it isn't a thing you want to see twice."

There were grumbles of agreement in the room, the loudest

121

from Phil, who felt bad about having said the name of *The Palatine*. Now he was agreeing with everything that anybody said.

I recalled the weird and flickering light I had seen from the life raft. I wondered what it was. The old man who had been out on the water half a century believed what he said and he did not tell me this for my amusement. It was no story just to pass a stormy night.

"Who wants a free paper?" asked the newspaper deliveryman. "I got some extras."

Everybody got a free paper, and sweaty Phil was overly grateful for his.

At first, I didn't look at the paper. My coffee and my sandwich had arrived and I was hungry.

"The damn Russians finally gived in," announced Phil. "They could have come to me thirty year ago and I'd have told them communism wouldn't work."

"You'd have saved them, Phil," said the other ferryman. "Saved them a whole lot of trouble."

"I would. I'd have done it for free."

"And then you could have saved the rest of the world because you're so damn smart."

"No cursing, please," said the old lady in the corner. She seemed to have forgotten her own husband's blasphemies. The raindrops were still beaded on her see-through plastic rain hat.

I had only half been paying attention to what they said, but now I looked at the paper. The headline said BERLIN WALL COMES DOWN. REUNIFICATION OF GERMANY BEGINS. I read it again, thinking I had misunderstood. The front-page picture showed people streaming through a gap in the wall, and others swinging at it with sledgehammers and knives, even clawing at it with their bare hands. I guessed that this was why the sub had failed to meet us. I started to read, heat spreading across my face and down my chest.

"You didn't know about this, did you?" Phil asked me. "I can tell from the look on your face."

I shook my head. I stared at the picture, the grainy black and white. The ragged tear in the huge concrete slabs of the Berlin Wall was like a hole punched through an artery. I tried to grasp what this meant. What would happen to my country now? What would happen to me? I had never thought that the Berlin Wall would come down in my lifetime, and it had never even occurred to me that communism would cease to govern the Soviet states. The thing I had thought most solid in the world had vanished. It was as if I also suddenly ceased to exist.

"The whole world knows about this by now," Phil told me.

I fumbled in my wallet for some money and laid some still-soaked bills on the table.

"Can I eat your sandwich if you don't want it anymore?" asked Phil.

I didn't answer him. I walked out and stood in the rain.

SIX HOURS LATER, the weather had calmed enough for the ferry to leave for Hyannis. I rode it out across the murky green chopped sea and was alone except for some stranded deliverymen, Phil from the diner, and his friend. I clung to a radiator, because I had no warm clothes. When I reached Hyannis, I took the bus to Providence and from there to Newport. By the time I reached my apartment, it was late afternoon. There was a note from Suleika on my door, saying she was all right and she would meet me in the parking lot behind Bad Joe's two hours from now. I felt foolish for the things that I had thought about her earlier. I took the note and folded it and put it in my wallet, telling myself I would look at it anytime I ever had any doubts about her again. I wrapped myself in all the warm clothes I could find and lay on my bed and began to shake.

When I finished shaking from the cold, I started shaking from

123

the memory of Liedke. Again I saw him flying through the air, like an obese and falling angel. I heard the sucking rise of *The Baby Blue*'s steel-plated stern as it cleared the water and Liedke's howl of terror and then the thump as the stern slammed back into the water and the silence, even in the howling of the wind, as the screaming suddenly stopped.

You think you can grow numb to other people's pain. You believe that reservoir of pity can be emptied out. But it fills up again and it will follow you. There is no place you can hide. I didn't even try. I told myself it was all in the past now. The next great chapter of my life was about to begin.

Five

I TRIED TO CONTACT SACHA AT AEROFLOT. I CALLED FROM
a pay phone on Thames Street next to the army/navy store and
the video-game arcade. I was transferred and put on hold. While
I waited, I listened to the grunt and squeak of video games coming from inside the arcade. Then a man's voice came on the line,
Russian but speaking good English. He told me that Sacha didn't
work there anymore. I asked whether there was a number where
he could be reached.

"He cannot be reached at the moment."

"Is there anyone who took his place?" I asked. "Specifically
anyone?"

"Ah," said the man cautiously.

"I was supposed to be in touch with him," I said.

"Ah," he said again.

"How bad is it?" I asked.

The man was quiet for a moment. Then he said, "Sir, I regret you will have to make your own travel arrangements home."

I hung up the phone. I considered getting on a plane and heading straight for the Russian embassy in Washington, but I knew I wouldn't go without Suleika.

I went home and sat at my kitchen table. Pale sun beamed through the old red and green and blue medicine bottles that Suleika and I had pulled up from time to time in the trawler nets. Lozenges of ruby, sapphire, and foggy emerald stretched across the tabletop and gently over my hands. I thought about the great concrete slabs of the Berlin Wall, bulldozed into the ground.

One hour later, I went out to meet Suleika in the parking lot behind Bad Joe's bar. We sat in her Camaro with the windows down. Cool breeze swirled inside the car.

"Why did you leave?" I asked her.

"I had to," she said. "I had all that money on me. I had to hide it someplace. I tried to wake you."

"I know," I told her. "But I thought I'd never see you again. Once you had that money . . ."

"It's our money. I had to hide it quickly. Did you honestly think I was just going to cut out on you?"

"I didn't know what to think. I guess I was just shaken up. What are you going to do now?" I asked, to change the subject.

"I've thought about it," she said, "and I'm not going to run. If they want me, they can come and get me, because they'll get me anyway, no matter where I am."

"But what will you do here? You have no boat." What will *we* do? I was thinking. *We* have no boat.

"We have," she said slowly, "two hundred and ten thousand dollars in cash." She reached over across my knees to the glove compartment and popped it open. She took out a bulky manila envelope wrapped in several rubber bands. Then she dropped it in my lap. "That's your share. A hundred and five thousand dollars."

I laughed nervously. "What if they come back for it?"

"I'll tell them it's with *The Baby Blue*. At the bottom of the sea. I'll tell them that Liedke kept the suitcases chained to his wrists and that was what got him killed. It's just too bad we didn't get the other suitcase. With that money I just gave you," said Suleika, "you can start a new life almost anywhere."

There we were, dancing around the subject again, talking about whether we should remain together when duty no longer obliged us to do so. We spoke of it without mentioning the subject, so that if one decided to leave, the other would not carry the burden of having shown too much emotion.

"The most dangerous thing would be for us to stay," I said, and for the first time used the word *us*.

Suleika paused. She reached across and took my hand. She held it as if she were reading my palm. "All right," she said. "Where would we go? I can't spend the rest of our life moving from place to place and worrying about being discovered."

I saw what she meant. We would be like an army in perpetual retreat. We had arrived here as the enemy, and we would always be the enemy. We would not be forgiven. But we had a life here now. It was better to remain and take our chances. Suleika, in her usual way, was asking me to stay by trying to persuade me to leave. Both of us knew we couldn't just part company. We belonged now in the same split world and there was no escaping it. I understood the labyrinth in which we lived. It was no dungeon into which we had been thrown and would spend our lives wandering its empty corridors. This labyrinth was a seductive place, where we wanted to be lost. Now I would pray for my old self to be forgotten. I would become the person I once pretended to be. I took the envelope of cash and put it back in the glove compartment.

Suleika and I agreed to be patient. Not to spend the money right away. Hard days of waiting lay ahead. There was no long embrace to seal our decision. The only thing that happened was that we both sighed at the same time. Then we laughed at the co-incidence and the relief that neither of us would have to face the future alone.

For the first time, I considered asking Suleika to marry me. I stopped myself from saying anything. Our lives seemed too un-certain. I would wait. The time would come, I thought. I would know when it was right.

WHEN I GOT back to my apartment, I found a man sitting at the top of the stairs smoking a cigarette. After my initial panic, I re-alized he was a fisherman and not one of the police or secret ser-vice agents I had been expecting. It was the scalloper who had stopped us in the fish house that night we went out in the storm, the drunk who cursed our boat.

"Gunther sent me here," he said. He looked down at his boots. He didn't want to meet my gaze. "Gunther heard about your boat going down." The fisherman was wearing jeans and a khaki shirt with a black leather vest. He inspected his cigarette, which had burned down to the filter, then set it on the stairs and ground it out with his boot. "I'm glad you showed up. Gunther told me not to leave until you did. I figured I might be here for a couple of days."

"What do you need?" I said from the bottom of the stairs, my neck a little stiff from looking up at such an angle.

"Need nothing. Matter of fact, I come to give you something."

"What's that?"

"A job. If you want it. Gunther says you can come work for him and Suleika as well."

"Why is he doing it?"

The man shrugged. "You can't ever figure out why Gunther does what he does. He might just fire you tomorrow and he might just hand over the whole damn dock. It keeps life interesting any-ways, and I expect you won't be buying a new boat anytime soon. The insurance companies always have a way of figuring out that

128

they don't owe you shit." His eyes narrowed when he talked about the insurance companies, as if he had locked horns with them before and lost.

I remembered that Suleika had told me *The Baby Blue* was not properly insured. "What about you?" I asked. "Are you working for Gunther now?"

"Oh, yeah," he said, and for the first time looked me in the eye.

"I thought you were a scalloper on one of the deep-sea crews."

He raised his head. "I was. But I've had nothing except bad luck in those few days since I saw you and your lady friend in the fish house that night of the storm. I lost my job. The captain gave it to his nephew. Now I don't even have the money to get home to Carolina. It's all because of what I said that night. I should have known better." He stood slowly and clumped downstairs with his stiff knee joint and passed me. Before he stepped outside, he called up to me, "If you want the job, you be on the dock in the morning." Then he walked out into the street.

I called Suleika. "Gunther has offered us a job."

"What did you say to him? Did you accept?"

"The trap boats are as good as any other job for now," I said. "I told Gunther I'd take the job. I said I would let you make up your own mind. I'm heading out with him tomorrow morning at five."

"Then I guess I am, too." She was quiet for a moment. "Fish," she said. "I wish they'd never been invented."

"I know you," I told her. "You can't keep off the water."

"Five o'clock, cheeky boy." Then she hung up.

THE TRAP BOAT was a different world from anything I'd known before. Apart from the world of the land, apart from the trawler-men, the trap boaters lived a strange, limbo existence. People were always coming and going. Men would show up for a week and then vanish and never reappear. Suleika and I were welcomed into the ranks of the regulars. Having worked the deep sea, we carried rank that other newcomers would never reach. We rode out each morning at 5:30 sharp in a fat wallowing boat called *The Martha.* Its broad planks were painted with a glossy dark green paint. The stacks on the engine house growled out black smoke as we rounded the Fort Getty Point and nosed out into the open water. The deck was covered with men in tattered flannel shirts, cold in the morning chill. Some days the work lasted from five until five and other days we were done by lunchtime. It all depended on the catch, and the pay was always the same for each day.

Gunther always wore a yellow raincoat. He stayed mostly in the wheelhouse, puffing cigars. Smoke poured from the wheelhouse as if the place were on fire. Having gone to all the trouble of sending a man to invite me and Suleika to work on *The Martha,* Gunther then completely ignored us for the first few weeks. We wondered whether he had forgotten that he offered us the job, but at the end of the first week, we collected our small manila envelope with bills and change inside and money taken out for taxes.

We worked all through the winter. The great changes that were happening in Europe seemed like a half-remembered dream. I forgot about them for days. Then, on my way home through the rainy, cobbled streets, I'd become convinced that there was someone waiting to arrest me at my apartment. Time after time, I felt that dread wash through me. But my apartment was always empty. Always just as I had left it. After awhile, the worry started to fade.

One morning in January, as we rode out to the nets on *The Martha,* we all started singing to keep ourselves warm. We took turns doing solos, yowling out whatever songs came to our minds. There were twelve of us on the crew, including Suleika and two other women. Some of them sang in their native Spanish, others in Italian. Suleika sang a lullaby in Russian and two men on the crew who spoke the language wept when they heard it. I had never heard that lullaby before and she never sang it again, as if the memories that it retrieved were painful to recall. Snow materialized out of the air. I watched it veering in toward me through my half-closed eyes.

When it was my turn, I sang the love song that my father had taught me from his U-boat days.

Gunther heard the singing and stuck his head out of the wheelhouse. He caught my eye. "You," he shouted at me over the singing and the engines. "Waiterkins or whatever your name is. Get in here."

I had a comfortable spot beside the smokestack. At least one side of my body was warm. It was only grudgingly that I clambered out over the flanneled backs and rubber boots of the fishermen and went to see what Gunther wanted. I watched my spot by the smokestack vanish as the crowd closed up around it. I knew I'd never get it back and I'd spend the rest of the trip freezing.

Gunther pulled me into the wheelhouse and shut the door behind me. The smell of his tobacco was sunk into the wood and paint and the choking damp ash of his breath. "I heard the singing," Gunther said. "What was that song?"

"Something I learned as a child," I answered.

"Where did it come from?" He had brought his face close to mine. His eyes did not contain their usual glassy madness. Over the weeks of observing him, I understood that he was much less crazy than people thought. He wanted us to believe he was insane. It gave him the distance he needed. Gunther grew tired of waiting for my reply. "It made me remember something," he said. "I was in the Coast Guard in World War Two. We used to ride around Narragansett Bay and check up on the naval gun emplacements, which are still around here on Jamestown and Dutch Island and Newport, except that they're all covered in weeds

131

now. We'd escort boats up and down the bay. And then we'd keep an eye out for periscopes. German subs, you know. In the first couple of years of the war, the U-boats sank a lot of stuff out there." He waved his hand out into the pasty gray morning. "But I wasn't in the Coast Guard then. I was in college."

"You were?" I couldn't help asking.

He squinted at me indignantly. "Dartmouth. Class of '46." Then he swung his head back to face the front, scanning the horizon for a sign of the snow-topped barrels that served as floats for the great labyrinth of nets. "Anyway, the military called me up in the spring of '44, made me break off my studies, and I was still in the Coast Guard when the war in the West ended in May of '45. There wasn't much for us to do. Nobody needed to be guarded anymore. I had been a sonar man. I listened for things creeping around under the water. There was no use for me. The war was still going on out in the East, but there never had been any threat from the Japanese where we were. So we were just lounging around. But then one day, this barge carrying coal exploded just off Newport. I forget now whether anyone was killed on it. I was sitting at a café on Thames Street when it happened. The explosion echoed all through the streets. We got down to our boat as quick as we could. It was just a little sixty-foot cutter. We were almost to the wreck by the time we realized that it had been torpedoed. We radioed for a destroyer. A sub-hunting boat. A navy plane out of Quonset spotted the sub. It was a German one, a type XVII, the best they built. The destroyer was close by and started unloading charges on it that we called hedgehogs because of the machine that fired them. These were like big bottle-shaped charges, twenty or thirty at a time. Splash, splash in the water and then the big white patches of froth coming up to the surface when they exploded. Except I couldn't see it on that day. I was busy tracking on the sonar. I could hear the sub's engine. The water was so shallow, only thirty fathoms, that I could even hear the clank of things moving around inside the sub. There wasn't any need for me to be tracking it. The destroyer had its own sonar crew. I was just eavesdropping. Well, they depth-charged the sub. And that sub got its engines or its props fucked up by one of the hedgehogs and it was just lying there on the bottom and the charges were raining down all around it. See, that destroyer crew hadn't seen any action in the whole war and they wanted some blood to finish up the show. It was only a matter of time before they cracked the sub's hull. And then I heard the damnedest thing. Heard it through my headphones on the sonar. I heard those people singing. Down there on the bottom. In the rocks and weeds and in their leaking sub and the water pouring in and no lights left. I heard them all singing. Singing while they waited to die. And do you know that was the weirdest, bravest thing I've ever known? I heard them singing right up to the end. I don't know what song it was. I never heard it again until you started singing it. Those men all died and that's a fact. They must not have heard that the war was over. Maybe their radios were out. Maybe they were too pissed off to quit. It's under us right now. The sub. It's right down under us now. This is the location. The bravest fucking thing, those guys, singing even when they knew they were going to die."

"Because they were going to die," I said. "They sang because they knew." I was thinking of my father. The voices of those doomed men down below became like the voice of my father, distant and unreachable and yet always there if I listened.

"How come you know that tune?" Gunther asked me. His voice was urgent, almost pleading. "Who are you?" The boat was going off course. We were heading right into the nets. If it hadn't been for that, and the fact that Gunther had to crank the wheel hard to correct our course, I don't know what I would have said. I could have told him most of the truth without placing my cover in any danger, but that wasn't the point. The danger was that I had shown him a face behind the face he thought he knew, and it unsettled him, and from then on he would never look at me the same way again. For Gunther, it was as if I had reached into his brain and hauled out of its delicate grayness one of his greatest secrets, a fragment of his own identity. I sang those few words without thinking of the consequence. I felt as if it wasn't me singing at all, but the ghosts of the Glory Boys, finding their forgotten voices in my own as Gunther's boat sliced the water far above their grave.

In later days, I would think back on that moment, and I wondered then if I would have been one of those men singing while the steel walls of the submarine caved in around them and the cold water bubbled up to their throats. I wondered if there might not have been a few men on that crew who were not singing, but who waited dry-eyed and in silence for their water-choking end to come. Not praying. Not weeping. Just waiting. I think I might have been one of those silent men, maybe not in the life I lived before but in the one I was living now. It is a brave thing to shout in the face of your own approaching death, but maybe a little too easy.

TIME PASSED. ALMOST a year went by.

Suleika and I merged with life on the docks and with those who worked the deep-sea boats. We started up our little business repairing nets on the weekends. We had a lot of work, because it was a job that the fishermen looked down on and wouldn't do themselves if they could help it. People came to count on us for fixing their nets. They'd snag an old wreck someplace off Martha's Vineyard, tearing their nets, and the crew would say, "Well, here's another job for you. We went and tore out our nets on your damn boat again." From then on, every snag on every net was jokingly blamed on the wreck of *The Baby Blue*. It was strange to work for such small amounts of money, "chicken feed," the dock boys called it, and all the while knowing we had huge amounts but couldn't spend it.

Now that we were together without the blanketing excuse of

duty, things grew more serious between us. As the weeks and months went by, people began to say our names together, as if they were only one name. The more time that stretched between us and the night the Berlin Wall came down, the safer we felt.

One day, almost unwillingly, Suleika said she loved me. She seemed relieved, as if she had not been sure of it until the words actually left her mouth. After that, she said it all the time.

I first made love to her late one September afternoon on the creaking cot in my apartment, with the cool breeze of autumn blowing through the mosquito-screened window and downstairs the fridge door–clunking, broom-swishing sounds of the Sicilians closing shop for the day, a little earlier than usual, until at last the sound of the radio with its endless jolly Italian music fell silent and we heard the quivering clang of the brass bell on the front door as they locked up. At the moment when I closed my eyes, my forehead touching her forehead, I had the sense of falling off a precipice so vast that I wondered if this was how it felt to die.

"You know," I said to Suleika on a Saturday afternoon as we fixed nets, "it's crazy you driving back and forth across the bay each morning. It takes time, not to mention the toll on the New-port bridge."

"Yes," she said without looking up, as if she weren't listening. But she was listening. She was waiting to see if I was talking about what she thought I was talking about.

"You should come and live with me," I said casually.

She sat on the net with her knees together, baseball cap laying an arc of shadow across her face. In the shadow, her blue eyes were glowing. "That would be too much trouble," she said.

"Of course. Trouble." I nodded and looked down. "Trouble for whom?"

"For you."

"It would not be trouble for me!" I shouted, catching us both by surprise.

"You need your privacy," she said.

I set down my work. I rubbed my chapped hands against my face, smelling the salty, fishy smell of the nets. "Look," I said. "Now look. We've been working together," I began. I could feel the words seizing up in my throat. "And I've begun to think." I looked at her, pleading with my eyes for her to stop making this so difficult. I wished we were back on *The Baby Blue,* where we never seemed to need our words so much.

She was smiling, no more than a tiny wrinkle in the corner of her mouth. She enjoyed making me work at this.

"Why do I have to be the one to say it?" I asked.

"Because," she said, "you thought it."

"You're thinking it, too!" I was completely exasperated. I set down the iron needle. My hand was cramped around its shape. "I'm going to quit for the day." I got to my feet, knees aching, feeling suddenly old, and started to walk away.

"You don't need to go," she said.

I turned around. "You wouldn't ever tell me to stay, would you? All you'd say was that I didn't need to go."

"If you know what I mean, then why make me say it any differently?"

"I'm not making you do anything, Suleika. If I even tried, you'd do the exact opposite, just out of habit."

"Stay," she said.

"No. There's no point in that now. I'm going into Bad Joe's," I announced.

"I'll be here when you get back," she said quietly.

I sat at my usual table. I was the only one there. While Biagio made a fresh pot of coffee, I drummed my fingers on the red-and-white-checked tablecloth. It seemed as if Suleika and I could go along fine for months, but every time we took a step closer toward actually being more of a couple, everything ground to a halt and we would talk as if we hardly knew each other. We moved along so slowly and cautiously that I figured we'd die of old age before we actually moved in together.

Biagio brought me the coffee. "You smell like the ocean," he told me.

"The ocean at low tide." I sipped the coffee and winced. "Forgive me for saying this, but the coffee is not very good."

"I know," he said. "Nobody seems to mind."

"It doesn't even taste like coffee." I didn't mean it. I was getting into an argument over something stupid and I couldn't help myself.

"It says coffee on the can." Biagio shrugged, refusing to be offended. He went back to his stool behind the bar. Sometimes he would sit with me at the table. Then he would no longer be Biagio the bartender. But today I was in a mood, so he stayed bartender. He gave me room to breathe.

"Don't be nice to me, Biagio. Don't play kissy-face."

"All right," he said calmly. "I will be impolite and ask you a personal question."

"That's more like it." The coffee rippled with my voice.

"It is a question," he repeated, "of a personal nature."

"Bring it on." I bounced the flat of my hand off the table.

"All right, I will, because you ask me to."

"I'm asking, Biagio. For crying out loud, don't make me beg, because I won't."

"When are you going to marry Suleika?"

I felt my neck muscles contract, giving me an instant headache. "What the hell kind of question is that?" It was the first time someone had asked me. Later, of course, I would be asked so often that it became a kind of joke. But just then it took the wind out of me. I guess I should have seen it coming. "I'm working on it," I said indignantly.

He made a *pfff* noise and said something in Italian.

"Well, Jesus, Biagio. If you know so much about it, how come you aren't married?"

"No interest. Only interested in watching you and her trying to say what you feel."

"So you watch us, do you?"

Another *pfff* noise from Biagio. "I hear everything. Sometimes I even hear what you are thinking."

I felt my shoulders slump. "All right, Biagio. The truth is, I . . ." I fell silent. I wiped my palm across my forehead as if to smooth away the wrinkles of my concentration. I couldn't tell him that all I thought about was the chaos that still surrounded Suleika and me. The great uncertainty. Suleika was starting to lose patience, but I could do nothing about it.

"She is afraid of being left again," said Biagio. "Don't forget she was married once before. Even though it wasn't Mathias's fault for dying, he still upped and left her. It doesn't matter how it happened. The fact is, it happened. Do you think she can go through another thing like that, a woman who keeps things so much to herself? She wouldn't ever tell you she was frightened, would she?"

"I doubt it."

"When you were out on your boat and it sank, did she ever say she was frightened?"

"No."

"And do you think she was frightened?"

"Yes."

"So you know she keeps things to herself."

"I always knew that."

"Then don't make her wait. You must be the one to make things go ahead. It is not about being old-fashioned. It is because she is scared, but she will never say it. What is the worst that could happen? She could say no."

"Yes," I said, "that would be about the worst." He was right. I would have to be the one. I didn't say any more to Biagio. To thank him would only have made things awkward between us. I put a dollar under my coffee cup and got up and walked toward the door. Before I went out into the parking lot, I turned to look at him. He had gone over to my table to clear away the coffee cup.

He had picked up my dollar bill and was folding it into the shape of a bird. He could do things like that.

WE MADE OUR peace, Suleika and I, the way we always did. She moved in a few days later. From then on, we spent only the weekends over in Jamestown at her place. I bought an iron-railed bed to take the place of the old army cot I had been sleeping on until then.

The news got around the docks about Suleika and me living together. It got to Bad Joe's and downstairs to the Sicilians in the pasta shop, who winked and nodded when they saw me. Soon all their customers knew. They winked and nodded, too. They said it was about time. The owner, Mr. DiRenzo, said he had even closed up shop early the first day that Suleika and I were together. He had probably heard us. When I blushed at the thought, Mr. DiRenzo smiled with his whole round face and tight curly gray hair and brown-green eyes. He slapped me on the back with his flour-powdered hand, leaving a print on my back like the war paint of an Apache.

Suleika and I often talked about the boat we would buy. We spent our weekends going to other ports and looking over boats that were for sale. We couldn't afford a new one, even with all of Liedke's cash. It was going to have to be something secondhand.

Eventually, Suleika and I decided that enough time had passed for us to be able to spend some of the money. In New Bedford, we picked up a ten-year-old steel-hulled sixty-five-foot dragger named *Ramona*. It had two small CAT diesels that squatted side by side in the engine room, and came complete with nets and a lazaret full of spare parts. The captain was retiring and he had cared for the boat well. He looked like a man who had spent his life on the water, his handsome flat-gray eyes webbed by wrinkled skin from years of being out under the blinding sun. His arms were thick and muscular and he walked with the plod of a fisherman, used to the deck rolling beneath his feet. He wore clean clothes, a zip-up jacket, plaid socks, and his new Dock-Sides with the too-white soles, the type you would wear only on land, and he seemed uncomfortable in them. As we stood next to the boat, the deal done now and figuring out some polite way to part company, he kept patting the iron bow. He seemed only half-aware of what he was doing. He couldn't quite bring himself to say good-bye to the boat, because he knew that somewhere in the metal flanks and coiled lines it possessed a certain kind of life. He was like an old cowboy giving up his horse, with the horse knowing it was being left and the man knowing he could never explain to the horse why he could no longer care for it. Eventually, he just turned away and started walking, out through the yellow-gray sun-heated dust of the dockyard. His wife was waiting for him in their car. I saw by the way she shifted over from the passenger seat into the driver's seat as he approached that his face must have shown how badly he was hurting. I wanted to run over there and tell him we would take good care of the boat and that when no one was around, I would tell the boat—yes, I would talk to it—about how the captain had grown old. I would explain it all, someplace out beyond the sight of land. But much as the old captain might have understood what I meant, and much as he might have wanted to thank me for it, he would not have been able to bring himself to acknowledge what I was saying. He would be as nuts for listening to me as I would have been for trying to explain myself.

Suleika and I rode the boat down to Newport. It was a breezy August afternoon. We opened up the throttle and the CATs hummed down below and we climbed fast over the gentle, snake-rippling waves.

The *Ramona* was small for a dragger, small like *The Baby Blue,* and it meant that we would probably be fishing close to shore. We would be what the Rhode Islanders called "buckeye fishermen." Buckeyes were a type of mullet that came by the tens of thousands to Narragansett Bay each year. That was fine with us.

Personally, I didn't care if I was never out of sight of land again as long as I lived.

We renamed our boat the *Liedke,* in honor of our most generous benefactor, and talked about how we would have liked him to work with us if he were still around. And then we would laugh, because he would never have worked on the boat. We had the *Liedke* repainted white, with a red bow line. People at Gunther's asked us what *Liedke* meant and Suleika went off on some story about how it was the name of a beautiful Russian princess in the time before the Russian Revolution. One of the dock boys liked the name so much that when he and his wife had a daughter, they named her Liedke. We wondered what the man would think if he knew he had named his precious daughter after a squat three-hundred-pound diamond smuggler. The dock boy often brought his daughter around to see the boat, and the funny thing was that, the way they said it, the name did have a pretty sound to it.

We told Gunther about our boat and how we would be quitting our jobs with him. Then we opened up a duffel bag and pulled out a magnum of Dom Pérignon and gave it to him as a way of saying good-bye and thank you. He held up the huge green bottle, tilting his body over to one side because it was too heavy for him. "Dom Puh-rig-non," he said in a loud voice. Then he threw the whole magnum into the oily water that sloshed around the pilings of his dock. "You guys," he said, "can come back and work for me if your boat sinks out from under you again." Then he walked back into the hut, where he smoked cigars and added up receipts.

Suleika and I looked at each other. Then we stared at the last fading rings of the splash where the magnum had disappeared.

"Do you think it's worth diving in to get it?" asked Suleika. The magnum had cost a small fortune.

I shook my head. "If that's where Gunther wants to keep his champagne, that's where he'll keep it." There was no sense asking Gunther or ourselves why he had thrown it in the bay. So we turned around and walked back to the *Liedke* and put out to sea, just like in the old days, which were not so old, after all.

More and more, we were putting the past behind us.

To prove this to myself, I became an American citizen, which Suleika had done years before. I got my blue passport and made the pledge of allegiance up at the statehouse in Providence, with its gold statue of a man with a spear on the roof. I held my hand over my heart and looked with a solemn face at the American flag and said the words: "One nation under God, with liberty and justice for all." And that day, I did a thing I hadn't planned to do, but suddenly at the last minute it became the most important thing I'd ever done. I changed my name. Did it all legal and tidy. Partly it was because nobody seemed able to get right the pronunciation of Wedekind. It's actually not such a bad name if you get it right, *Vay-duh-kint,* but people like Gunther and everybody else, it seemed, could make the word sound bad in fifty different ways. I changed it to the name that sounded closest in English. Watkins. Paul Watkins. Everybody could say that. I would never have to spell it on the phone.

As we drove back to Newport, Suleika said that me changing my name was like dying and being born again all in the same day. "And in a town called Providence, as well," she added.

But it would take more than just changing my name. I didn't realize this until one year later, when the crew of a Wanchese scalloper named *The Argosy* pulled up a human skull in one of their dredges while they ploughed the deep water east of Nantucket. They rode into Newport in a pouring rainstorm. The crew stood on the bow, rebel-yelling in that terrifying high-pitched wail "Woh-hoo-ey! Hoo-ey! Hoo-ey!" Their sweat-stained clothes were drenched in fish blood and grease. They looked like something out of a nightmare.

They put the skull on a broomstick and waved it over their heads as they approached the dock, singing their happy death song. The lower jaw was missing from the skull, as were most of the teeth. Some fillings showed in the few molars that remained. The sockets were rimmed with algae and barnacles studded the forehead.

I thought it might be Liedke. That was, after all, where *The Baby Blue* had gone down. At first, I hoped to God it wasn't him. But then I wondered if the fat man might not have found some humor in the way the crewmen danced around the skull, as if the bony face still held some kind of life that they could not understand but knew was there. Perhaps he would have liked this final send-off, which ended when the skull slipped off the broomstick and fell onto the salt-hardened planks of Gunther's dock with a sound like an earthenware pot breaking on a tiled kitchen floor. Some of its teeth fell out. Then the captain picked it up and pitched it far out over the harbor. The skull spun, grinning, end over end, until it splashed into the bay and disappeared.

Over the next few days, I could not get the image of the skull out of my head. I focused on the picture of those little peg teeth that had fallen out of the jaw and were scooted away with a toe of a fisherman's boot until they fell between the planks into the harbor. One last memory from Afghanistan was surfacing, like a shark with wide-open jaws and hollow black eyes rising from the murky green water.

SINCE THE COLLAPSE of his business at Diaghilev, Ingo's fame had inverted into ridicule. The most outcast members of the camp turned on him with a sadism created from relief. Now there was someone even lower on the ladder than themselves.

Ingo was given the new job of interrogating mujahideen prisoners who were brought into the camp on their way to a larger POW compound. For them, the same as for us, Diaghilev was a place of transit. Everyone was always going someplace else. The information that could be extracted from the mujahideen was very important, but it had to be done quickly. They were interrogated as soon as they arrived. The job was given to Ingo because it was the least desirable job in the camp. The previous interrogator had committed suicide, leaving behind an interpreter who spoke both Russian and Afghan. Ingo had no idea how to get information out of prisoners, but he learned.

Meanwhile, I used the excuse of Ingo's arrest to assume that my services were no longer required by GRU. I'd heard nothing from them anyway. Now, I told myself, I'm just like everybody else down here—*peyanitsi*—a bit of a drunk.

After weeks of failure, Ingo suddenly began to get results from his interrogated prisoners. Neatly typed reports appeared on Volkov's desk. They contained large amounts of accurate information—the locations of mujahideen camps, ammunition stashes, upcoming campaigns. Ridicule changed to curiosity. Until now, no one had ever had much luck interrogating the mujahideen.

It would be a long time before people found out how he accomplished this. When they did, Ingo Budde would win for himself a different kind of fame.

He moved his place of business to an abandoned aircraft hangar at the edge of the compound. It was a leaky, corrugated-iron-roofed hut. A fence of razor wire was built around the building. Apart from a few guards and the prisoners, no one was allowed in. Rumors began to spread. Ingo refused to talk about them with me. He warned me not to mention it again. The only clue I ever received was once when I saw the interpreter walking away from the hangar with tears running down his face.

One night soon after that, Ingo and I were drinking vodka out of the bottle, no longer bothering with dainty things like glasses or even the tin mugs that came with our mess kits. Not the Stolichnaya of the good old days, either. This was the stuff I had once used as windshield washer fluid. We sat on our cots, drinking grimly and steadily.

Ingo started rocking slowly back and forth. The bunk creaked with each shift of his body. He looked like a mental patient. "I'm not going to heaven," he said. Then he grinned at me. It was an ugly baring of his teeth.

I laughed. "We'll all go to hell," I said. "We'll outflank the devil and catch him by surprise."

"I'm not joking," said Ingo. "I woke up this morning and knew it for a fact. You know, the way some people can see their own deaths approaching. The way a drowning man sees his own life pass before him."

I sat up as straight as I could. "What are you talking about? Drowning men. Death approaching. Gibberish." I stood up and had no sensation of anything below the knees. If I'd taken one step forward, I would have fallen on my face. Then, with my vodka courage, I said something I never should have said. "Will you, Ingo Budde, once and for all tell me what the hell has been going on in your little house of a thousand questions?"

Ingo calmly set his bottle on the floor. Then he stood and walked toward me. "I warned you," he said.

"Yes, but . . ." I gestured vaguely in the air.

"Didn't I warn you?" he asked again.

I realized that things had suddenly become very serious, but my vodka-fuzzy thoughts could not catch up. "Ingo," I said, trying to sound in control, "now listen to me, Ingo. . . ." The next thing I recall was flying through the air, curious at first as to how I got to be this way. Then, just as it came to me that Ingo had thrown me across the room, I crashed into the metal cabinets where we kept our clothes. I had some sense of being hurt, but my nerves had all been dulled by the vodka. I found that I could not get up. I seemed to have vertigo. I flapped my arms, but it was useless.

Ingo was looming over me. "You want to know what I do?" He grabbed hold of my jaw and forced my mouth open by digging his fingers hard into my cheeks. His breath was stale from cigarettes. "Open your mouth, damn you! I'll show you what happens in there. Open your damn mouth before I carve up your cheeks!"

"Ingo, it's Paulie," I tried to say, because it seemed he no longer recognized me. "It's your old pal Paulie."

He squinted, as if surprised that I knew his name. As if he wasn't even sure of his own name. "What I do?" he echoed himself. "What I do? Terrible things! Things that when I am doing them, I cannot even believe it is me!" He slid one hand behind his back. "Terrible things." He held something in front of my face. I couldn't tell what it was. It looked like a leather-wrapped piece of broomstick about the length of his hand. Then suddenly, the thing in his hand seemed to jump and it became three times as long. I understood now. It was a spring-loaded cosh with a heavy bolt welded to the end. Using a cosh like that, Ingo could crack a man's head open with a flick of his wrist. The leather wrapping was grooved to the shape of his clenched fist. The bolt and the coils of the spring were crusted with blood. He waved the spring stem in front of my eyes. Dried blood crumbled black onto my shirt.

"Jesus, Ingo," I said.

"This is only what I start with," he shouted. "The rest is too awful for you to know." Suddenly, the rage filtered out of his face, leaving the skin strangely pale and luminescent. "I will not tell you," he said calmly, but exhausted, "because I am your friend." He walked over and sat down on his bunk again.

Two weeks later, when things were returning to normal between us, Ingo woke me early in the morning. "Volkov wants to see you," he whispered.

My blood was fizzy with sleep. "Who?" I asked him. "What's going on?"

Ingo handed me a cup of kvass. It's a kind of tea made with burned bread. It doesn't sound good, but in fact its taste is very comforting. "There's some jeep broken down in the hills. It was part of a convoy. Ilyushin was acting as an escort for them and his truck broke down. He's still up there with it. Volkov wants you to go up there and fix the truck, and he wants me to go with you."

Sleep dissolved around me. I began to assemble in my head the various things I would need—toolbox, jumper cables, weapons checked out of the armory. You weren't allowed to leave the camp without a gun. I sat up, leaving the warmth of my sleeping bag. My bare feet touched the freezing floor. I heard a soft rain falling on our tent. The sound of boots squelching in mud reached us from outside.

Fifteen minutes later, we were standing in front of Volkov in his small and smoky office.

Volkov was immaculately dressed, as always. He sipped the smoke from his cigarette. His supply of contraband had not been interrupted. Ilyushin had simply taken over where Ingo left off. To Volkov, it all seemed to have a certain inevitability, like the changing of a season. He even seemed vaguely amused that Ingo would be a member of a rescue party for Ilyushin. His lips twitched, as if he were trying to choke down a smile.

"We'll just need your signature on the vehicle-requisition papers, sir," said Ingo, handing him a clipboard with the papers attached. The old familiarity was gone.

Volkov looked through the papers, flipping up the first few pages.

Ingo stood waiting. He touched the tips of his fingers together as if he were about to pray. His nails were rimmed with black dirt.

I remembered Ingo's old words about Volkov: "I have that bastard in my pocket." So much had changed since then.

Volkov signed the papers and then leaned far back in his chair, yawning and stretching, as if lifting the pen had taken all his strength. He ran his long-fingered hand across his smoothed-back hair without disturbing a strand. "We traded a batch of your interrogated prisoners yesterday, Mr. Budde," said Volkov. He sucked in more Marlboro. The pleasure he took in those gusts of bluish smoke was indecent. It was as if, in the moment that each rush of nicotine hummed in his brain, he found himself lying with some White Russian woman.

"Traded them?" asked Ingo warily. "Traded them for what?"

"Other prisoners!" Volkov snorted. "Ours!"

Ingo's face went cloudy. "All my prisoners? Even the ones . . ."

"Yes, the ones you worked over. Some of them. That's why I mention it. I would appreciate it, and I'm sure they would, too, if you would not disfigure them quite so thoroughly. Am I making myself clear?"

Something seemed to break inside Ingo. "You set this in motion, sir!" he blurted out. "You gave me the job of screwing talk out of those Afghans, when that's not what I do. I'm a tradesman. But you weren't happy with that. You let those Speznas people come for me. Then afterward, you give me the worst job in the camp. And I did the job well. I did what you asked, and now you criticize me for it? You treat this like a game, sir. Like some tsarist parlor game."

"That's enough!" snapped Volkov. It didn't matter if he had been made to see his own hypocrisy. At the mention of the Tsar, a nerve had been laid bare.

"I saved Russian lives with that information." Ingo shoved his words into Volkov's thin face. "Russian lives!"

"Yes, but there are limits. That's all I'm saying. Now get out of here, Mr. Budde. I have to speak with the lieutenant about his motor pool."

When Ingo was gone, I heard the sigh of relief that Volkov wheezed out of his hawk-beak nose. I knew that the motor pool had nothing to do with his reason for holding me back.

"I got a call," he said. "The GRU director in Kabul wants to know why you've stopped sending reports."

"Because there's nothing more to say about Ingo Budde. They told me to find out whether he was setting up a drug operation and I told them no. I don't have anything more to tell them."

"I understand," he said, "that your conscience might have gotten the better of you." Volkov leaned across the desk. "But let me give you a piece of advice. Let them decide when you have done enough. Keep sending the letters. If there's nothing to report, then just say so. You see, if they have the letter in hand, they have what they asked from you. That way, you won't get into trouble."

He was right. I saw that immediately. "Thank you, sir," I said.

"Thank you," he replied, "for your selective memory loss."

I straightened up and smiled.

Ingo and I drove out of the motor pool, having drawn our pistols from the armory. The other soldiers were just emerging from their tents, most already smoking, bare-chested and with towels wrapped around their necks. They stretched and headed for the wash troughs, toothbrushes and disposable razors jutting from their pockets.

The road was dappled with frost. The sun hadn't yet reached our valley. It cut over our heads and lit up the mountains on the other side, where the light was sharp on the snow and flinty crags. I was at the wheel. Ingo drummed his mittened hands on his knees. He was smiling. It was infectious. I started smiling, too. We were leaving the camp, even if only for a while.

Ingo and I rode up into the hills, waiting for the moment when we would leave the shadow of the valley and break out into the sun. I wanted so badly to feel it against my face. It was as if I'd lived my life until now in nothing but shadows and cold. There was something hypnotic about the sheer and flaky-stone cliffs, all woven colors of gray and brown and glittering veins of white crystal. The cold had saved huge icicles that hung down over ledges in the rock. They dripped silty rivers down the middle of the road. I could feel the engine straining as we climbed and climbed. I drove completely blinded by the brassy sunlight, up stretches of road that seemed to be in flames. The crystals in the rock burst and danced like fireworks. I felt the warmth

149

against my winter-pale cheeks and breathed in deeply, as if the air itself were made more pure by the light. We didn't think about time. We forgot the danger we were in.

It was two hours before we found the jeep. The vehicle lay on its side in a gulley beside the road. Ingo saw it first as we rounded a bend in the road. At that precise moment, I had been checking the dashboard instruments to see if our own Zovi was overheating.

"Stop!" Ingo shouted. He waved his left arm at me, slapping me on the shoulder, not taking his eyes from the wreck.

I hit the brakes hard and as we slewed across the road, I tugged at the emergency brake to keep us from going over the edge. Ingo dived out one side and I climbed out the other. I knew that the first thing we had to do was find some rocks to stick behind the back wheels of our Zovi to stop it from rolling backward. "Christ!" I shouted, "Volkov didn't say anything about the damn machine being flipped! We'll need a crane to get it out of there."

"There's no one here," said Ingo, climbing out of the jeep. He stood on the road, heavy black zigzag-treaded combat boots stirring the gravel.

The chugging engine of the Zovi was all around us. I cut the ignition. The echo died away, but I still felt its vibrations in my bones. I glanced at the walls of rock that rose above us. Shrubs clung to the crevices. Water dripped out from hidden springs. The wind picked up the rivulets of water and threw them out into the air, so drops of rain fell on us from a clear blue sky.

I got out and walked over to the flipped Zovi. Its heavy undercarriage was a mass of pipes and lug-treaded tires and mud-splattered metal. It looked like a giant reptile. I peered around. "I don't understand where they went," I said.

Ingo was already climbing back into the jeep. It was too quiet in this place. "Let's go," he said. "Let Ilyushin find his own damned way home."

I turned the key and felt the engine's vibrations shuddering up through the gearshift and the steering wheel. I cranked our jeep around until it was facing back down the hill. It was then, even over the rumble of the engine, that I heard a cascade of gravel down the sloping walls of rock. Through the glare of sunlight reflected off the tiny snowmelt waterfalls, I saw a man sliding down toward the road, booted heels dug in and seeming to skate over the plates of shale. He was an Afghan. He wore a filthy pink-brown dresslike thing and a vest made of animal fur and a shapeless cap with a wide, folded brim. Clutched against his chest was a Kalashnikov submachine gun. I saw the black shrub of his beard and his teeth bared with concentration. He wasn't looking at me. He kept his eyes on his feet as he navigated the slide. There were others also coming down the walls, as if they had materialized from the rock, as if they were a part of it.

I took my pistol from its holster, twisted around, set my arm out straight across the top of the seat, and fired the entire magazine at the first sliding man I had seen. I didn't think about doing this. I just did it. The man gave no sign of being shot, but at the point when he should have hit the ditch, ready to jump up onto the road, his legs buckled under him and he collapsed into a heap of filthy clothing. For a moment, it looked as if he had vanished completely.

The other men scrambled up from the ditch and into the road. There were at least a dozen. They marched toward me, Kalashnikovs held at waist level, shouting. They were all bearded. Some wore pieces of Russian combat gear—faded canvas ammo pouches and black boots chafed to white suede, the toes curled up from being too big for the people who wore them now. They closed in on me. They were coming from all sides.

Their shouting confused me. I knew I had to destroy the pistol. That had been drummed into me during training. If you are going to be captured, ruin everything you have, soak your ammunition, dent the cartridges so that they can't be used, take the slide out of your gun and throw it away, burn your rations, burn your maps, smash your binoculars and radios. All I had time to do was throw the empty gun into the ditch, where it was quickly picked out and squabbled over by the Afghans.

The men were all around me. The muzzles of Kalashnikovs were jabbed into my ribs. I saw the dull black holes at the ends of the barrels, the way the blueing had been rubbed down to bare steel. They were still shouting. They shoved me out of my seat with their guns. Some pushed me one way. Others kicked me in a different direction. I had my hands raised to the level of my shoulders.

One Afghan took two steps back and the others seemed to melt away. He shouted at me and gestured at the ditch, where the man I had shot still lay untouched. His legs were tucked under him. At first, I saw no blood. Then I noticed that one of his cheekbones had shifted toward his nose. His forehead looked crumpled. The jaw stuck out grotesquely, tilted to one side. One of his sandals had come off. The soles of his feet were so thick that they had grown a crust on them. The black hair flowed from his disfigured head like rivulets of ink. Bullets had gouged the deep reddish brown of the shale, leaving it white and splintered. Only then did I notice any blood. Tiny droplets of it lay like shiny pebbles on the rock. The water downstream from the body was pink with diluted blood. The Afghan who had shouted at me turned over the corpse with his foot. The dead man slopped over onto his face and I saw where the bullets had impacted against his head and back and buttocks. The Afghan raised the Kalashnikov to his shoulder and aimed at me, squinting one eye shut as he sighted down the barrel.

It occurred to me that there would be no pain. I shut my eyes and flinched and I heard the distinctive clanking bang of a round fired from a Kalashnikov.

I felt nothing. I opened my eyes.

The man who had been about to shoot me whirled off his feet and fell onto the road. His gun clattered into the ditch. Immediately, he sat up. He had been shot in the shoulder. He kept his arm hooked into his side. He began to jabber at someone who stood behind me.

I still didn't know if I'd been shot. I looked down at my chest and saw no blood. There was no pain. Only the chilling of my sweat.

A hand grabbed my arm and spun me around. I found myself looking at a tall man in Afghan clothes, with a thin face deeply pocked by old acne scars, some of which was hidden by a scrubby beard. But he was no Afghan. His skin was too pale. In the rise of his cheekbones and the way his eyes were not as deep-set, he looked European to me.

The Afghan who had been shot in the shoulder was trying to get to his feet. He was cursing and waving his good hand, keeping his other arm tight against his body. His voice rose to a grizzling whine. Someone helped him to his feet and now the man began to cry, sobbing in a rage and shaking his fist at the European, who took no notice.

The other Afghans were milling around. They found themselves flat rocks to sit on or crouched on the road, smoking the last of my cigarettes. Their eyes darted back and forth between these two men. They were waiting for something to happen, but it soon became clear that the wounded man lacked the courage to do anything more than curse.

"My name is Mohammed," the European said to me. He spoke in Russian, but it was not his native language. I wondered if he was a deserter from the Soviets. A German maybe. A Czech. For now, I couldn't place him. Wherever he came from, he was in charge. To be a foreigner among armed men is hard enough, but to shoot one of them and then calmly turn your back on the rest required a kind of leadership I'd never seen before. "Stay close to me," he said, "or they'll kill you."

As he led me down the road, I saw Ingo with his hands in the air, surrounded by Afghans. They were emptying his pockets and tugging the binoculars from around his neck.

Mohammed barked at the Afghans, who stood back from Ingo but kept the things they'd taken. They all disappeared under the wide folds of their robes. "Which of you has higher rank?" he asked us.

"I do," I said. I wanted to add, And like hell your name is Mohammed.

Mohammed shouted something to a group of Afghans who had just finished rigging a grenade underneath the driver's seat of our jeep, which they left standing in the middle of the road. The other Afghans climbed to their feet and kicked their shale-rock seats back into the ditches.

I looked across at Ingo. His eyes met mine. Both of us were thinking the same thing. We should have killed ourselves while we had the chance.

The Afghans led us up a narrow path off the road and into the hills. I couldn't actually see the trail until I was on it. I was made to carry the Afghan I had killed. He didn't weigh much, but he was soaking wet. I carried him in a fireman's lift, the legs and arms sprawling down on either side of me. The weight of his body was hard and cold across my back. His face lolled back and forth in the corner of my vision.

I didn't think much about the fact that I had killed him. No pity or guilt. I wondered where those emotions had gone.

We climbed steadily. My calves and thighs cramped. At times, they locked and I had to stop. At first, the Afghans behind pushed me on, but after awhile, they used me as an excuse to rest themselves. The sun was sharp in my eyes. We crossed snowfields where the thin top crust of ice would hold me until I put my full weight onto one foot. Then I would sink in up to my knees. I was thirsty and covered in sweat. I breathed through my teeth so as not to smell the man I carried. The others were tired, too. Ingo moved ahead of me without looking back.

We knew instinctively that the Afghans were looking for an excuse to kill us. Only Mohammed kept us alive, and for what, I couldn't guess. The man he had shot in the shoulder kept up a stream of muttered curses and whining until Mohammed walked back from his place at the head of the line. At first, it looked as if he meant to walk right past the whiner. He didn't look at the man. But as he came level, he suddenly swung the flat of his Kalashnikov stock into the face of the whiner, who collapsed into the snow with a broken nose. Then Mohammed picked up the other man's gun and walked back to the head of the line. We started moving again. No one had spoken. The whiner refused to get up. He wailed at us and waved his one good arm as we disappeared over the horizon. But as soon as we were out of sight, he came running. He kept his mouth shut for the rest of the journey.

From the arcing path of the sun, I knew we were marching north. We traveled most of the day. There were no roads, only paths marked by small piles of stones. We climbed to the edge of a precipice, the wind cold and sharp, and then followed a trail down into another snow-clogged valley. There was no sign of life as far as I could see. But this time, as we descended, I could smell fires burning. Men walked out from an underhang of rock onto the floor of the valley: mujahideen. They squinted up at us, teeth bared in their dark faces.

Their camp was tucked against the rock. They slept under sheets of opaque plastic, which were tied to stones and used as screens, behind which they made beds for themselves on the rock ledges. There were several fires burning, fed by piles of gnarled sticks. Their guns lay all over the place, as did their food, which consisted of Russian infantry mess tins filled with rice and what looked like clots of tar. There was a red sauce that some of the men kept in little bowls. They balled the rice with the fingers of their right hands and dipped it in the sauce and ate, packing the rice carefully into each crevice of their mouths. A few curly-tailed dogs trotted from group to group, begging for food.

Under one ledge, I noticed a green wooden box about the length of a man but too narrow for a coffin, which it otherwise resembled. A man squatted beside it, Kalashnikov across his knees. I saw white-stenciled letters on the box that appeared to be in English, but I was too far away to see them clearly. When he saw Mohammed, the man came walking out. He was smiling. He was no Afghan, either. He had a short fuzz of blond hair and a squared-off face. He shook Mohammed's hand and the two of them laughed about something. I tried hard to understand what language they were speaking, but with the wind in this little valley, I couldn't hear. The blond man glanced at us, the smile still on his face, but his eyes went dull. Then he turned away.

Mohammed told me to set the dead man down. I dropped slowly to my knees and rolled him off my shoulders. I expected that I would be killed now. The idea had been growing in my head for some time. But no one paid much attention to the dead man. A few mujahideen went over and looked at him. They looked at Ingo and me, but without the curiosity I had expected. They avoided making eye contact.

The whiner crawled into his space in the rock and lay with his back to us. A man went over to him, carrying a Russian medical kit of the type used in armored vehicles. He touched the whiner, who turned around and slapped his hand away. The medic laughed at him and walked away and then the whiner called him back.

We were taken to a hut that lay between the rocks and down a narrow path. The hut was made of the same gnarled sticks that were being fed into the fire, woven together horizontally and vertically. The door was from a house, faded blue paint on the wood. From the scratches along its surface, I guessed it had been used as a sled on its way to this camp. The roof was corrugated iron.

It appeared to be an old shepherd's hut. As I came near to it, I could smell excrement.

We were shoved inside the hut and the door was locked with a chain and padlock. A guard sat down cross-legged outside the door with his back to us, my service pistol cradled in his lap.

It was very dark in the hut. There wasn't room to stand up. The place was ankle-deep in shit. I didn't know whether it was human or animal. It covered the ground in a half-frozen glue. There was nothing I could do to avoid the smell, so I just breathed it in until I was used to it. At first, I couldn't see anything. I crouched by the door while my eyes grew used to the dark. Ingo crouched next to me, shivering. We didn't speak. When my eyes grew used to the dark, I realized that there was someone else in the hut. The person lay spread-eagled in the shit, almost submerged in it.

I stood, my joints aching, resting my hand on Ingo's shoulder to push myself up. Ingo rested his hand on mine and gave it a gentle slap. We still hadn't spoken. I walked across to the spread-eagled man. It was Ilyushin. I assumed he was dead. I reached down to touch him and as soon as my fingers brushed against his face, he screamed. His body rose up from the ooze and he flung himself against the woven stick wall and clung to it as if the floor had disappeared and there was a thousand-foot crevasse beneath us. The noise that came out of him was not human. It was a wheezing, spitting, delirious moan. It horrified me so much that I didn't dare go near him again. I crouched down by Ingo and we both watched, both more afraid now than we had been before.

The guard was peering through one of the gaps in the walls. He watched for a moment and then returned to his place, only a little farther away. The sunlight made a spider's web of beams, which appeared so solid that I had to force myself to pass through them when I moved around, feeling their faint touch of warmth.

We were kept for two days in the hut. The guards changed and sometimes glanced in to see that we were still there, but otherwise they left us alone. We were not fed or given anything to drink. Ingo had brought some compressed food bars with him, a hard-packed mush of dates and crushed nuts. They hadn't been found by the Afghans because he kept them tucked between his shirt and undershirt. The only way you could eat these pressed food bars in winter was if they were soft from body heat. Otherwise, you'd break your teeth on them. Ingo tore off a piece and gave it to me. Then he slopped through the muck to give a piece to Ilyushin, but Ilyushin lashed out with his feet, spraying us with clods of shit. He gripped the sticks that made up the shed, as if Ingo meant to drag him out. So we left Ilyushin alone and he wouldn't answer us when we softly called his name. We kept to our side of the hut and after awhile, Ilyushin fell asleep. He thrashed around in his dreams.

The smells of cooking lasted all day and into the night. There seemed to be no organized mealtime, or any organized meal, either. It was just whatever they could scrounge up, and fights often broke out between those who were begging for food and those who shooed away the beggars with curses and clenched fists.

Everyone was armed. They almost never set down their guns. Even when they were eating, they kept their guns across their laps. The one time I did see an Afghan set down his gun, when he took a nap in one of the slab beds hacked into the stone of the cliff, another Afghan stole it and I watched him frantically using a knife to scrape the finish off the wooden stock and then to rub the blueing off the barrel with gasoline so the gun would be unrecognizable to its original owner.

I thought about the fact that I had never heard of Afghans allowing Soviets to surrender, except in a few cases of outright desertion by some of the Russian Muslim soldiers, who felt more sympathy for the Afghans than they did for the Red Army.

At the end of the second day, there was a lot of activity in the camp. Mohammed set up a radio with a large dish antenna out in the snow beyond the shadow of the cliff. When he talked into the microphone, he was speaking English. I guessed now that he might be an American, maybe CIA.

The nights were the worst. The shit froze our feet to the ground. My lungs were so full of the odor that I found I could no longer smell it. Cold leached away the pockets of warmth between the quilted lining of my jacket and my skin. When the last warmth was gone, uncontrollable shivering walked up my spine and trembled in my body like an earthquake aftershock. Through the punctured tin roof of the hut, I could always see the stars. The sky was deep navy and shimmering. I smelled the smoke of the fires and tried to imagine the warmth that they were giving out.

Late on the second night, Ingo unstuck himself from the ice that formed around his boots. It seemed he couldn't stand the thought of being frozen there. He trod across the ice, which creaked and crunched under his boot steps, until he reached the edge of the hut. He looked out across the field of snow. His face was cobalt in the night. "It will be all right," he said. He spoke with such conviction, as if he had just seen something out there on the snow. I rose up off my aching haunches and looked out to where he had been staring, but nothing was there except the smooth field of snow.

Then I asked Ingo something that had been on my mind all day. "Do you remember Bader?"

Ingo turned and looked at me. His eyes shined like marbles. "Bader? The guy who died of the drug overdose? Of course! Why?"

"I want to know"—I had to clench my jaw muscles every couple of seconds to stop my teeth from chattering—"if you sold him those drugs."

"Have you gone mad?" said Ingo, his voice rising. "I don't want to talk about him now."

At the sound, dogs barked in the camp. For a moment, both of us held our breath, waiting for one of the Afghans to approach. When nothing happened, Ingo came and sat beside me. "Why the hell do you need to know a thing like that at a time like this?" he whispered. "Are you just delirious? What the hell difference does it make?" His shoulders shook in the cold. He wrapped his arms around his legs and set his forehead against his knees.

"It makes a difference to me, Ingo."

"Well, it's stupid to talk about that. Why don't we talk about getting out of here?"

"Just tell me, Ingo."

"I didn't. Are you happy?"

"Is that the truth?"

"Of course it's the damned truth!" he rasped at me.

I didn't believe him. His agitation, even here, gave him away. I looked through the wooden cage and out across the snow.

"What?" he asked.

"I didn't say anything."

"You don't believe me."

Now I looked at him. Our faces were close. Even over the stench of the hut, I could smell his breath and the old sweat on his body. "No, Ingo. I guess I don't."

"What's it to you, anyway?" he blurted out.

I shook my head. "I don't think you'd understand, Ingo."

"No." He brought his face even closer. "It's you who wouldn't understand. It's complicated. Not some movie where everyone is either good or bad. But you like to think the world is like that, don't you?"

"You have only two choices now," I told him. "You can say nothing and know I hold you responsible for Bader's death. Or you can explain to me what is so complicated." I was glad to feel anger. It made me forget about the cold.

It seemed like a long time before he answered. I had begun to lose consciousness, when suddenly he began to speak.

"I was approached," he said. "Last year. People saw that I was doing well at selling blue jeans and cigarettes and whatever else I could scrounge up. I had contacts. That's all I am, really. A contact man. I find out what people want and then I find some-one who can give it to them. So as I say, I was approached"—he sighed—"by this man. He said he wanted to go into business with me. Now when someone comes up to you and starts saying a thing like that, you know what's coming next? Threats. Black-mail. Extortion. And that's what it was. Usually, I can get out from under that stuff. Do a little blackmail of my own. You see, Paulie, I have to know so many people. I have to keep them all in balance, all happy. I'm like a man trying to run too many puppets in a puppet show, all at the same time."

I thought of Ingo with strings dangling from his fingers as he made the smiling puppets dance.

"This man said he had some prime narcotics for me to sell. He had a regular supply. All coming out of the Soviet Union, out of Kazakhstan or somewhere. Heroin, opium. Hard-hitter stuff. He had things organized. How much I would buy it for. How much I would make. He said we were like-minded. But I told the guy I didn't sell drugs. 'I could have been selling the stuff a long time before now,' I told him. 'What the hell do I need you for?' I asked."

"Why wouldn't you sell drugs? I mean, you sell just about everything else."

Again there was a pause. "Because it's the same as at Di-aghilev. There are layers of what's legal and what's not. With cer-tain things, you can get people to look the other way. But not narcotics. That's the difference between a black marketeer, which I am, and a gangster, which I am not. If you want to deal in drugs, you'd better have a private army to back you up. And in one sense, that's what this guy had. He left me no choice. So, yes, I did sell Bader the drugs."

"Who was the man? Someone I know?"

"I guess it doesn't hurt to tell you now. It was Markus," said Ingo, "that little man everyone loves back at school."

"Not possible," I said, choking on the words.

"You think what you like, Paulie. I'm telling you the truth. He's a Stasi man."

I kept my head still, staring hard and unfocused at the night.

"Do you think the Stasi would have taken my word over his? Do you think I had a choice? He said he could get me busted. Busted for selling what he ordered me to sell. Simple, isn't it, when you know all the angles? It was all going along the way he wanted it until Bader went and killed his stupid self. Markus panicked. He told me to stop selling the stuff and he and I spent a long night flushing everything we had down the toilet. Then I got sent to Diaghilev and I haven't heard from him since. When I get back," said Ingo, "I'm going to kill that little man."

I breathed out sharply through my nose to show I thought he was being funny.

"I'm serious," he whispered.

"I hope you do kill him," I said.

The next morning, they came for us. Through the haze of my half sleep, I heard their footsteps crunching through the snow. The lock on the door was undone after much fumbling with the key and after a lighter had been held against the padlock to thaw ice that had jammed in the keyhole. Then the chain that held the door shut was pulled through with a long, clanking rattle.

It was Mohammed and his blond-haired friend. They walked into the hut and looked down at us. They had scarves tied so tightly against their mouths that I could see the outline of their lips. They were disgusted by the smell, which I had almost forgotten.

We were led out into the snow. Mohammed stopped to wipe the shit off his boots against the side of the hut.

The other man didn't stop. He just kept striding on.

The light was so bright that I couldn't see where I was going. My legs were cramped and I had trouble walking. I could make out the silhouettes of the sentries perched on the top of the cliff. I saw the stretched-out shadows of their Kalashnikovs and the curved new-moon magazines. There was a lot of blood on the ground where we were led. A dappled trail of it led back to the hut. The blood had melted into the snow, turning it rosewater pink.

The blond man frog-marched Ilyushin out into the snow.

It was warm on the field. I felt the sun on my neck and the back of my head. I saw the Afghans, maybe thirty of them, peering out from under their makeshift tents and from the rocky ledges where they had spent the night. Even the curly-tailed dogs were studying us, with sharp eyes and muzzles raised and nostrils flexing to catch our scent.

I looked at Ingo but could tell nothing from his face. His eyes were almost shut against the glare.

Mohammed told me and Ingo to stop. Ilyushin was hauled past us. He thrashed about, but in a hopeless way that reminded me of a child who knows there is nothing to be done. The blond man dumped him at Mohammed's feet.

All around, the sun was sparkling gold and orange and blue off the crystals of the snow. The sky was pale and without clouds.

I thought about the camp, and how the Russians would be making their way to the mess tent, goose bumps on their tattooed arms from the morning chill. I tried to think about anything but what was actually happening.

Mohammed took hold of Ilyushin's short-cropped hair and yanked his head back until the tendons in his neck were stretched hard against the flesh.

Ilyushin's lips were tightly closed. Tears dripped down his face and vanished into the dirty cloth of his quilted jacket. He made no move to stop Mohammed.

I wondered how badly they had hurt him already.

Mohammed grabbed hold of Ilyushin's jaw and tried to make him open his mouth. But Ilyushin, snuffling and moaning, kept it shut. The blond man stepped in. He pinched Ilyushin's nose and we all watched Ilyushin's bloodlessly pale face turn red until

163

he gasped, and then Mohammed jammed his fingers into Ilyushin's mouth. Keeping one hand knotted in Ilyushin's hair, he used the other to pry open his jaw.

Mohammed turned to Ingo. "We know who you are," he said. "You're the interrogator from Diaghilev. Some of these men here"—he waved his hand at the cliff wall and the squatter's camp of plastic-sheeted shelters—"were set free in a prisoner exchange last week. They recognized you instantly."

"I've never interrogated anyone in my life," said Ingo. His face had gone so pale that anyone could see he was lying.

"You have been identified!" shouted Mohammed. His eyes were wild with outrage. "You are a waste of a life."

"It's not me!" Ingo raised his voice.

I didn't dare to glance across at Ingo now. The expression on my own face would broadcast his great lie.

"It is not me!" Ingo barked out the words.

Mohammed still had hold of Ilyushin's dirty blond hair. The tendons strained in Ilyushin's neck. But Mohammed seemed to have forgotten about the man at his feet. A particle of doubt had lodged in his mind. It glimmered weirdly in his eyes. Perhaps they had the wrong man after all. He spoke very softly, almost lovingly, to the blond man.

The blond man took off running. A minute later, he came back with an Afghan who stumbled through the snow. He was a ragged, thin-shouldered man, flecks of gray in his unshaven beard. He was terrified. He would not look Ingo in the face. He grimaced against the painful brightness. He appeared almost impossibly old, like an Egyptian mummy come to life.

Mohammed discarded Ilyushin and clasped the raggedy man's arm, strong fingers sinking through the cloth and latching onto the flesh and bone. He asked the man a question in a level, threatening voice, as if prepared to turn all his rage on this scarecrow if there had been some kind of mistake.

Ingo stood with his nostrils flaring, swaying drunkenly back and forward. He stared at the man, and I knew he was trying to recall the face.

The old man fixed his eyes on the silhouette of Ingo. Then he edged a little closer. The man reached out cautiously, ready to recoil, and touched his shaking fingers to the broadness of Ingo's chin. Gently, he made Ingo turn his head to the side.

Ingo allowed his head to be turned, sweat running off his face.

Even Ilyushin looked up from his slump, knees sunk into the snow, hands lying useless and palm-up on his lap.

The raggedy man backed away from Ingo, raising a hand and pointing to single him out. He mumbled out an accusation. His speech was slurred and trapped in the phlegm of his throat.

The doubt vanished from Mohammed's eyes. "You will see for yourself!" he shouted in Ingo's face. "You will see your own friends suffer! You will suffer the way you made this man suffer!"

Suddenly, Mohammed turned to me, as if seeing me for the first time. "Who are you?" he asked.

I couldn't speak. There was no moisture in my throat. My tongue had swollen and stuck to the roof of my mouth. I just started coughing.

The raggedy man sidestepped toward Ingo like a crab. Bolder now. Insisting. His hand was raised and pointing, the yellowy nail like the scale of a fish balanced on the end of his index finger.

At a sign from Mohammed, one of the Afghan guards produced a large rusted iron file. It was the kind I had seen used for filing down the heads of nails in house construction back home.

"No!" shouted Ingo, but he did not move.

The blond man grabbed hold of Ilyushin. They wrenched back his head so far, I thought his neck would break. When Ilyushin screamed, they rammed the file into his mouth, choking him on the rusted iron.

The blond man filed Ilyushin's teeth down to the gums.

I turned my head away and Mohammed's shout forced me back. I caught sight of the ragged man, standing off to one side.

The muscles of his face were clenched. Between his parted lips, I saw the stumps of bone that had been his teeth before Ingo grated them down.

The blond man stopped his work on Ilyushin. Ilyushin's gums were ripped and bloody. The pink softness of exposed nerves showed at the center of each tooth.

Ilyushin's tears ran out over the hands of the blond man, who held him. As Ilyushin sobbed, his head shook slightly.

Then I noticed that the blond man was crying, too.

"This is for you," Mohammed said, pulling back on Ilyushin's hair so that his face leered up at Ingo. "You did this."

Ilyushin slowly closed his mouth. Bloody saliva dribbled down his chin.

I took a step forward to help him. I had my arms held out. I barely knew what I was doing. I had almost reached Ilyushin when Mohammed pulled a pistol from somewhere in the folds of his clothing. He pointed it at my face.

Ilyushin gagged into the snow.

Mohammed cocked back the hammer of the pistol, still pointing it at me.

I was looking right into his eyes.

Then, without hesitation, Mohammed set the gun against the top of Ilyushin's head, a movement that required him to bend his wrist almost double. He pulled the trigger. His hand jumped with the gunshot.

Ilyushin slapped facedown into the snow at our feet. Smoke came out of the bullet hole in the top of his head. His hair burned. He melted the snow with his blood.

The sound of the shot was not loud. It was a dull snap, like a dud firecracker, and the noise skittered off the rocks and back to us and returned to the rocks and disappeared.

I felt a kind of relief that Ilyushin was no longer in pain. Now I was only impatient for them to finish me off. The thought of it no longer troubled me.

Ingo's eyes bulged. "I"—his voice boomed across the snow-field—"am Ingo Budde!" He called out his name as if it were the last line of a magic spell. "Ingo Budde!"

Mohammed cocked his head to one side, curious but unafraid. The pistol still dangled in his hand.

"Ingo Budde!" howled Ingo across the blinding snow. "Nobody kills Ingo Budde"—he gasped for breath—"except Ingo Budde!"

When the echo of his shout had finally died away among the sparkling rocks, there was only the sound of the wind over the crags at the top of the cliff. The long robes of the mujahideen billowed in the breeze. Their shadows were like banners on the ground.

Mohammed turned and spoke to the blond man, who unshouldered the Kalashnikov he had been carrying. He pointed it at me and then swung the barrel toward the hut, showing that this was where I should go.

"What about me?" asked Ingo. His voice was hollow. The voice that a statue might have.

"You stay," said Mohammed.

The blond man locked me in the hut. Then he trudged back out into the snow. I squatted down in the corner and began to shake.

Through the slats of the hut, I saw Ingo shouting at Mohammed. The Afghans stood restlessly by the cliff face. They didn't know any more than I did why Mohammed would allow himself to be shouted at by a prisoner. The yelling continued for some time, with Mohammed growing more and more agitated.

"It's very simple!" Ingo shouted. "You can get ten of your people out of captivity for each one of us. Make an exchange. The way you did before." Ingo paused. "Don't be a fool! Twenty men! What use are we to you if we are dead?"

Mohammed seemed to be considering this for a moment. Then he snapped at the blond man, who moved so rapidly in what he did next that I could tell it was a relief for him to be in motion. He swung the butt of his gun into Ingo's back and side and when Ingo dropped, howling, the blond man used his Kalashnikov on Ingo's back the way a man uses an ax to cut wood. Ingo held up his hands and the blond man broke them and would have beaten Ingo to death if Mohammed had not made him stop.

Ingo rolled on the ground, hands to his face. His fingers were crooked and snapped.

Mohammed straddled Ingo, sitting on his chest like a bully in a playground fight. He beat Ingo's hands aside and took his jaw and jammed the rat-tail file through his closed lips and wrecked his teeth with sharp and vicious raking motions.

I heard Ingo's gurgling scream. I put my hands to my ears and began to scream as well.

When the job was done, Mohammed stood up and threw the file to one side. He waved his hand at the blond man and walked away, crazy-eyed out by himself across the snow.

The blond man took hold of Ingo's feet and rolled him over. Then he began to kick at Ingo, slamming the heel of his boot down on Ingo's back and head. When he had finished, he dragged Ingo back to the hut. He threw Ingo inside and left us there.

I gathered Ingo in my arms and carried him to the far corner of the hut. He shook his head from side to side. When he breathed, the flaps of his torn lips spattered me with blood. All night I sat with Ingo. There wasn't anything else I could do for him. He thrashed around and talked without making sense. His tongue lisped softly across the wreckage of his teeth. I didn't try to calm him. It seemed to me that the only thing keeping him alive was his anger.

I felt sure we would both be killed in the morning. We had been kept alive for symbolic reasons. For those same reasons, we would be executed. I waited for my life to parade past me in a drowning man's slide show. But it never happened. There were people I should have thought about that night but did not. Instead, my mind was consumed with thoughts of Ingo as he lay in my arms. It seemed I could recall with perfect clarity all the time we had spent together, from our childhoods together all the way up to the present. As the night grew darker and darker, clouds piled up on the horizon, snuffing out the stars. It snowed. Wind scratched around the door, blowing through the cracks and filling the hut with a moaning sound. It echoed Ingo's own moaning, as if some invisible creature that lived in these hills was crying to him out of sympathy. I huddled close to him, smelling the cooking fires by the cliff. Later in the night, it stopped snowing and the sky cleared. It became much colder then. Sometimes I saw the arcs of falling meteors, burning up as they entered the atmosphere. I thought about their heat, and for seconds at a time, this dream of heat would keep me warm. And sometimes through the hole in the roof, I saw bright spots of orange-yellow, like planes flying overhead, but from their steadiness and speed, I knew they were satellites. I imagined them, gleaming from the sun and filled with the voices of thousands of telephone conversations. It was as if I could hear all the voices myself—languages I'd never known before.

I have never told anyone about this before, but that night I traveled far beyond the confines of my body. I ranged across space and out among the satellites. I felt neither cold nor hunger nor sound. I saw far beyond the veil of my own life, seeing things that I was never meant to see. When at last, in the brassy dawn, I settled back into my skin, I no longer feared what would happen to me in the coming day.

I was led from the hut. Ingo stayed behind, his body stiff and cold. I knew he was dead. I started walking out into the snow, toward the gentle mound under which I knew Ilyushin's corpse was lying. The dusting of snow had made everything clean. I was defiant as I walked into the killing field. I will show you how to die, I thought. I felt already dead. My execution would be nothing more than a formality.

Then someone called to me. Called me by name. By my first name, even. It was a strange act of gentleness, which caught me by surprise.

When I turned around, I saw Mohammed sitting by a smoldering fire on a seat made of flat rocks. He waved me over to him. He was holding my military passbook.

I walked into the middle of the Afghan camp, past stacked Kalashnikovs and leather bandoliers of ammunition hanging from knives stabbed into cracks in the rock. I felt the stares of the Afghans like the fluttering of moths against my face. I walked to where Mohammed was sitting. He gestured to another stone seat on the other side of the fire, over which a coarse woolen blanket had been thrown.

I sat. I didn't understand.

Mohammed handed over a Russian mess tin filled with a white paste like baby food, into which dates and sunflower seeds had been stirred. His hand moved over the fire, disturbing the thin veils of slowly rising smoke.

I held the mess tin. I didn't dare to eat.

But Mohammed waved at me again.

I scooped out some of the baby food with the fingers of my right hand. I put it in my mouth. The sugar from the dates sent a charge like electricity through my body.

Mohammed gave me water in a felt-covered canteen. It was melted snow, almost freezing, painful to drink.

"Do you feel better?" he asked me. He handed me back my passbook.

I took the passbook and stuffed it in my pocket. I could not meet his gaze.

"Things have changed." He raised his mess tin to me in a toast. He drank a mouthful of whatever was inside and spat it into the fire, as if this was part of his salute. "I see you have noticed our treasure," he said. "Come and see."

My face had been turned toward the green box that lay by itself under a ledge, safe from rain and wind. I had not actually been looking at the box, but Mohammed insisted that I accompany him as he walked over to it. The box was scraped up. It had obviously been hauled a long way, probably by hand, all over these mountains. Nearby, the blond man was sleeping, cocooned in a sleeping bag. The barrel of a Kalashnikov poked from the top of the bag.

Mohammed squatted down and opened the box. Inside it was a missile, about five feet long and thicker than a man's leg, painted green drab with yellow writing on various parts of its shell. I could see from the way it was built that the weapon was designed to be fired from the shoulder. The aiming apparatus and the trigger were all built close together on the left-hand side.

"It's a Stinger," said Mohammed quietly, so as not to wake the blond man. "We took down one of your helicopters with one of these the other day."

"Yes," I said, "I know about that."

"There's plenty more where this came from," Mohammed told me. "Mention that to your friends when you get back to Diaghilev."

Without returning to the hut, I was blindfolded and led out of the camp. I assumed I was being traded, but I didn't believe it until I actually climbed into a Russian truck. It was waiting for me on the same road where I had been captured by the mujahideen. Half a dozen Afghans were handed over to Mohammed, who whispered in my ear, "Stay away." He undid the rope that had been tied above my elbows, pulling my arms painfully behind my back.

I thought I was being taken back to Diaghilev, but instead, we went right by it and I was bundled on board a Soviet troop-transport plane. No explanation was offered by the political commissar who accompanied me throughout the trip.

Within twenty-four hours, I was at Tatianawald military installation, where it was explained to me that I had been given up for dead and that my name had appeared on the casualty list. It provided me, I was told, with a unique opportunity. I could continue my work for the Stasi and GRU/KGB in America—or I could go back to Afghanistan.

Seven months later, I left for the United States.

SOMETHING CHANGED IN me after I relived the story of my capture. Before, I had been troubled by a sense of fragility. I would find myself looking at my hands and wondering how it was that my bones even held together. I was haunted by the image of my body coming apart. Now those nightmares lost their grip on me. They scattered like birds flushed from hiding in the tall grass and disappeared over the horizon.

Seasons passed. For a long time, we had luck. We had luck the way the Vikings thought of luck—like a talent, a gift you could not give away. Good catches, the nets bulging heavy with fish. Good weather, rain gentle when it fell and land always nearby when the iron-belly clouds sent out their lightning bolts. No trouble with the boat, the deliriously shaking rust-bubbled engines refusing to die or break down. No sickness, no fever dreams to send me back into the mountains of Afghanistan. No nightmares that came true. Nothing to drive us apart. My accent merged into the fluent but badly pronounced English that everyone spoke on the docks. I earned respect from the other fishermen and women, simply by doing my job.

Only one thing came along to remind us that we were still separate from others around us. We fit in because of what they didn't know.

One New Year's Eve, Suleika and I went out to sea. The fish prices would be high when we returned. Most crews stayed home with their families for the holidays. But with us, wherever we were, that was our family. The water was rough with winter waves, longer and more drawn out than the short swells of the summer. Boats can't ride the winter sea as easily. Worst of all is if you catch what the New Englanders called "a gray-beard roller." It is a huge wave that rises and rises like a mountain heaving out of the water. A boat will ride a gray beard to its foamy crest, then plunge into its trough, gathering speed until there is too much force to stop it from riding under at the depth of the wave. The whole boat disappears underwater, down and down. Nothing but old life jackets and scraps of wood come to the surface.

The *Liedke* was icing up. If too much ice formed on our rigging, the boat could capsize. We took turns thrashing at the cables with hammers to knock off the huge castings of ice. They crashed onto the deck like fallen chandeliers and shattered. But the fishing was good—huge fat winter fluke with their beautiful hunter's green and orange–flecked backs, cod, and yellowtail flounder by the hundredweight.

Around midnight, we turned on the television. I had to hold the aerial and keep twisting it around to keep the reception from slipping. Channel 12 in Providence was televising different New Year's parties all around the state of Rhode Island. We were about twelve miles off the coast and we could pick up the signal pretty clearly as long as I kept moving the aerial. There was even a party in Newport, right on Thames Street. The road was decked out with lights and Chinese lanterns and tinsel and all the bars were open. We saw Biagio standing in the doorway to his bar, which was crowded inside. For days, he had been down at the Narrow River digging for his famous oysters in the ice and frozen mud. Now his arthritis was so bad, he could barely stand, which we knew was why he stayed leaning in the doorway to the bar, smiling a toothy, nervous grin at the cyclops eye of the TV camera. He waved at the viewers, waved at the people in the street, at his own bossy Wurlitzer, at the plastic lobsters and the fishing net on

173

the walls. He waved at so much, he appeared to be having a seizure.

Suleika and I were caught up in the laughter and the music. For a moment, we forgot that we were not there with Biagio, in the warmth of the crowded bar, everything bustling and happy and the jukebox amusing itself in the corner. Then, as the signal faded out momentarily, we remembered where we were, and the howling of the wind through the rigging and the pounding of the waves on the hull reached us in the little cabin.

"It's all right," I said quickly. "I'll get it back in a second." I fiddled with the aerial, trying to find the picture and return us to the sound of Bad Joe's bar on New Year's Eve. But the signal was lost, and there was only the gray dust of static on the screen.

Suleika turned off the set. Darkness gulped light from the screen, leaving a fading white dot at the center.

I thought of how alone we were, not just now but almost all the time. We were as separated from the people around us as if we were watching them on the TV, and what they did not know about us made us even more removed from them. It should perhaps have been a sad moment for us, but instead, I felt an overwhelming closeness to Suleika. It was as if we were already married, not by ceremony but by circumstance.

We turned in for the night. We spooned together in her narrow bunk, old Hudson Bay blankets piled on top of us and sharing one scrawny feather pillow. I let her feel my weight against her stomach and her chest. I kissed her neck, where she was too sensitive to be kissed at other times. Her hands raked through the short hair on the back of my head and she squeezed hard at the muscles in my shoulders. When she took off her T-shirt, the smell of her body waved up into my face. It blinded me to everything except her softness and her warmth. I felt my body mix with hers. This swirl of heat and sweat became something of its own, apart from both of us. Her breathing changed with mine. We forgot about the ice that sculpted itself against the portholes, like cataracts on a person going blind. In me was a hovering emptiness that lifted me out of myself and threw me back and lifted me again. One after another, my senses shut down, until there was only the hovering, half in, half out of my body, in which I could no longer recognize myself. Her teeth clamped tight together. Her head pressed back into the pillow. I heard a faint noise in her throat, which rose into her mouth and disappeared in a breath that she breathed into me. One last time, I tumbled back inside the framework of my bones. I became aware of everything around me. The roughness of the blankets. My cramped legs and arms. The ocean. The unfamiliar beating of my heart. For a long time, Suleika lay there with her eyes closed, unreachable, it seemed to me. All around her, even in the darkness, was that strange electric clarity. Finally, she opened her eyes and smiled. Her hands moved through my hair again. Her breathing grew slower and she slept.

I slipped gently from the bunk and tucked the blankets in around her. Then I put on my clothes and went out into the night. I broke the ice where it had formed. When that was done, I went back inside and lay on the floor, rather than wake her again. The *Liedke* bobbed and twisted on the winter waves. I had no fear of the storm. I lay still but did not sleep. I kept us safe until morning.

We had luck, Suleika and I. Viking luck. The best and greatest kind. And when we lost our luck, as we did that day of the killing at Bad Joe's, we lost it like the Vikings—completely, and for reasons only the capricious gods could understand.

Six

THE MAN I SAW COMMIT MURDER THAT AFTERNOON IN BAD
Joe's bar was Ingo Budde, who I had thought was rotting on
some mountain in Afghanistan. The more times I replayed in my
head the moment when our eyes had met, the more certain I became that it was Ingo.

Police swarmed around the bar. They blocked off the lower
end of Thames Street. Tourists gathered by the front of the building. Faces peered in through the window, fogging the glass. Some
of them pressed cameras against the window and took pictures.
Flashes silvered the air. Behind the bar, uniformed officers
shooed away curious fishermen, who stood up on the toes of their
rubber boots and craned their sun-creased necks to get a better
look.

Suleika and I stood in the parking lot, by the sour-smelling
Dumpster.

A plainclothes officer approached us. "I'm Lieutenant Buffington," he said. "Newport Police." He was short but athletic-looking, his chest wide like the chest of a bull. His hair was combed straight back on his head, and greased, so that it resembled a heavy coat of lacquer. As he stood in front of us, he rested one hand against the small of his back, as if he were in pain. When he did this, I saw a small-caliber revolver in a leather holster clipped to his belt.

"You know who this guy was?" He waved his hand at Mudge's body, which still lay on the floor of Bad Joe's. Through the open door, we could see that blood had spread around the corpse, making islands of the chair and table legs and the fingertips of his right hand, which touched the floor and were reflected in the blood that was now growing dark and dull and thick as it dried.

"Samuel Mudge," I said. "That's what he told us."

"Have you ever seen him before?"

Suleika and I both shook our heads.

"What did he do? Start a fight? Was he drunk when he walked in? Did he know the guy who killed him?" Buffington fired questions until he had no breath left.

"He just walked in," said Suleika. "He was minding his own business." Suleika's features looked pinched and tired, the way they had done when I first met her.

Biagio still sat behind the bar. He held his face in front of his hands. His nose peeked out between his fingers. He looked like a child playing peekaboo.

"I can't get a damned word out of that bartender in there," said Buffington.

"Mudge said he was part of that trade commission conference up in Providence," I offered up.

"All right," said Buffington. He took out his notebook. "Now we're getting somewhere."

But if we were getting somewhere, that was as far as we got. He wrote down what we told him, but he shook his head as the tiny pencil moved across the little pages of his book.

An ambulance rolled down into the parking lot, tires crackling over the gravel.

Police photographers crouched over the body, flash units blasting. When the photographers left the building by the back door, they walked past us. Their cameras whirred as they re-wound the film. They tracked bloody footprints out into the parking lot.

"Okay to bag him?" asked the woman in charge of the ambulance. She held up a black body bag. I had seen her before, too. She used to run a little concession truck with silver sides that sold doughnuts and coffee to people on the docks. Now she drove the ambulance and seemed to find none of this gore any more disturbing than handing out Ring-Dings from her truck.

"Bag him," said Buffington.

The ambulance crew, three in all, lifted Mudge into the bag and zipped it shut. Then they carried him out, hunched over and shuffling because of the weight. The blood drained from their hands as they held on to the black plastic straps. They slid the body onto a stretcher and then heaved it into the ambulance, whose lights still turned with a whirring noise.

By now there must have been over a hundred people milling around the street. A news van arrived. Two cameramen spilled out like commandos.

Buffington took our address and phone number. "How did he get hold of that spike?" he asked me.

"We were fixing the net right outside the back door here." Suleika gestured to the heap of net. "We were sitting on those milk crates. We use the spikes to fix the net."

"How come you just left it lying there? That spike was a dangerous weapon."

"You find me something on this dock that isn't dangerous," I told him. "There're enough fish knives and hammers and bolt cutters lying around to make finding a weapon simply a matter of choice."

Buffington looked down toward the water. His eyes scanned the tangle of cables and plate steel and wood and nylon nets that made up the boats. "Why didn't the man use a gun?" he asked, as much to himself as to us. "It would have been easier."

"Maybe he didn't have a gun," I said.

"Didn't have a gun?" asked Buffington. "In *America*?"

After Buffington let us go, saying that he would need to talk to us again, I knew I had to tell Suleika about Ingo. I kept waiting for some reversal of certainty to enter my brain, as if my silence would stop it from being the truth.

We dragged the nets down to the dock and returned the ones we had repaired back onto the various boats. We still had about three hours of work ahead of us. But we couldn't just pick up where we had left off. Not after what we had seen. For a while, we stood there, deaf to the bustle of the dockyard and the heavy slap of waves against the pilings.

"Let's fix the nets," said Suleika.

I fetched another spike from the lazaret of the *Liedke*. We sat down in the sun, against the side of the fish house, and finished the repairs.

"Are you all right?" I kept asking her.

"Yes," she said. "Stop asking."

By the time we had finished, it was evening. The clouds were ribbed like sand when the wind is blowing down the beach. It would rain before long.

"We should go home," said Suleika.

"I think I know who that was," I blurted out.

"Who are you talking about?" she asked. She was winding the loose lengths of repair nylon back onto the spool.

"The man who did the killing."

Very carefully and slowly, Suleika set down the spool on the chafed wood planks of the dock. She rested her boot on the spool to stop it from rolling away. "You do not know him," she said without looking at me. "You are upset. That's all."

Suleika had been afraid all along that I did know the man. She had seen the way he caught my eye before he left the bar.

I explained. I left nothing out. She knew about Ingo from the stories I had told her. Knew as much about him as I did. When I had finished telling her, I sat back against the wall of the fish house. The metal was still warm from the sun. I smelled the tar paper on the roof. A breeze off the water carried the scent of approaching summer.

"You're wrong about Ingo," she said. "And if you aren't wrong, I won't forgive you for being right."

Suleika and I sat on the dock, through the brass and gold and copper of the sunset until it grew dark, moving only when the night watchman's gentle footsteps drew close and he fired the mercury beam of his flashlight in our faces. We sat huddled like two scruffy owls, paralyzed by the brightness.

"Oh hey," he said, and turned off the light. He held up the flashlight as if it were a gun whose trigger he had almost pulled. The old man's name was Lester. He lived in a gray boat permanently moored at the dock. He was Gunther's watchdog. Lester was smoking a cigarette, which he flicked away. The butt trailed sparks like a bottle rocket until it vanished into the water. "When you see Gunther next," he said, "tell him I was doing my job." Then Lester teetered away on his rickety bones, his feet loose in his boots.

Suleika and I walked back to my apartment, through bell jars of yellow-orange light thrown down by the streetlamps. "You are wrong," she whispered to me. "I am telling you for a fact."

I didn't argue. I had said all I could to convince her. Nothing short of seeing Ingo herself would change her mind. But if I was right, we would see him again. There was a reason he had chosen my marlin spike to do the killing. It was a message. Half a message. The rest would follow soon.

A WEEK HAD gone by since the murder.

The news was filled with reports of Mudge's death. He had been assistant to a man named Chester Todd, who ran a relief organization for Bosnian refugees. The organization was called Project Safe Haven. They had come to the trade conference to appeal for funds. There was speculation that Mudge had been killed by a member of the Serbian Secret Service. The Serbs denied this and accused the Croats. It went round and round.

The police came back three or four times to Bad Joe's, which had remained closed during the investigation. Each time, along with Biagio, they interviewed Suleika and me. They asked the same questions over and over. They made us act out where we had been and where Mudge had been.

Biagio was slowly calming down. "Do you think," he asked me, "that I should close down the bar for good?"

"No," I said.

"Well, do you think, then, that I should feel bad about more people coming here after what happened?"

"Wait and see if they come. If they do, then you can feel bad." I thought about the bar where my old friend Bader had killed himself—the Cyclone. The place didn't close, but it was a long time before people felt right about going in there again.

It felt strange to be going back to work, almost as if nothing had happened. A dozen times a day, I would stop what I was doing and look around me, expecting to see Ingo standing there. As the days passed, I began to convince myself that I had not seen him after all. I thought about the legend of the doppelgänger— that some people have a double, who roams the earth in search of its lost twin. What you saw, I told myself, was Ingo's doppelgänger. That monster is too late. Ingo is long gone. You held him in your arms when he died. He is gone. He is gone.

He was not gone.

When I returned home from work that day, Ingo was waiting for me in my apartment. Ingo Budde. Back from the grave. As if he'd never been away. He lay there on my bed, still wearing his boots, his big hands folded on his stomach. I knew it was Ingo even before my eyes could frame his silhouette in the dusty light through the window. He wore a short-sleeved polyester shirt with shoulder straps and sharp-creased khaki trousers. He had started to grow a beard, which fanned across his face in a black scruff. He smiled the broad smile that I remembered.

I stood in the doorway. "Oh my God," I said. A pillowy fog swirled around me. My face grew suddenly hot.

"Not God," replied Ingo. "Only me." He was enjoying my confusion.

I didn't go into the room. I just stood there. "I knew it was you," I said. I was having trouble breathing. "Then all this week, I thought I was going crazy. Jesus Christ, Ingo."

"Not Jesus, either." He swung his feet to the floor, folded his hands, and rested his elbows on his knees. "Didn't I tell you, Paulie? Don't you remember?" His voice was a boom of confidence. "You and I are the only ones in this world who aren't crazy."

"What are you doing here?" The arteries thumped in my neck. "How can you even be alive?"

"Paulie," he said, drawing out the word: Paulieeee. "It's like I told them back in Afghanistan. Nobody kills Ingo except Ingo." He waved a hand at me, motioning me closer. "Shouldn't you come inside?"

I rubbed my hands slowly across my face, smelling the rust of the boat ground into my palm. "Oh my God," I said again.

He tapped on the bed rail. His fingernails clicked against the iron. "I'm sorry to give you a surprise, Paulie. When I'm finished talking, you'll understand why."

I felt his nervous energy again, filling the air like static.

"I'm not a ghost," he said. "And I am thirsty."

I walked into the room. Numbly, I shook his hand. I could not focus on his grinning face.

Ingo got up from the bed and went straight to the fridge. He already knew the layout of the room. He pulled out a carton of milk and sat down at the kitchen table. He reached across and slapped his palm down on the bare wood to show I should sit down, as well.

While I sat there in silence, Ingo explained why he was still alive and what had happened since we'd last seen each other. He had woken up in the mujahideen hut and found me gone. The guards told him I had been traded in a prisoner exchange several days before. Soon afterward, another exchange was offered by the Russians. Since Ingo was the only one the mujahideen had at the time, he was reluctantly handed over and sent back to Di-aghilev. At first, they kept him in the infirmary, which was in fact the same corrugated iron hut in which Ingo had held his interro-gations of the mujahideen. The place had been converted in his absence. He made trips into Kabul, where a dentist attached to the Russian air force worked on his teeth. He slept deeply and had to be woken by a man standing several paces back, calling his name. If anybody touched him while he was still asleep, he at-tacked them. After a month, Ingo was pronounced fit to return to duty. He was sent back to work, but no longer as the chief in-terrogator. That task had already been assigned to someone else. They had him changing tires on the Zovis at the motor pool, but he worked too slowly. He would fall asleep and the officer in charge of the pool would find him curled up among the empty packing crates. It was no use punishing him. Only his body had been cured. From there, they moved him on to the kitchens, where he boiled rice. He couldn't even manage that. It got so he couldn't even dress himself. He wouldn't leave his tent. The soldiers showed him what was in some ways their greatest disrespect. They pitied him. In the end, he was shipped back and given a medical discharge.

As he talked, I studied the way time had rounded off his features, reddened his face, and plucked away some of his hair. It was as if my mind were making space for him again. It wasn't just the space of him sitting there in front of me. I had to reach back, like drilling a mine shaft through my brain, to the place in time where I had left him for dead. In my memory, I refleshed his bones and creased his face with age, like marking soft clay with a knife. But I could only bury Ingo once in my mind. Now that he had returned, he still belonged in the in-between place. He would always be there from now on.

Ingo sensed this. He wiped at his face, as if to smear away the shadows that the light cast on his skin. He tried to make jokes, but just beneath the surface was the frustration that he could not get back what he'd lost. It seemed to bulge against the soft shell of his body, as if something were moving inside him and at any moment would tear its way through. He got up and began to pace the room, walking in circles around where I sat at the kitchen table. He ran his fingers across the books on my shelves. "A woman lives here," he said.

"Yes. Her name is Suleika." She was still on the boat, taking a nap. I had left her a note, saying I'd return after taking a shower at the apartment.

"Suleika. Suleika," Ingo echoed the name. "Well, I'm sure she's very nice." He poked his head into my bedroom and laughed. "Still making your bed like a soldier. Or does she do that for you now?"

"I make the bed," I said quietly. I went over and tucked the blankets back in, to make it as if he had never been here.

Ingo smiled while he watched this. When I had finished, he

took a coin from his pocket and dropped it onto the blanket and watched it bounce. That was a trick the sergeants used to do in boot camp to see if the sheets were tucked in tightly enough. "Yes, this is your work. I can tell." He walked back into the kitchen, sighing and shaking his head. He seemed disappointed to have found me in such humble surroundings. The truth must have collided with some fantasy he had invented. "I would have come sooner," he said, "but I've been busy making plans."

"Why have you come here?" I asked. It was like speaking to someone in a dream. Each word to him might be my last. I might wake to find him gone and myself alone in this house.

"Paulie," he whispered coarsely. It was the voice of some-one giving up a secret. "I've come all this way. Aren't you glad to see me?"

"Ingo," I said, "I don't know what to think. For Christ's sake, you killed a man right in front of me."

"I certainly did." His jaw muscles clenched as he said the words. "You killed a man once." He drank some milk. His Adam's apple bobbed in his throat.

"That was in a war. Why did you kill Samuel Mudge?" I asked. "What did he ever do to you?"

"What did he do?" Ingo fired back the question. His eyes were glassy. "He filed down my fucking teeth is what he did." Ingo pulled back his lips in a grimace and bared the false teeth. He tapped his fingernail against them. *Tick-tick-tick* against the porcelain. "He gave me these. He caused me so much pain that I barely feel pain anymore." Ingo paused. He straightened up, composing himself. When he spoke again, his rage had gone away. "You didn't recognize him, did you?" He answered for me. "Of course you didn't, Paulie. You'd have killed him yourself if you had."

"You can't know that was him." I stared at Ingo in amaze-ment. "That was years ago. It was a lifetime from here."

"It was him," said Ingo with the calm of absolute certainty. He reached into his wallet and pulled from it a piece of a newspaper. He handed it over.

The clipping was from the *Frankfurter Allgemeine*. It was an article, dated three weeks previously, about the conference here in Providence and the German representatives who would be taking part. There was a picture of two men greeting a German representative from Audi. One of the two men was Samuel Mudge. "So?" I said. "So one of these guys is Mudge. So?"

He set down the milk. "Look at the other man in the picture."

I looked. The photo was grainy but clear. I saw a tall, thin man with a narrow face and a close-cropped dark beard. It was Mohammed. Except that now his name, according to the article, was Chester Todd. He was the organizer of Project Safe Haven. I would not have known it was Mohammed if Ingo had not told me of the connection. Now I recognized Mudge, as well. He was the blond man in the snowfield. Ingo was right. There was no doubt in my mind.

"You know who it is," said Ingo.

"Yes," I answered, the word barely forming on my lips.

"Good!" Ingo banged the table, satisfied. "Now," he commanded. "Now we can talk! I've come here to do you a favor."

That was a lie. Ingo didn't do favors.

Late-afternoon sunlight beamed through the kitchen window. It lit up the space between us, sepia tinting the air.

"What happened when you got sent home, Ingo?" I made my voice gentle, like speaking to a child.

"I wasn't quite myself." He raised his eyes and glanced at me. Then he snuffled a weak laugh. "Actually, it was a little worse than that. I was in some kind of hospital."

"For your teeth," I said. "All that dental work."

"No, Paulie. Not for my teeth. I was at Grodek."

"Oh." I looked down. Grodek was a notorious mental institution outside Dresden. The patients there, often political prisoners, were kept drugged for months at a time.

"As you can see, I'm fine now." He shifted the milk carton back and forth across the ridges of the wooden tabletop. He watched the movements, as if following the swing of a watch on a chain, hypnotizing himself. "I was there for a couple of years. I don't remember very much. By the time I got out, the Berlin Wall was down. I didn't want to go back home. I had to start over someplace, so I went west, like a million others. I worked for a while in Hamburg. I drifted around." He picked at his teeth while he talked. It was hard to understand him. His false teeth had given him a slight lisp. "I didn't have my engineering degree. Not sure I ever really wanted one anyway. I settled into the only kind of life I knew."

"Black market," I said.

He nodded. "As you well know. And"—he sighed—"I was arrested in Denmark for selling stolen Soviet weapons, mortars in fact, two of them, to a man I thought was an Iranian member of Hezballah. It turned out he was Iranian all right, but he was also working for Interpol. I was extradited back to Germany. The sentence I received was actually quite reasonable. Only five years. Of course, I ratted out every last contact I could name in order to get the sentence reduced, but that didn't matter to me."

"I'm sorry for you, Ingo." As soon as I'd said it, I knew I shouldn't have.

He shuddered. His head twisted with the force of it. "I don't need you to be sorry for me. The thing is," he said, "while I was in prison, I began to think about how I'd ended up there. How certain people had taken advantage of me. I began to get resentful. You understand, of course."

"Of course," I said cautiously.

"I thought about Markus. What he did to me. Then I thought about those two Americans in Afghanistan. What they did to me."

"How do you know they were American?"

"I heard them talking while I was lying there in that hut. I knew they were American. They were CIA, I expect. I don't know. I really don't care. In prison, it got so all I could think about was setting things straight. So when I got out, I started with Markus."

"What did you do to him?"

"What the hell do you think I did?" Anger flared into his voice again. He could not control it.

"Why didn't you just let it rest?" Even as I spoke, I heard the hypocrisy in my own words. I didn't blame him for wanting Markus and the Americans dead. But there was all the difference in the world between wanting them killed and coming halfway around the world to do the job.

He ignored my question. "I was lucky," he said, raising his eyebrows as if still surprised at his good fortune. "It only took me a month to track down Markus. He had a teaching post in the West. University of Bonn. I buried him in a box in the woods called the Kottonforst, outside a town called Bad Godesberg. After I buried him and I was walking away, I could still hear him. He was offering me money."

My face was covered in sweat.

He slid the milk across to me, bumping over the wood. "Don't be upset, Paulie. Have a drink. Markus got off easier than I had planned. It was the others who took time. I'd almost given up when I saw that newspaper clipping. I had to sell most of what I owned to get here."

"And me?" I asked. "How did you know where I was?"

"I've known that for years. I got Markus to tell me."

"What else did he tell you?" My throat was dry. I was thirsty, but I didn't want to drink the milk that he had been drinking.

"Nothing." Ingo shook his head. "After that, I was too busy shoveling earth to hear what else he said."

I thought of Markus beating at the splintery walls of the box and the thump of dirt as it covered him up.

"I'd been here for about a week before you saw me. I watched you for a couple of days. From a safe distance of course. Then I went up to Providence to shadow Mudge and Todd. When Mudge was doing his tour of the state on his day off, I trailed him through about half a dozen towns until he got to Newport. He was wandering around like a lost soul, so I went up and bumped into him and we even got to talking for a while. He asked me where he could get something to eat and I sent him right into your bar. I offered to buy him some lunch, but he didn't want that. I found him quite rude. You know, Paulie"—his thoughts were wandering—"I was surprised to find you here. I thought you would have moved on by now. This isn't much of a life."

"I decided not to move on." I remembered that day when Suleika and I sat in her car and made up our minds. I recalled the exact coolness of the breeze. "We decided," I said. "And we like it here."

"Ah, yes." He craned his head around, taking in the faint perfume of Suleika's soap and her body and each detail of her presence here that caught his eye. "The pleasures of the flesh."

"So, Ingo," I said, "you want to do me a favor."

He watched me for a few seconds before he spoke. "We're going to kill Todd," he said. "We are going to set things straight."

This is not Ingo, I thought. It is some beast in the frame of his body. It is his doppelgänger. I imagined myself striking him in the chest with the flat of my hand. I pictured his ribs collapsing into a stinking emptiness inside him. "You don't need my help for that," I said.

"It's not about help," he answered. "Aren't you angry at what they did to us? Don't you want to make them pay?"

"Yes," I said. "I do." I stood and looked down at his heavy shoulders and his thinning hair. I rested my knuckles on the tabletop. "But I don't want to risk throwing away what I have now. I don't want to set the record straight at the price of screwing up

189

everything else. I'm sorry for you, Ingo." I knew he didn't want to hear it. "I'm angry, but I'm not that angry."

He looked at me with a weariness in his salt-fire blue eyes. Without getting up from his chair, he reached across to the windowsill and picked up the sea-foam green telephone. He lifted it over to the table and when he set it down, the bell inside clanged faintly. "So call the police," he said. "Tell them what I did."

"You know I won't call the police."

"You'd have to explain how you know me. Why you're in America. It would all come out. The truth."

"I'd spend the rest of my life in prison." I finished his thought. "And so would Suleika."

"What you have here"—he fanned his arms around the room—"is a dream. You are not Paul Watkins. You are not the person you claim to be. The only thing real in this room is Ingo Budde. With me here," he continued, "you have to stop pretending who you are."

"Why couldn't you have just showed up and we could have gotten drunk and told stories and you wouldn't have hundreds of police out looking for you? Why couldn't you have done that?" I paused. "No," I said, realizing the foolishness of what I was saying. I knew who I was talking to. "Of course you wouldn't do that. Not when there're debts to be paid. It's an unfinished transaction, isn't it, Ingo? And I know how much you hate unfinished business."

"Yes," said Ingo, for the first time sounding like himself again. "That's what I hate the most. I'll make you a deal. You help me with Todd. Then I'll go away, if that's what you want."

"And what if I don't want to take that risk? It's bad enough that I'm here talking to you now."

He picked up the receiver and butted it across to me with the heel of his palm. The coiled extension cord stretched out between us. "Then call the police. Or maybe I should call them."

When I just stood there, trapped as he knew he would trap

me, Ingo smiled and set the receiver back in its cradle. He got up and slapped me on the back. "You'll see I'm right," he said. He headed out the door. His heavy footsteps clumped downstairs and then the door clicked shut.

SULEIKA HAD JUST woken up. She was making herself some coffee in the galley of the *Liedke.* She looked up through her mussy hair as I walked into the room. "Oh no," she said when she saw my expression.

We sat down at the galley table. I told her what had happened. This time she didn't try to convince me I was wrong. "Does he know about the reports you wrote on him?" she asked when I had paused for breath.

"I don't think so. I don't know."

"If he knows, Paul, he'll probably try to kill you as well."

The coffee machine spluttered on the counter. The smell of it drifted past my face. "I think if Ingo knew about it, he would have done me in already."

Suleika went to fetch the coffee. She set two tin mugs on the counter. "And what about this other man? This Todd man. Does he really deserve to die?"

"He did some awful things. So did his friend Mudge. But we all did awful things over there."

"Are you going to help him?" She set the coffee down in front of me.

I watched the little ghosts that twisted on the shiny black liquid. "I'm going to do whatever it takes for us to keep what we have."

"We could run."

"We could have run before." I reached across the glitter-top table and rested my hands on hers. "But we didn't, because we knew we would spend the rest of our lives looking over our shoulders. If I run now, Ingo will come after me. And I know this man. He will not quit. If I help him, he'll leave us alone."

"How do you know?"

"Because that's the way his mind works. That's how he would pay me back for helping him. He would need to pay me back. He couldn't stand to owe me for my help."

"Why does he need you to help him?"

"I don't know," I said. "Whatever the reason, he's got it all planned out." I got up and walked to the open galley door. Heat shimmered up off the *Liedke*'s deck.

"Didn't you two used to be friends?" she asked.

"We were friends," I told her, "but only when business had been taken care of first."

"So he wasn't much of a friend."

"Neither was I." I leaned against the metal of the door frame. The white paint was blistered with rust. "I wrote those reports."

"But you cleared him." There was the sound of her hand slapping flat on the table. "What you wrote saved him!"

"It doesn't matter. What matters is that I wrote the reports."

"You had no choice."

"I have no choice now, either." I turned and looked back at her. "He said that everything we had here was only a dream."

"So what if it's a dream," she asked, "as long as we're living it?"

"You should go someplace for a while," I said.

"I will not," she answered.

"Please, Suleika."

"Don't ask me again." Her hands had crept to the edges of the table. She gripped the corners, as if to anchor herself to the world.

TWO DAYS LATER, Ingo and I walked into the Providence convention center, posing as journalists from the German magazine *Stern*. We had an appointment to interview Chester Todd. Ingo would do the interview and I would photograph Todd afterward. That was all I knew.

"I have to get close to him," Ingo said on the way over. We were driving in a rented car. Ingo wore a suit. He had shaved off the scruff on his chin but had left a thin mustache on his upper lip.

"You can't do it there. For Christ's sake, Ingo." It crossed my mind that maybe he wanted to be caught. For both of us to be caught.

"Now then, Paulie. Didn't I say I had this figured out?" He didn't take his eyes off the road. "I have to get him to trust me. Otherwise, I can't get him where I want him."

I hadn't slept much since our last meeting. I punted ideas back and forth in my head until I was dizzy. I had trouble facing the fact that Ingo was alive. Even with him sitting beside me now, I still felt a veil between his presence and the truth. I kept thinking about what he had said—that my life was a dream. Only he was real. Not pretending to be something else. I thought about the man I had killed in Afghanistan, the way I had carried him into the hills and dumped his body like a sack of rocks at the feet of his friends. I wondered if I could do it again. I had no choice. Ingo had made sure of that before he ever came to me. That was what Ingo did. He made sure.

Ingo fished two Papirossi cigarettes from his pocket and set them between his lips. He lit them with the mushroom-shaped lighter in the car's dashboard. He pinched the cardboard tubes and handed one to me. "A little souvenir," he said.

I breathed in the smoke and winced as the musty reek of it brought back the smell of other things, the waterproofing of our tent in Afghanistan, the damp, sweaty smell of all the food at Diaghilev, the faint medicinal taste of Tarkhuna vodka in my spit. "Jesus," I said. "Did we really used to smoke these things?"

"In great quantity."

I had a few more puffs and then gave up. My eyes were watering. "Oh, I can't finish this."

Ingo took the cigarette away and smoked both at the same time.

"This project," I said.

"Project Safe Haven." Ingo rolled the words sarcastically off his tongue. "Just another front for smuggling arms."

"Are you sure?"

"I know all that I need to know about Todd."

We kept quiet after that.

The entrance to the convention center was a short semicircular drive, in the middle of which was a roof held up by Greek-looking pillars. Large plate-glass windows showed a lush plant-filled foyer on the other side. A uniformed guard opened our doors and a valet took our key and parked our car.

I carried with me a camera and a nylon bag filled with spare lenses and film. Ingo had bought it at a pawnshop. He made sure I knew how to work the equipment. I wore clothes that I had bought from the Salvation Army store and that I would throw away afterward.

There was a large escalator a few paces beyond the entrance, across a polished marble floor. As Ingo and I went up the escalator, I looked down at clusters of seats, a table laid out with coffee urns and cake, and a man in a tuxedo playing the piano. The room was dotted with stiffly dressed men and women who sat by themselves, smoking or reading portfolios. They looked tired. The convention had been going on for two weeks. In three days, it would be over.

Ingo had two press cards from *Stern* magazine. I didn't ask where they had come from. He showed them to a woman at the reception desk, which was parked at the top of the escalator. Ingo was polite and soft-spoken. The woman made a call and said that Mr. Todd was expecting us. She gave us passes that were green laminated cards, and she told us where to find Chester Todd.

I felt myself trembling as we walked down the carpeted corridor toward Todd's room. Ingo walked quickly, the tail of his trench coat swishing against his legs. We passed door after door, each one with a number screwed in brass to the front and with a tiny bubble-eyed peephole. Maids with loaded laundry carts pushed past.

We reached Todd's door just as he was opening it. He carried a tray with some room-service food on it. The plate was still half-loaded with an omelette and sliced-up strawberry garnish. "Oh, hello," he said. "I'm sorry. I was just having a late breakfast. I would have had us meet in a conference room, but they were all booked." He put the tray down and shook our hands while Ingo introduced us.

His hair was graying. That was the first difference I noticed. His acne-scarred skin sagged. He looked pale. He did not seem dangerous, only apologetic as he walked us into his room, trying to tidy it as he went, stuffing a hairbrush into a drawer, kicking a pair of slippers under the bed. The room smelled of his breakfast and the mugginess of his sleep.

I would never have recognized Todd. My memory of him was so wound into the sharp light and the cold, the stench of the hut and the flaked rock of the cliffs that I could never have separated him from that place enough to know him anywhere else. I had worried that Todd himself might recognize us, but now the worry passed. It was too long ago. This place too many worlds away.

"I did an interview with the *Frankfurter Allgemeine*," said Todd, "about a month ago." He was arranging some chairs around a little table with a too-big lamp planted on it. The curtains had been drawn and now he pulled them back, revealing the skyline of Providence.

We all grimaced in the brightness.

"Will this do?" asked Todd. "I really should have found us a conference room."

"This is fine," said Ingo. "This will be perfect. Do you mind if I take off my coat?"

Todd helped him off with his coat and the two of them sat down at the table.

I sat down on the bed. Todd had tried unsuccessfully to tuck the sheets back into their original creases. I held the camera on my lap. When I raised my head, I saw myself in the large mirror directly opposite. I looked frightened and old.

Ingo pulled something from the pocket of his suit jacket. I thought it was a gun at first. My heart clenched and unclenched so hard it seemed to have exploded in my chest. But I saw it was only a small pocket recorder. Ingo switched it on and leaned back in his chair. He was confident.

This is Ingo's universe, I thought. A place where he always knows what is going to happen next.

While they talked, I felt the muscles tighten in the back of my neck. Ingo was going on about how important Project Safe Haven was and how the German participation in the Bosnian crisis had been slow and inadequate. Germans, said Ingo, should be inspired to begin their own relief efforts.

"Yes," Todd was saying. "Yes, exactly." He spoke with great seriousness.

I had believed Ingo when he said that Todd was running a front organization to smuggle arms into Bosnia. I just assumed that because of what I knew about Todd's past. But now I began to wonder if perhaps the project was legitimate. Maybe Todd had changed. I looked at Ingo, trying to detect whether the thought might have crossed his mind also.

They talked for a long time. Todd spoke about the need for privatization, a guaranteed minimum wage for Bosnian workers, profit sharing, and the establishment of trade unions. "In the meantime," he said, "the best we can do is provide some of the basic needs for survival. Medicine. Clothing. Food. And the vehicles to get them there. Until essential services are restored, none of these other issues can be addressed."

"Why not just smuggle in guns?" asked Ingo.

There was a pause. "What?" said Todd.

I watched a drop of sweat splash onto the shiny black surface of the camera on my lap.

"There are rumors," said Ingo, "that this is just a front for shipping arms. I'm sure you've heard of them."

Todd shrugged. He looked a little dazed. "Well, actually, no, I had not."

"Such an approach"—Ingo drew out the word *approach*—"is not entirely without reason. We must be open to all things. Perhaps the time for rational discussion has not yet arrived."

Todd sat back slowly, pinching his chin between his thumb and index finger. "All right," he said. "For the sake of argument, I'll try to answer that."

"Yes," said Ingo, "please answer that."

He's going to kill Todd right here, I thought. Right here in this room. I felt myself withdrawing far inside my body.

"I have some experience," said Todd, "of what happens when rational discussion is obliterated. There will always be people who say there is not time for discussion. And it may be that what I am doing now is only to make up for the mistakes I made before."

"What mistakes?"

For God's sake, Ingo, I was thinking. But there was no way to stop him. Ingo had probably imagined this conversation a hundred times when he was in prison. Now he was determined to live it out.

"It doesn't matter," said Todd. "What matters is the work I'm doing now. No weapons. No sides. Just the basic tools to allow the people of Bosnia to get on with their lives."

"We were sorry," said Ingo, "to hear about the death of your assistant, Mr. . . . ." He pretended to forget the name. "Mr. . . . ."

"Mudge," said Todd. He looked a little dazed. "Yes, I don't understand that at all. We had been together, working together, a long time. I don't understand," he said again. "The police tell me it was a professional job, and then there were all those accusations between the Serbs and the Croats. To tell you the truth, I think Sam just got himself in a fight. He had a temper. When he lost it, even he didn't know what he was going to do next. I still can't get it into my head that he's not around anymore. I think the shock hasn't hit me yet."

I had sunk so deep inside myself that Ingo had to call me a couple of times before I started and jumped to my feet.

"Let's do some photos," he said. He made a big production of repositioning the furniture and standing back and repositioning it again. He seemed frustrated.

I didn't understand what was so important about the damned photo. Let's just take it and get the hell out of here, I thought.

"It's not going to work in here," said Ingo. "Mr. Todd, are you busy for the next few hours?"

"Well, I do have a presentation to make. That's in about half an hour. Here's no good for the photo?"

Ingo clicked his tongue. "No, not really. We're a color magazine. We do need some quality shots."

"Of course," said Todd. "Well, how about tomorrow?"

Ingo clapped his hands almost silently together. "Perfect!" He arranged to meet Todd very early the next morning, because that was the only time he had free.

We shook hands again in the hallway. It was empty except for the three of us.

"I'm sorry about some of those questions," said Ingo. "You understand, of course."

Todd closed his eyes and nodded once. "Absolutely. Just doing your job." He shook our hands once more.

INGO PULLED OUT fast onto the road. "It's all set," he said. "You did well, Paulie. Do you see why I needed you? It wouldn't have looked right if I didn't have a second man along as a photographer." He set his dry-skinned hand on the back of my neck and squeezed hard. "You did well!"

We drove for a while in silence, but then I had to talk. "Ingo, what if Project Safe Haven is legitimate?"

He shrugged with a great crumpling of his shoulders. "What if it is?"

"Can you not think of the work he's doing now as some sort of penance?"

"Penance?" Ingo exploded. His spit splattered on the steering wheel and the windshield. "I don't care about anything he's done since that day out in the snow. There's no point you feeling sympathy for that man because he is already dead."

"What happens now?"

"Is there an out-of-the-way place where you can dock your boat?"

I thought for a minute and then said, "There's an old fish house I know. It's about a quarter of a mile down from the one I dock at now. The dock is rotten, but I suppose I could pull up to it."

"Fine. Then that's where you'll be tomorrow morning at seven A.M. We're going for a little boat ride with Mr. Todd." He pulled the car over at the bottom of Thames Street. "Best if you walk home from here," he said. "This girl of yours . . ." he began.

"She doesn't know anything," I lied.

"Clever boy." He tapped an index finger against his nose.

I undid my seat belt and opened the door just a crack. "When this is over, Ingo . . ."

"Yes, yes, I know," he said impatiently. "I'm gone. Poof! Like a puff of Papirossi smoke. You can pretend I'm dead again. Just do as you're told, Paulie. Just be there tomorrow. Then you can go back to your woman and your dream."

WHEN I GOT back to the apartment, Suleika was there. She was standing by the kitchen window, looking out into the street.

I told her how it had gone.

Her face was stony while she listened.

When I had finished talking, she pulled the little drawer out of the kitchen table and took from it a government .45 pistol. She set it flat in front of me. "Kill him," she said.

"Where the hell did you get that?" I asked. The blueing on the .45's squared-off barrel had been rubbed down to the steel. The checkered grips were cracked. This gun had been around a long time.

"It belonged to Mathias. I want you to kill Ingo Budde. I don't care if you used to be friends. I don't care if you think that you owe him some loyalty. Kill him when he comes to the boat tomorrow. Kill him when you're out on the water. I don't care. But I want you to kill him. Will you do that? Will you kill him? Because if you won't, I will. It's the only way he's going to leave us alone. He's not just going to go away."

I heard Ingo's voice again: "Poof! Like a puff of Papirossi smoke."

"At first"—Suleika's words tumbled out, as fast and desperate as when I had first met her, that hot day at Logan Airport— "I didn't want anyone to get hurt. Then I decided that I didn't care who died, as long as we got to keep our life here. And now I don't even care about that. I just don't want you to get hurt. And if you don't kill him, you are going to get killed yourself. Kill him, Paul." She picked up the gun and held it out to me. "Kill him with this."

"Keep your voice down," I said.

She grabbed hold of my shirt and the skin of my chest beneath that and she gripped it so tightly that my teeth gritted together and I cried out.

"Are you going to do it?" she hissed.

I lifted the gun gently out of her hand. "I said I'd do whatever it took."

She released me and stood back. "I'm telling you what it will take. You think of your father," she said. "You think of what he would have done."

She was right about my father, who would have snuffed out Ingo's life the second Ingo tried to blackmail him. My father would have risked everything rather than submit to that. For him, it would have been a question of honor. All debts would have been canceled. Compassion shoved aside.

"Do you want me to stay?" she asked.

"No," I said quietly. I knew we might talk ourselves out of what had to be done, and into some plan that would not work. This was the only way. I promised I would come find her at her house when I was done. I said I'd be back sometime tomorrow afternoon. I told her to wait. Then I kissed her good-bye. I told her she should leave now.

"All right," she said and kissed me again and then left. When she had gone, I put the gun back into the kitchen drawer and lay down on the bed.

I didn't sleep again that night. I still felt the pain of her hands clawed into my flesh. I pulled away my shirt and saw the red bloom of burst blood vessels. When I couldn't stand lying still anymore, I went to the kitchen table and checked the gun. I slid out the magazine. It was full. There were spots of turquoise verdigris on the stubby brass cartridges. With a toothbrush soaked in oil, I scrubbed each of the bullets until the cartridges were smooth and polished and the copper heads were shiny. Then I wiped off the oil with a cloth. I checked the action of the gun, moving the slide back and forth. Then I set it on the table in front of me and rested my head on my folded hands.

I was glad when the sun finally came up. It gleamed weakly off the fog-damp rooftops. I took the ice trays from the freezer and knocked the cubes into the sink. Then I ran the tap and washed my face in the freezing water. I didn't eat. I pulled on my diesel-smelling clothes. I pulled on my salt-stained boots and rolled the pistol inside my rain slicker. Then I went down to the dock and fired up the engine of the *Liedke* in the still morning air.

Seven

It had clouded over by the time I reached the abandoned fish house with its bird shit–spattered roof and rotten pier.
The fog, which normally burned off in the first hour of sun, still
lingered around the pilings and across the cracked tarmac of the
fish house lot, where weeds grew up between the splits. There
was no one around. The fish house blocked off any view from the
road.

I tied up the boat. Before I had even secured the lines, Ingo
showed up in his rented car. The wheels crackled over the gravel.
Ingo was the only one I could see in the car. He turned it around
and backed up as close as he could to the boat. Then he cut the
engine.

It was quiet. Fog swirled in around us.

Ingo got out of the car. He was wearing the same clothes as the
day before. His face looked very pale. The hair was wet around
his forehead, as if he had been sweating heavily.

I stood on the bow, one of the heavy mooring ropes still in my hand. I had untucked my shirt and set the gun in the back of my jeans. I could feel the weight of it and the metal against my skin.

"Are you ready?" asked Ingo.

I nodded. I noticed that his knuckles were bloody.

Ingo walked around to the trunk. He popped it open.

Slowly, like something mechanical, Chester Todd rose from the belly of the trunk until he was sitting. His face was painted with blood. The collar of his shirt was dyed scarlet. His lips were torn open. Clumps of his hair were missing. His nose was skewed to one side and broken. His eyes were filmed with red. He was looking right at me. Todd opened the wreckage of his mouth. The cry that came from him was shrill and inhuman.

I felt it. The sound raked through my nerves.

Then the noise suddenly quit as Ingo wheeled around, smashed Todd in the face with his fist, and knocked him out. Ingo wrapped Todd in the plastic sheeting that he had laid out on the floor of the trunk. He picked him up and carried him across the rickety boards of the dock and dumped him onto the deck of the *Liedke*. Then he jumped down himself in a waft of trench coat. He pointed to the ice hatch. "What's down there?" he said. He didn't wait for my answer. He heaved off the hatch cover and peered in. "Good," he said. I could see Todd's hands and the top of his head showing through the heavy plastic sheeting. His polished city shoes stuck out the other end. A little comb and a neatly folded handkerchief had fallen from Todd's coat and now lay on the deck. Ingo picked them up and put them in his own pocket. He lowered Todd's body down as far as he could into the ice hold, then dropped him the rest of the way. "I'm not finished with Todd yet," he said.

"Ingo," I said, "you're a fucking animal."

He turned on me. "Did you think it would be pretty?" he asked. His voice was gravelly with anger. "Don't forget what he did, Paulie. Now be a good boy and take us out to sea."

Just then, I saw someone appear at the end of the alleyway that led out into the fish house parking lot. My heart kicked. It was Suleika. She was walking quickly toward us, her face without expression.

"Who is that?" Ingo snapped at me.

"Suleika," I said, too stunned to say anything else.

"What's she doing here?" demanded Ingo.

"I don't know," I said.

He could tell from the look on my face that I was telling the truth. "I'll handle this." Ingo hauled himself up onto the dock and his heavy steps shook the rotten planks as he walked out to meet her. The trench coat swished around his legs.

As soon as he had turned his back, I pulled out the pistol. I flicked off the safety with the side of my thumb.

Suleika and Ingo drew closer. The distance vanished between them.

"The little lady!" exclaimed Ingo. He bared his teeth in a smile. His hands were open at his sides, as if he meant to embrace her. "I'm pleased to meet you, finally. My name is Ingo Budde."

Suleika's arm swung out from behind her back. Locked in her clenched hand was the fish club with its hobnailed tip. She smacked Ingo across the side of the head and spun him around so hard he ended up facing her again. She flailed her arm the other way and hit him once more. His legs buckled. He hit the ground hard on his back and grunted as the air punched out of his lungs. He rolled over and tried to get up. His movements were groggy. Suleika stood over him, breathing heavily. If she hit him again, she would kill him. Ingo was on his hands and knees, shaking his head slowly. Then his arms gave way and he planted his face on the ground. He tipped over onto his side and lay still. Only now did Suleika look across at me. "You wouldn't have done it," she said.

"I guess we'll never know," I told her. I put away the gun. I was stunned at what I had just seen. I believed Suleika to be capable of violence, but only in moments of panic, if she was cornered and threatened and didn't have time to think about what she was doing. But she had thought about this. She had gone to the boat and fetched the club, which she had used to dispatch hundreds of fish over the years. She knew how to use it. The weight of it in her hand. The exact arc of its swing, and the knowledge of its lethal force. It was on purpose that she had not killed him. She could have split Ingo's skull the first time she hit him.

While Suleika untied us from the dock, I carried Ingo onto the boat. He was unconscious but alive, bleeding from one ear, his nose, and a split lip. The bruises on his head were already starting to swell. I bound him with nylon line from the net-repair spool. I tied his feet and his hands and above his elbows so that they were locked behind his back. Then I put a strip of wide electrical tape over his mouth and tied him by the neck to a cleat on the side of the wheelhouse. Once that was done, I covered him with a heavy gray canvas tarp.

Suleika steered us out to sea. There were few other boats out. I didn't need to ask where we were headed. I knew from the loran coordinates that she was making for a place called "the Sink." It is a sharp dip in the ocean floor about a mile and a half off Moonstone Beach in South County, Rhode Island. It goes down hundreds of feet. Trawlermen avoid it because the steep sides of the dip cause their nets to trail and the steel "doors" that keep the net open to flip or drag the net shut. We didn't talk. I just sat next to her and we both stared out into the gray morning, the engine vibrating up through our feet.

"Hold on to the wheel," said Suleika. "I'm going out on deck."

Her voice caught me by surprise. I had grown used to the silence. "No," I told her. "I'll do it."

I slipped down from my chair and was dizzy and sick as I headed out on deck.

"Do it quickly," she called after me. "We'll be there soon."

We were hugging the shoreline, about a third of a mile from the beach, past Narragansett, Scarborough Beach, Matunuck, up toward Quonochontaug. The shoreline was dotted with little summer cottages, most of them still empty because it was too early in the season. The shore faded in and out of the fog. There was no wind, so the diesel fumes blew across the deck and made me breathe through clenched teeth. When I pulled back the tarp, Ingo was looking at me. The blood from his nose had dried in a streaked crust across the silver electrical tape. He was crying. I crouched down next to him and pulled off the tape.

He choked and spluttered. His face was wet with tears. "Oh no," he was saying, softly to himself, "Oh no. What will happen to me now?"

"Ingo," I said. "I want to tell you something."

"Oh no. Oh no. Poor Ingo," he murmured, as if he had become detached from his own body.

"Ingo, listen." I took hold of his arm.

He looked at me.

"Ingo, when we were in Afghanistan . . ." I faltered. "When we were there . . ." Again I faltered. "I worked for the Stasi, Ingo. They sent me to write reports on you." I told him what I had done. My hand slipped from his arm and I looked down at the deck. I told him everything.

I heard him then.

He was laughing through his tears. "I know," he said. "I read each report before Volkov sent them out."

I sat back against the steel apron of the boat. "What do you mean, you read them?"

"Volkov," he said. He sniffed and then coughed out another laugh. "I told you I owned that man."

"Why didn't you say anything?"

"You were writing such nice things about me, I didn't want you to stop. Besides, what would you have done if I did tell you?"

206

"I don't know."

"You see? I knew what you were going through. I knew what Markus did. I didn't blame you for that, especially after I read the reports."

I raked my fingers through my hair. "All this time, Ingo. I swear to God."

"What's going to happen to me?" he asked. He wasn't laughing now.

For a long time, we just looked at each other.

After a while, I spoke. "What were you going to do, Ingo? After you'd killed Todd, what were you going to do?"

He let his head fall back against the wheelhouse. He bumped the back of his head a couple of times, front teeth biting his split lower lip. "I wasn't going to do anything. I thought we should do this together."

I pulled the gun out of my jeans and drew back the slide so that one of the bullets popped out and rolled across the deck.

"No!" Ingo shouted. His face crumpled. He blinked rapidly and pressed his head back against the wheelhouse. "No!" He turned his face to the side, false teeth bared and gritted. "Jesus, Paulie. Don't."

"Stop lying to me, Ingo."

"I'm not lying." His eyes were shut tight, deep creases fanning out from the corners of his eyelids.

"If you lie to me, Ingo, I'm going to shoot you right now."

He writhed in the knots that held him, straining and grunting with fear.

"Tell me the truth, Ingo. I swear, it's the only chance you've got."

"You're going to kill me anyway."

"Look at me, Ingo." Diesel fumes were sour in my mouth.

He cracked open one eye. He was breathing hard.

"Your only chance," I said. I glanced through the cloudy plastic screen of the wheelhouse door. Suleika stood at the wheel, her hands locked around the pins, as if she were holding our course through a hurricane and not the still water that we cut through now. She was waiting. I knew the muscles would be tight around her eyes. Her breathing would be shallow, dragged through the whiteness of her clenched teeth.

I looked at Ingo. His face was gray and sweaty. His lips had dried into cracked slivers of flesh. Now is the time to kill him, I thought. Now that he knows he's going to die and his senses are shutting down and something like his ghost is hammering at the thin walls of his body, trying to get out. In my mind, I could already smell the cordite smoke and hear the jangle of the empty cartridge as it hit the deck and his blood was already pooling in the deck-plate dents, dripping out through the scuppers, and dragging crazy lines down the hull into the sea. It was as if it had already happened, but the gun was still in my hand, the magazine still full, the sea air still an undisturbed emptiness in my lungs.

It was quiet except for the engine. The heavy, smooth, gray water slid by us. A thin strip of beach seemed to ripple out of the fog, like a snake slithering along beside us. Trees bunched down to the sand. Just then, Ingo began to speak. "I was going to make sure you got blamed for Todd's death. I was going to leave traces here on the boat for the police to find. I'd call it in. By then, I'd be far away. Even if they didn't convict you over Todd, they'd find out who you really are. You'd end up in jail, anyway."

"Why? If you didn't blame me for the reports. Why?"

"Because you left me." His face was red now from the nylon twine that dug into his neck. It caught against his Adam's apple when he swallowed. "I woke up in that hut and you were gone. You could have made them take me with you. You could have said something. You could have done something. You said you wouldn't leave me. That means no matter what."

"No, Ingo, I . . ." I thought back to that night, remembering how cold he was in my arms.

"You said you wouldn't leave me," he said again.

208

"I thought you were dead." I remembered my relief when I believed he was no longer in pain.

"Well, you should have made sure! You were the only friend I had."

I went over to the rack where we kept the fish knives. They were long and wooden-handled, with blades that curved slightly upward. I drew one out and checked that it was sharp.

Ingo tried to see what I was doing. He craned his neck around, eyes twisting in their sockets. The nylon dug into his throat. "What are you doing?" he asked. The panic returned to his voice.

"Don't move," I said. "Let's make this quick."

"Please, Paulie," he whispered.

I cut the line around his throat and the lines that bound his feet. I kept the gun in my other hand. "Get up slowly," I said.

Still with his hands bound behind his back, he struggled to his feet. "I told you the truth," he said. "I did what you wanted."

We were standing side by side, looking out to sea through the pearly fog. I found myself thinking of my father. I wondered if he and I would have been friends, if he had stayed alive.

Ingo was crying again. "Oh God," he said.

With one slash of the knife, I cut the line that bound his hands. I set my fist against his back between the shoulder blades, the gun still locked in my hand. I shoved him hard, putting my whole body behind it. He fell forward, arms spread, caught his shins on the low apron of the boat, and cartwheeled into the water. He barely made a splash. When he came up, gasping with the sudden cold, the boat was already leaving him behind. He thrashed wildly, looking around him. The wake of the *Liedke* bobbed him up and down.

I walked to the stern.

He was watching me, wide-eyed, with surprise to find himself still breathing. The trench coat billowed around him, sculpting itself to the waves.

"So long, Ingo," I called to him. The distance between us was growing. The white slather of wake payed out from the *Liedke.*

Ingo rolled his head, taking in the eggshell sky and the gray sweep of the waves around him. His senses crept cautiously back to life. His face grew suddenly calm with relief. He was alive, and only now did he believe it. He raised one hand, the nylon line still wrapped around it like a many-banded bracelet. He understood what I had given him and he understood why. All debts were canceled now. He let his arm slap down again into the water. Then, with slow determination and the clumsy straight-armed crawl of a poor swimmer, he began to make his way toward the shore, which nestled in the fog a few hundred yards away.

The wheelhouse door slammed. Suleika lunged at me. "You bastard!" she shouted. She tried to grab the gun out of my hand.

It flipped out of my grasp and tumbled into the water.

She stared at me, enraged. Then she kicked me so hard in the shin that I dropped to my knees. "What is it with you?" she shouted.

I tried to get to my feet, but she put the heel of her boot against my shoulder and pushed me over again.

"What the hell is it with you and that man?" she asked.

This time, I made it to my feet. I leaned against the wheelhouse, still wincing from the pain that throbbed out of my shinbone.

For a while, we both watched the figure splashing toward shore. Then the fog swallowed him up.

"I had to take the chance," I said.

Suleika glared at me. She swallowed one sharp breath. Then she blinked rapidly two or three times, as if someone had blown smoke in her eyes. Her anger was fading. She could not hold it down. A part of her had known that I would let him go, even before I did. And she had allowed it to happen, even as she steered us out to the place she planned for Ingo's grave.

Suleika walked back inside the wheelhouse. She spun the wheel and the *Liedke* returned to its course.

CHESTER TODD WAS dead.

I tied the plastic sheeting around him and lifted his body out of the ice room. Then I took a seventy-five-pound anchor from the lazaret and strapped it to him with rope.

We stopped over the Sink. There were no other boats around. Not even on the radar. I loosed Todd over the side. He went down fast in the metallic gray-blue sea. Pockets of air that had been trapped inside the plastic sheeting streamed out in silver bubbles, but only for a little while. Then the water was still again.

I hosed the blood out of the ice room and off the deck. Then I washed it off my hands. It clung to my skin. I scraped it away with my nails.

BY THE TIME we made it back to Newport, Suleika and I had agreed that we would go away for a while. We would take the boat south, as if we were moving to another port to fish for the season, the way many boats did this time of year.

We gathered up our papers and some clothes and all our money, which we kept in a Tupperware box behind a wooden slat that served to anchor the radiator to the wall. We bought some groceries and tanked up the *Liedke*. Then we went up to Bad Joe's and told Biagio that we were leaving. We gave him the keys to our house and the apartment, and money to take care of the rent.

"Of course, of course," said Biagio, without really paying attention. He was sitting on top of the bar. He held his arms out, thumbs cocked on his hands, measuring the space like a director framing a shot. "I've been thinking about wicker again."

"Yes," I told him, "maybe the time is right."

We thought about saying good-bye to Gunther, but he wasn't

in his office. It wouldn't make a difference to him, anyway. People came into his life and disappeared again. He never seemed to feel any differently about them at the end than he had at the beginning.

We headed south, putting in at places like Cape May, New Jersey, Norfolk, Virginia, and Hatteras, where they fly the Confederate flag. We sailed on down to the Florida Keys. At night, we left the portholes open. A warm breeze blew in off the Gulf of Mexico.

Each time as we pulled into port, I expected to see Ingo standing there waiting for me, or the police. But he never was there, and neither was anyone else. I will always wonder what happened to him.

At Key Biscayne, Suleika and I got a priest to marry us on the deck of the *Liedke*. We bought a ring made from the melted-down gold of a sixteenth-century Spanish dubloon, which had been found in the wreck of a conquistador galleon, just off the key. The next day, we sold the *Liedke* to a Puerto Rican shrimping captain with a tattoo of an anchor on his forehead. He said he was going to rename the boat *Mariposa*. Suleika and I spent a month hopping through the islands of the Caribbean, through Saint Thomas and Saint Martin, Tortola and Bequia, and eventually passing into Mexico through Cozumel.

We reached the Mayan temple of Tulum and walked around its crumbling stones. We found the beach with the flour-fine white sand that my father had seen from the deck of his submarine more than half a century before. Suleika and I decided we would stay here. We rented a little cabana on the beach south of Tulum.

It was here that I began to write. At first, it was only to get things straight in my head, but as the first words fanned out across the page, I could feel my old self dying. Then I knew I had to finish what I'd started.

Each morning, while Suleika reads in her hammock or goes

for a walk on the beach to see if anything interesting has washed up on the shore, I sit down in my shorts and sandals at this rickety table with its chipped blue paint that matches the shutters. I write with a pencil on cheap gray-white notepads. They are the only paper I can find in the village of Tulum. In the afternoons, I put my head down on my arms and fall asleep. When I wake up, I look out of the glassless window at the ruins of the temple in the distance. I can tell how long I've slept from the way the light is shining on its stones. In the twilight, I watch pelicans fly just above the crests of breaking waves.

These are my days.

Sometimes, when I am writing, I notice that my hands have grown a shade darker from the sun, except for the webs between my fingers, where the Northman's pale shows through.

After sunset, I write again by candlelight, because this place has no electricity. Night crowds up against the shutters. The breeze through the palm trees sounds like rain. The sound of the ocean is so loud that it seems to be rushing toward me.

Before we turn in, Suleika and I walk down to the sea. We go in up to our waists and watch our bodies outlined with the electric green phosphorescence that you get down here in the Yucatán. Sometimes Suleika will head back into the house and I stay there a while longer. The bright sparks swirl around me. My body is coming apart, atom by atom, slipping away into the ocean. I am disappearing. I am myself again.

The author would like to thank Professor Hector Morales of the
Cobá Archaeological Facility, Cobá, Quintana Roo, Mexico,
for his help in forwarding this manuscript
to the publishers.